Andrea Kuhn Boeshaar has done it again! This talented author captures readers' attention on "Page One" and holds them spellbound right through to "The End." *Unwilling Warrior* is a beautifully written story of triumph over tragedy and disappointment that will sometimes (literally!) leave you breathless. I'm adding this one to my "Keepers" shelf, and I think you will too.

—LOREE LOUGH
AUTHOR OF *LOVE FINDS YOU IN NORTH POLE, ALASKA*;
TALES OF THE HEART; AND *PREVAILING LOVE*

Andrea Kuhn Boeshaar has successfully entertained readers through the years with poignant stories that touch the heart and thrill the soul. *Unwilling Warrior* is one of those stories that the reader will not soon forget.

—DIANN MILLS
AUTHOR OF *SWORN TO PROTECT*
AND *A WOMAN CALLED SAGE*

Andrea Boeshaar is the real deal. From the hand of a master of the craft of writing, *Unwilling Warrior* is a must-read!

—KATHLEEN Y'BARBO
AUTHOR OF *THE CONFIDENTIAL LIFE OF EUGENIA COOPER* AND
BELOVED COUNTERFEIT

In *Unwilling Warrior*, amidst a Civil War backdrop, you'll witness two believers engaging in a fight to make right—against both friend and foe. From riches to ruin to *real* riches, you'll enjoy Ben and Valerie's journey.

—PAMELA TRACY
RITA FINALIST AND WINNER OF THE ACFW 2009 BOOK OF THE
YEAR FOR SHORT ROMANTIC SUSPENSE

Andrea Boeshaar pens a compelling historical romance woven with believable characters who quickly draw the reader into their world. A tender romance laced with both uncertainty and intrigue that hooks you in the beginning and propels you on to the end. I highly recommend *Unwilling Warrior* to all lovers of romance. It won't disappoint.

—MIRALEE FERRELL
AUTHOR OF *FINDING JEENA* AND
LOVE FINDS YOU IN BRIDAL VEIL, OREGON

UNWILLING WARRIOR

Seasons of Redemption

BOOK ONE

ANDREA KUHN BOESHAAR

REALMS
A STRANG COMPANY

Most STRANG COMMUNICATIONS BOOK GROUP products are available at special quantity discounts for bulk purchase for sales promotions, premiums, fund-raising, and educational needs. For details, write Strang Communications Book Group, 600 Rinehart Road, Lake Mary, Florida 32746, or telephone (407) 333-0600.

UNWILLING WARRIOR by Andrea Kuhn Boeshaar
Published by Realms
A Strang Company
600 Rinehart Road
Lake Mary, Florida 32746
www.strangbookgroup.com

All Scripture quotations are from the King James Version of the Bible.

The characters portrayed in this book are fictitious unless they are historical figures explicitly named. Otherwise, any resemblance to actual people, whether living or dead, is coincidental.

Cover design by Bill Johnson

Library of Congress Cataloging-in-Publication Data

Boeshaar, Andrea.
  Unwilling warrior / by Andrea Kuhn Boeshaar.
     p. cm.
  ISBN 978-1-59979-985-8
  1. Marriage--Fiction. I. Title.
  PS3552.O4257U59 2010
  813'.54--dc22

                                    2010001453

First Edition

10 11 12 13 14 — 9 8 7 6 5 4 3 2 1
Printed in the United States of America

In memory of my father, Roy L. Kuhn—a true
Civil War buff.

Also, to my husband, Daniel—who is an
encourager to a high-maintenance me!

Special thanks to my son Benjamin, who let me
use his name.

And a shout out to Bob Zeller, president of
the Center for Civil War Photography, and his
book, *The Blue and Gray in Black and White:
A History of Civil War Photography* (Praeger,
2007).

Cast thy burden upon the LORD, and he shall sustain thee.

—PSALM 55:22

ONE

New Orleans, December 1861

RAINDROPS SPLATTERED AGAINST THE GARDEN'S COBBLE-stone walkway, forming puddles in low-lying areas. Above, the heavens seemed to mourn in tearful shades of gray. Staring out the floor-to-ceiling window, Valerie Fontaine realized she'd forgotten the dreariness of the season. She'd been back in New Orleans only a week, arriving Christmas Eve, but now she questioned her decision to leave Miss C. J. Hollingsworth's Finishing School for Young Ladies, a year-round boarding school in Virginia where she'd studied for the last sixteen months. She let out a long, slow sigh. Life here at home was—well, worse than the weather.

Closing the shutters, she stepped away and hugged her knitted shawl more tightly around her shoulders. She strolled from the solarium to the parlor, steeling herself against her father's continuing tirade. But at least they were talking now. He hadn't said more than six words to her since she'd been home. "You should have stayed at school." She had thought Father would be glad to see her, given that it was their first Christmas without Mama.

But such wasn't the case. Instead of spending the holiday with her, he'd been at his gentlemen's club almost continuously. His actions hurt Valerie deeply. Nevertheless, he was the only family she had left now.

"You should have stayed at school," Edward Fontaine muttered as he poured himself another scotch. His third.

"Yes, so you've stated. But isn't it obvious why I came home? I'm grieving, and I need the love and support of my father." She gave him a once-over, from the tip of his polished shoes to his shiny, straight black hair. "And it might not seem like it, but I think you need me too."

"Need you? I should say not!" He teetered slightly but caught her reaction. "And don't roll those pretty blue eyes at me either."

Valerie turned toward the roaring hearth so he wouldn't see her exasperated expression.

Holding out her hands, she warmed them by the fire. Although temperatures registered well above the freezing mark, the cold and dampness had a way of seeping into her bones. She shivered.

"I told you, *ma fille*, your efforts, as you call them, aren't needed."

She flicked him a glance. "I think perhaps they are." She sensed her father mourned Mama's death too. However, drowning himself in scotch would hardly help, and he'd lose his good standing in society if anyone found out about his...*weakness*. Did neighbors and friends already know?

"Bah!"

Valerie turned to watch as he seated himself in a floral-patterned, Louis XV wingback chair.

"You were to stay in Virginia and complete your education." Father gave a derisive snort. "I doubt Miss Hollingsworth will give me a refund on your tuition."

Valerie placed her hands on her hips. "How can you value money over my well-being?"

"This is not a question of one or the other. These are dangerous times…there are plans that you know nothing of…"

"What plans?" Curious, Valerie tipped her head.

Silence.

"Father?"

He lifted his gaze to hers, and she saw a flicker of something in his eyes—regret perhaps? Then his face hardened. "My plans were for you to stay in school and marry a young man from an established family."

Valerie groaned. Running her hands down the wide skirt of her black dress, she gathered the muslin in clenched fists of frustration. How could she make him understand? She simply had to follow her heart and come home. Otherwise, she surely would have stayed at Miss Hollingsworth's, as many students did. On most holidays, like this one, time constraints restricted travel. School let out the Friday before Christmas and began next week, on the sixth of January. However, Valerie didn't plan on returning, and her reasons to leave boarding school ran deep.

She lifted her fingertips to her temples as a headache formed. "Father, school proved too much for me after Mama's untimely death. I tried to make it, stayed all last summer, but after the war broke out I had to come home."

"Silly girl. You risked your life traveling through that part of the country. Did you think I wanted to bury a daughter too?"

"No, of course not. But I thought you would have wanted to see me at Christmastime."

He didn't comment on her remark. "So, what am I going to do with you? I can't very well send you back. It's too dangerous."

"It's not as if I need a nanny." Indignation pulsed through Valerie's veins. "I'm almost nineteen, and I can take care of myself—and manage the household for you too."

"I manage my own household."

Hardly! she quipped inwardly. Thankfully for him, Adalia,

their precious and loyal maid, had seen to almost everything since Mama died.

But Valerie wouldn't tell her father that. She'd learned neither retorts nor reasoning did much good when he'd been imbibing—which was frequently of late.

She watched as he swallowed the dark golden liquid, emptying the crystal tumbler in his hand. He made a sorrowful sight, to be sure. And yet Valerie knew her father was an honorable man, a capable man who owned and operated a large business. Her grandfather had started Fontaine Shipping when he had come from France. Father grew up near the docks and learned everything about ships and cargo, importing and exporting, and then he took over the business after he had finished his education at Harvard. Grandpapa had been so proud. And now Father secured his importance among the international shipping community as well as in New Orleans's society.

Or at least that's the way she had remembered him.

"I see I'll have to marry you off myself."

"Oh, Father, I'll marry when I'm good and ready. Right now I can't think of a single man I'm even remotely interested in."

"And what of James Ladden?" Father asked

"James is…a friend. That's all." Valerie moved to the burgundy-colored settee. Gathering her black hoop skirts, she sat down. Her fingers played across the rose-patterned, embroidered armrest. Her father's gaze seemed troubled. She shifted. "Perhaps I should ask Chastean to bring you some coffee."

He gave her a blank look, as though she'd spoken in a foreign tongue.

"Our cook…will bring you some coffee."

He held up his empty scotch glass and said, "I'm fine with this."

Valerie sighed when he rose to pour another drink. His fourth. How she wished she could hide that scotch bottle!

"We're having a houseguest tonight," he said.

"What?" Her jaw slacked at the surprising news.

"You heard me." He eyed the amber potion glistening in his glass. "A houseguest."

"Who is it?"

He lifted his slim shoulders and wagged his dark head. "Last name's McCabe. Don't know his first. He's the son of an acquaintance." He looked her way. "I extended the invitation before I knew you would burst in from school unannounced."

Valerie chose to ignore the slight. "Where did you meet him, or rather, his father?"

Father's gaze met hers. His brown bloodshot eyes watered slightly, and his Adam's apple bobbed several times as if he were struggling to contain his emotions. "I met him," he continued in a pinched voice, "just after your mother passed away."

Valerie swallowed an anguished lump of her own. He'd so rarely spoken of Mama since her death.

Her mind drifted back to that terrible day she'd received the news. She'd been at school, getting ready to paint with the other girls when a telegram had been delivered. The weighty sorrow that descended then returned now as she recalled the words: YOUR MOTHER TOOK ILL WITH A FEVER ON 23 JUNE 1861 AND HAS DIED. YOU HAVE OUR SYMPATHIES AND OUR PRAYERS. The telegram was signed Mrs. Vincent Dupont, the doctor's wife.

Upon returning home, Valerie learned that a tropical storm had detained the family physician when her mother had taken ill. He hadn't been able to reach Mama in time to help her.

Valerie had never gotten a chance to say good-bye or even attend Mama's funeral.

"I miss her too." Valerie whispered the admission, hoping this time it wouldn't fall on deaf ears.

But Father drained his glass and poured another. Number five.

"Our guest will be arriving sometime tonight. I'll be out. I've left instructions with Adalia."

"You won't be here to greet him?" Valerie swiped away an errant tear and squared her shoulders.

"Not tonight." He suddenly hollered for his coat, hat, and walking stick.

"Where are you going?" Stunned, Valerie strode toward him.

"The club. For supper."

"Again? But I had so hoped you'd come to the Donahues' tonight and celebrate the coming of the New Year with me."

"You should know right now, *ma fille*, that *hope* is a useless word in the English vocabulary. All of mine died with your mother."

Valerie's breath caught at the admission, tears obscuring her vision as the portly British maid, who'd been part of the family ever since Valerie could recall, entered the room carrying Father's belongings. He donned his winter coat.

"I hadn't planned to stay home to entertain a houseguest."

"I don't expect you to." He moved into the foyer and adjusted his black top hat. "Adalia will show him to his room, and you can go to your party."

"But—"

He swung open the front door and disappeared, closing it behind him before Valerie could speak again. All she could do was stand there, stunned.

At last she exhaled, her lower lip extended so the puff of air soared upward and wafted over the strands on her forehead. "Oh, this is a fine mess." She folded her arms.

"You needn't worry. I'll be sure to tidy the gentleman's room."

"I know you will." Valerie smiled at the good-natured woman. "Thank you."

"You're welcome, dearie. But here now—" Adalia bustled

across the room and slipped one arm around Valerie's shoulders. "Don't look so glum."

"I can't help it." Valerie's bottom lip quivered as she peered into the maid's bright green eyes. "My father has no room in his life for me, Adalia. I'm a burden to him." She paused. "Maybe I always have been, but I never noticed because of Mama."

Adalia patted her shoulder.

When the moment passed, Valerie straightened. "Well, Father said I can go to the party. I've been looking forward to it."

"Go. I'll take care of Mr. McCabe. Now you'd best be getting yourself ready."

Valerie gazed down at her dark skirts. "And another thing. I'm tired of this dreary mourning garb. It's been six months."

"That it has, and you've fulfilled your societal obligations and behaved as any good daughter would." Holding her by the shoulders, she turned Valerie so they stood face-to-face. "I don't think I'm out of place to say that y' mother'd want each of us to go on with our living. So go and have fun tonight. As for y' father's guest, he can occupy himself in the library. Plenty o' books in there."

Valerie sighed, remembering some of Father's former houseguests. "He's probably some eccentric old geezer who'll just want to read and go to sleep anyway."

Adalia snorted. Her eyes twinkled with amusement. "We've seen our share of those over the years, now haven't we?"

"Yes." A smile crept across Valerie's face. "We certainly have at that."

Beneath the bright glow from her bedroom's wall sconces, Valerie studied her reflection. She selected a sapphire-blue silk gown with satin trim around its off-the-shoulder neckline. The flouncy creation matched the color of her eyes and complemented her pale complexion. Adalia had expertly swept up Valerie's dark brown hair into a becoming chignon, although several tendrils rebelliously escaped and curled around her face.

"Pretty as a princess, y' are. Just like y' mother." Adalia stood back to admire her. "You look just like her."

"Thank you." Valerie took the compliment as high praise. "But do you think I seem a bit pale?" She pinched her cheeks until they turned a rosy pink.

"Not anymore." Adalia placed her hands on her hips. Valerie smiled, then chuckled. Adalia turned and folded an article of clothing on Valerie's four-poster bed. "Now, you be sure to catch the latest gossip, dearie. Chastean and I are dependin' on you."

Valerie whirled from the full-length mirror in a swish of silk. "Why, Adalia, I don't listen to gossip."

"'Tis such a pity. We'll be needin' something to talk about while we stir our soap."

"Mama's soap." Valerie's grin faded as wistfulness set in. She'd almost forgotten how she and Mama used to create the specially scented soaps from garden herbs and the essential oils that Father had shipped in from around the world. The practice had started with a church bazaar for which Mama had to bring something she'd made, something unique.

She called her little square bars "Psalm 55 Soap" after her favorite passage of Scripture. Mama gave them to friends or left them near the basin in the guest room with a handwritten portion of that psalm. Feeling a sudden deep determination to hang on to the memory, Valerie decided to somehow keep her mother's custom alive.

"We'll make a new batch soon," she said.

"Good, 'cause we're down to the last few bars of the lavender rose."

One of Valerie's favorites. "They're from the last batch Mama made?"

Adalia replied with a remorseful bob of her gray-blonde head.

That weighty sorrow descended again. Valerie's shoulders sagged.

Several long, reverent seconds ticked by, and finally Adalia picked up where she'd left off. "I'm particularly interested in hearing if Mrs. Field's wayward daughter married that sailor she ran away with." She fidgeted with Valerie's dress. "So listen up."

"I'll do no such thing. Besides, James told me yesterday that Nora Mae married the man in a private ceremony."

"Y' don't say!"

Valerie turned to her. "I shouldn't have even repeated that, except there's nothing wrong with saying a wedding took place, right?"

"Right."

Valerie narrowed her gaze. Maybe she had succumbed to gossiping after all.

"Now you'd best get downstairs." Adalia wisely changed the subject. "Mr. Ladden'll be here soon, and you know how impatient that one gets if he has to wait even a minute."

"You go on down. I'll be there in a bit." Valerie wanted to check her reflection one last time.

"Don't tarry."

"I won't."

The maid left, and Valerie checked her reflection once more. It felt good to shed those black mourning clothes. She thought of all her friends she hadn't seen in the almost year and a half since she'd been away at Miss C. J. Hollingsworth's. They'd always been such fun-loving girls. Valerie smiled, thinking about how they used to laugh together with chatter of balls and beaus and fashion.

Would it be the same when they saw each other again tonight?

Sadness spilled over her when she thought things might have changed. She felt so removed from those subjects now. They seemed trite, considering her present circumstances. She'd never imagined her life without Mama. But here her future lay, stretched out before her in grim uncertainty.

Cast thy burden upon the LORD, and he shall sustain thee…

Valerie smiled as part of Mama's favorite psalm waltzed across her mind. Drawing in a deep breath, she plucked her satin shawl from where it lay on her canopy bed. She pulled it around her bare shoulders, admiring its ivory softness, and fixed her mind on the gala. She'd laugh and dance, and maybe some semblance of joy would return to her life.

Leaving her bedroom, Valerie made her way down the stairs to the parlor. As it happened, she turned out to be the one who did the waiting. It seemed forever before she heard James's carriage pull up in front of the house.

At long last he entered the foyer, looking dapper in his overcoat with its fur-trimmed collar. He shed it and handed the garment, along with his hat, to Adalia. Valerie noted his foggy-gray dress coat, waistcoat, and matching trousers. The flame-red curls on his head, usually unruly, were combed neatly back.

"Why, James Ladden, don't you look handsome!" She held out her hand in greeting, and he took it at once.

"Thank you, honey. I'll have you know this suit is cut from the best cloth money can buy."

"It's quite…nice." Valerie felt a bit wounded that he didn't remark on her gown or the style of her hair.

Instead James puffed out his chest and smiled. "We have some time before we have to go." He ambled across the parlor's large Persian carpet. "Perhaps a drink to warm the blood would be appropriate."

"Yes, of course. I'll call for Adalia." She flicked a glance at him, hoping he didn't imbibe like Father. This was, after all, their first public outing together. A moment later she decided to serve hot cider in spite of the fact he hinted at something stronger.

She looked at him again. James had been a childhood friend, an auburn-headed prankster who annoyed her by putting twigs in her braided hair and calling her names. He threw slimy, creepy-crawly creatures at her and laughed when she screamed in terror. But then James matured into a dashing young man, and when he discovered that she'd come home from school, he offered to escort her to every social event in New Orleans beginning this New Year's Eve. She'd accepted because…well, it was a kind offer, and James seemed to have transformed into a gentleman.

"Is your father home?"

"No, he chose to ring in the New Year at the club."

"He won't be at the Donahues', then?"

Valerie shook her head.

"I had hoped to speak with him tonight about an important subject." His frown turned to a smile. "You."

"Me?"

"I have courtship on my mind."

His news surprised her. "I thought we were just friends, James."

"We are. But the way you look tonight makes me wish we were more."

So he'd noticed. That was something anyway. However, his backhanded flattering didn't change her feelings for him. But unwilling to hurt him, she chose her words with care. "I am fond of you. It's just—"

"Y' father's houseguest just arrived." Adalia poked her head into the room. "What would you like me to do with him, dearie?"

Valerie grimaced. "Oh, yes…" She'd almost forgotten about the man. "Show him in." Looking back at James, she said, "Excuse me for a few minutes."

"What's this?" He stepped forward, frowning his displeasure. "What houseguest?"

"Forgive me. My father only told me at the last minute." She moved toward the door. "I must see to him. It won't take too long."

Putting on her best hostess's smile, Valerie strolled into the foyer in time to see a tall but shadowy figure of a man coming down the hallway. He must have entered through the back way. Over his shoulder he carried a large satchel and, in the opposite hand, a valise. As he neared, she saw that he was soaked to the skin. Rain dripped from the wide brim hat.

"Good evening." He set his burdens down with a *thunk* onto the tiled floor. "Name's Benjamin McCabe."

"Valerie Fontaine." She held out her hand to him. He took it politely, and Valerie felt how cold he was. He also appeared young, in his midtwenties. Hardly the old codger she and Adalia had envisioned.

"Miss Fontaine, I must say you look…lovely this evening." He spoke in a velvet baritone, and yet Valerie heard a hint of a twang in his voice.

"Why, thank you." It had been more of a compliment than what she'd received from James.

He shifted his stance. "The liveryman is seeing to my wagon." He gave a backward nod. "I trust it will be safe in the stables. Most of my equipment—"

"Your wagon will be just fine," Valerie assured him. "Willie is a very capable attendant."

An awkward moment passed as Valerie tried to get a better view of the man standing there in the dim, candlelit entryway.

"I apologize for dripping rain on your floor." Mr. McCabe glanced down at the puddle forming beneath him. "That last downpour caught me."

"No need to apologize. But I imagine you'd like to get out of your wet clothes. Adalia here—" She inclined her head toward the maid. "—will show you to your room."

The man nodded his gratitude, taking hold of his baggage again. "It won't take me long to change. I take it dinner is to be a formal affair?" He glanced over her attire once more.

"Oh, well…" Of course he'd be expecting dinner. He was an invited guest. "Actually, there's a gala tonight at the home of some friends. You're more than welcome to join us." The offer rolled off her tongue before she could think better of it.

"That's a fine invite." She saw his smile in the partial darkness. "Yes, I'd like that." With one last mannerly bow, he shouldered his satchel again and followed Adalia up the stairs.

Valerie pivoted around, facing the parlor. She squared her shoulders and returned to James.

But her thoughts followed the new stranger up the stairs—who was he to her father? And why had he come to see him?

Two

HAD HE EVER SEEN EYES THAT PARTICULAR SHADE OF blue? Maybe. On a perfect Missouri summer day when the corn grew high in the fields and there wasn't a cloud in the sky.

Idiot! Ben admonished himself. He couldn't allow himself to get blindsided by another beautiful woman. Not like he had by Miss Gwyneth Merriweather. No sir. He wasn't about to lose his common sense over a woman a second time. He had to focus on finding his brother.

Ben's heart grew heavy. Luke went missing after the battle at Bull Run. Not a word from him. Nothing since. It wasn't like Luke, not to at least write to their mother in Jericho Junction.

He had to be alive. Luke's name hadn't appeared on any lists of the wounded or killed. Ben scoured each and every one of those printed columns the newspapers published. However, the question nagged him: If Luke was alive and well, why hadn't he tried to contact their parents in Missouri?

Setting his valise on the neatly made bed, he glanced around the tastefully decorated room. The Federal style furniture gave it a stately feel. As comfortable as these quarters appeared, he would be here for only a few days, just long enough to keep his promise to his father. Then he'd get back on the trail in his quest to find Luke while photographing battles and skirmishes with his partner Clint Culver.

He brought his mind back to the task at hand. Rummaging

through his things, he found his best clothes, noting that they were wrinkled beyond compare.

"Allow me, sir."

Ben turned to see a slim, well-dressed gentleman at the doorway of his bedroom. An educated light shone from the man's eyes.

"I'm Ephraim," he said in a formal tone. "Miss Fontaine sent me in case you'd need some assistance."

"Well…" Ben stared at the rumpled garments in his hand. "Looks like these have been through a war all their own."

"Not to worry, sir." The valet gave a stiff incline of his head. "I shall have your things pressed while you wash up."

"That'd be some kind of blessing. Thanks."

A smile tugged at the corners of Ephraim's thin lips. "You're welcome, sir." With that, the lanky man strode purposefully from the bedroom, garments slung over one forearm.

Ben stared at the empty doorway in the servant's wake. It seemed the valet was a hired man, just like the British maid. He hadn't seen any slaves around. Ben's opinion of the Fontaines went up a few pegs.

He crossed the expanse of the room to the polished mahogany chest of drawers on which the porcelain washbasin stood. Beside it lay a bar of soap, tied with a fabric ribbon. The small card attached to it read: *Cast thy burden upon the Lord, and he shall sustain thee.*

He smiled at the encouraging passage, trying to recall where in the Bible he'd read those words. Psalms? Then he took a whiff of the bar, and his senses came to life at the woodsy and spicy mix. He felt a second wind coming on.

"James, I can't abandon my father's guest."

"But—" James began to protest.

She sent him her sweetest smile, and he raised his hands in a gesture of defeat. "There's something else, James."

"Oh?" He arched his brows.

"I invited Mr. McCabe to come with us tonight."

"What?"

Adalia suddenly bustled into the room, carrying a tray containing a carafe of hot cider and two cups and saucers. Valerie let out a sigh of relief. She hoped James wouldn't argue further. Then the maid poured out some of the cinnamon-spiced mixture.

Sitting in the armchair, Valerie lifted the cup and saucer from the tray. "Some hot cider, James? Chastean's best."

He snorted. "A glass of bourbon would suit me just fine."

"I'm not serving bourbon."

Adalia snickered softly as she left the room.

Valerie decided to change the subject lest James become insistent. "I was reading in the newspaper that oil of every kind is getting scarce and that we need to do our part to conserve by using candles. It appears that most folks can't afford store-bought ones anymore, so the article suggested making one's own tapers." She sipped from her demitasse cup. "The article gave instructions on how to make good candles, and I cut out the recipe...just in case."

"You shouldn't be reading the newspaper," James groused. "It's not healthy for women to read such goings-on. Keeps them up all hours of the night fretting."

"I sleep quite soundly." Valerie arched a brow, wondering how he knew what kept women awake all night. No matter. Setting the cup in its saucer, she discounted the remark and continued to prattle on about everything from candle making to cannon fire in order to keep James from discussing either his taste for alcoholic beverages or courtship.

A long while later Mr. McCabe reappeared, and Valerie thought he made for an impressive figure, standing there in the doorway.

He wore a long, shiny black dress coat and waistcoat. His trousers were of a contrasting fabric, a charcoal gray in color, and he wore a crisp white shirt and a dark cravat tied in a floppy bow.

"I apologize for keeping you waiting." He gave her a polite half bow before entering the parlor.

"Quite all right." She took in the handsome stranger's straight blond hair, parted neatly to one side, and his eyes—why, his eyes were the exact color of her father's scotch. Golden brown.

A slow smile worked its way across his face, and Valerie realized he had caught her appraising him.

She lowered her gaze while an embarrassed blush spread across her face.

James cleared his throat. "Valerie, honey, where are your manners? Aren't you going to introduce us?" He strode toward her guest.

"Forgive me." She set aside her cup and stood. "Mr. McCabe, this is James Ladden, my escort for this evening and my, um…*friend*." She ignored James's sudden scowl then couldn't help noticing that their guest stood a good half a head taller than James. His shoulders were wider as well.

He extended his right hand in greeting. "A pleasure, Mr. Ladden."

"Yes…nice meeting you too, McCabe." There was no mistaking the clipped tone in James's voice.

"I hope I'm not imposing by coming along." Mr. McCabe looked from James to Valerie.

"Not in the least," she replied before James could answer.

"Well, good."

Was that amusement she saw in his gaze? Their mysterious guest moved to the hearth where he warmed his hands. She remembered his cold grip. "But if you're not up to it, Mr. McCabe, we could stay home. I could have our cook prepare—"

"Valerie." There was an edge to James's voice, and she wondered if their guest detected it too. But then he softened his tone. "The Donahues are expecting us, honey."

Mr. McCabe turned from the brick fireplace and eyed James, but he spoke to her. "Thank you, but I'm feeling just fine, Miss Fontaine, and looking forward to this evening."

The remark almost sounded like a challenge, but when she searched his features for traces of offense, she found none.

A soft light entered his eyes as his gaze came to rest on her, followed by a wry grin that tugged at the corners of his nicely shaped mouth.

"Valerie!"

The second warning in James's tone surprised her. Only too late Valerie realized she'd been ogling their guest again. Rude and inappropriate…it just wasn't like her.

Tearing her gaze away, she couldn't deny the man's inexplicable allure.

"Seriously," he repeated, "no need to stay in. I'd enjoy a celebration tonight."

"Well, then, it's settled." She pushed out a smile of her own.

Minutes later Adalia brought in their outerwear, and Valerie secured her velvet bonnet beneath her chin. As they left the house, the trusted maid whispered, "Have y'self some fun, dearie."

"Yes, I plan to."

They exchanged conspiratorial smiles.

The coachman assisted Valerie into the carriage, and, once seated, she began the task of straightening her skirts. Mr. McCabe climbed in next and seated himself beside her. He shifted one way then the other in an effort to make himself more comfortable. Valerie could feel the roughness of his woolen overcoat as it brushed against her forearm. He smelled of the cedar and sage, one of her mother's more masculine-scented soaps that he evidently used to freshen up. She inhaled again, hoping for a second whiff. The scent was one of Valerie's favorites for men. Mama had come up with the concoction of herbs as a surprise for Father, although he never became fond of it. He preferred a more subtle and sweet fragrance that he acquired from Paris.

"I hope I'm not squishing the life out of you, Miss Fontaine." Mr. McCabe flashed a charming grin.

"Not at all." In fact, the warmth emanating from his body proved far more effective at quelling the night's chill than her cape.

James boarded and, sitting across from them, frowned at the arrangement. "Look here, McCabe—"

"We're so glad you could join us," Valerie put in quickly. "Isn't that right, James?" Her father would be appalled if he learned James acted rudely to an invited houseguest. "*Right, James?*" She repeated the words with a bit more force.

He pressed his lips together in acquiescence.

They rode for a good mile in silence until Valerie couldn't stand it anymore. She began making small talk with Mr. McCabe since James seemed to be brooding.

"The weather has really been quite awful."

"I know." A note of amusement carried in his voice.

"Of course you do. You said you've been traveling all day."

"Mm-hmm. My partner, Clint Culver, and I have been following various Confederate regiments all over the Confederate States."

"Do tell." James leaned forward, looking suddenly very interested. "Which troops?"

Mr. McCabe listed them by name. "Third Regiment, Arkansas, Second Georgia Infantry, although those men are just getting organized…"

"You're a Confederate?"

"No. But I'm not a Federal either. I'm a freelance photographer, and I'm looking for my brother. He went missing after the battle at Bull Run."

"That's awful!" Valerie couldn't imagine the angst he felt. "You have no idea as to his whereabouts?"

Mr. McCabe shook his head.

"Is he in the infantry?" James asked as he leaned forward on his knees. The carriage rocked to and fro.

"No, he's a preacher. We were traveling together. My partner, Clint Culver, his wife, Luke, and me. We...Clint and I were photographing the troops, and Luke was ministering to the men's spiritual needs—when we lost touch. Somehow we got separated."

"Hmm..." James sat back, appearing thoughtful.

"I'm ever so sorry to hear it, Mr. McCabe," Valerie said. "I pray you find him soon."

"Prayers appreciated." He turned to look at her, the intimacy of his gaze causing her face to flame.

James cleared his throat. "So tell me what you've heard in the field, McCabe."

"Heard plenty." He looked across the way at him. "What sort of information are you looking for?"

"Nothing in particular. But surely you've conversed with military officers if you've photographed them. What do they have to say?"

"Could we please talk about something else?" Valerie asked. "I'm tired of hearing about the war. It feels like the end of the world sometimes, and it scares me." She gazed into the surrounding darkness. "But I don't want to think about that tonight. Tonight I plan to enjoy myself." She shifted slightly, her arm pressed tightly against Mr. McCabe's. "Besides, I'm in the company of two handsome gentlemen. I'll be the envy of every lady at the party."

"Well, I'd say so." The lilt to Mr. McCabe's voice said he'd found her remark amusing. "With or without us 'handsome gentlemen.'"

Valerie blushed at the compliment as she noted James's look of challenge aimed at their guest. Was he jealous? Angry? Both? She couldn't be sure.

The carriage continued to roll through the streets of the neighborhood, finally turning onto the lane that led to the Donahues' expansive home. Despite the rain and fog, candlelight shone like beacons from the tall front windows. Live oaks lined the circular brick drive, their gnarled limbs forming an eerie-looking canopy.

At last the conveyance pulled to a halt at the front entrance, and Valerie alighted with the assistance of the coachman. She gazed around the first floor gallery, admiring the bows of holly and the large evergreen wreaths. How she used to enjoy decorating for the holidays with Mama—

She quickly pushed back the onslaught of memories.

Mr. McCabe and James climbed from the carriage, and the three of them made their way up the stairs to the portico. At the door they were greeted with hugs and handshakes and ushered into the house.

Valerie breathed in awe as she took in the foyer with its tinsel and glitter. Her gaze swept over the evergreen bows tied to the balustrade with red velvet ribbons and the three shimmering Christmas trees that stood aglow with candles on every branch.

"Well, Valerie Fontaine…" Elicia Donahue, dressed in red silk with white satin trim, strolled over to greet her. "I'm glad you could come to our party tonight."

Valerie embraced her longtime friend. They hadn't seen each other in almost a year and a half, and while Valerie wrote often, Elicia wasn't in the habit of corresponding.

"Everything looks so lovely," Valerie said. "Your family did an expert job with the decorations this year."

"Why, thank you." A pleased smile stretched across Elicia's face before her hazel eyes moved to James. "You handsome devil, how nice to see you again."

He grinned while a spark of mischief entered his gaze, and he bowed over Elicia's gloved hand.

"And who might this be?" she asked, taking a step toward Mr. McCabe.

"Benjamin McCabe at your service." He too gave a courteous bow.

"Mr. McCabe is an acquaintance of my father," Valerie explained to her friend who had now locked arms with her. "He'll be staying with us for a bit."

"How very nice." Elicia smiled. "Welcome to our home, Mr. McCabe."

"Thank you kindly," he replied with another of his lazy grins that Valerie found quite charming.

"Well, now if y'all will come with me," she drawled, "there are more people to meet and greet." Elicia showed them to the bedecked ballroom where a small ensemble of musicians was playing a lively waltz. As they entered the room, several other friends came up to greet Valerie. She hadn't seen them since returning from school.

Wistfulness stole over Valerie as she watched men and women, dressed in all their finery, dance beneath crystal chandeliers. Several Confederate soldiers in uniform took turns around the dance floor, their lovely ladies held close to their hearts.

"My, my, this is a sight for my country boy eyes," Mr. McCabe remarked.

Valerie turned to him. "You've never attended a ball?"

"I've attended plenty, but none like this." He turned to her. "This is quite the elaborate affair."

"I'll take that as a compliment." Elicia regarded him with an appreciative glance.

A moment of hesitation followed. Valerie sensed that Elicia wanted to say more to Mr. McCabe, but his attention was caught up in the revelry.

"Elicia, honey," James said. "I think I see Gabe over there, flirting with Iris Hackelbarth."

"What!" Her expression indicated her sudden displeasure. "Where is that scoundrel?"

"I'll escort you," James said. "Perhaps we will locate some champagne on the way too."

"You're teasing me."

James chuckled.

"I should have known." Elicia glanced at Valerie. "Some people never change, and it appears James is one of them."

"Hmm…" So had she misjudged him too?

Holding one of Elicia's gloved hands, James encircled her waist with the other arm and led her across the room.

"Some escort," Mr. McCabe murmured near her ear.

"Some friend," Valerie replied on a tart note.

She glanced at Mr. McCabe, and they shared a laugh. It didn't bother her in the least that James and Elicia had strode off together. "Are you hungry?" she finally asked. She pointed out the long table at the far side of the ballroom that was piled high with all manner of delectable foods.

"You must have read my mind, Miss Fontaine. I'm starved."

"Well, please, help yourself. I'll find us a table." She gazed off in James's direction. "I'm sure James will be a gentleman and make up a plate for me before he joins us." Her words belied the wondering inside.

"All right, then. I'll see you at the table." After a polite incline of his head, he took off across the room.

Valerie just stood there, watching him go. What was it about him that captivated her so?

As Ben helped himself to a mountainous plate of food, he kept a watchful eye on a certain Mr. James Ladden. There was something about the man that prickled the hair on Ben's neck. Even now as Ladden stood talking with three other rather dubious-looking men, Ben had a hunch they weren't planning a church picnic.

He worked his way down to the end of the table where the red-haired dandy and his friends stood. Delectable aromas of roasted meats caused his stomach to protest its emptiness all the more. Still he took his time and strained to hear what the well-dressed group was up to. Ladden drank liberally from an elegant long-stemmed glass.

Moving on down the table, Ben had just added a piece of corn bread to his plate when the name "Allan Pinkerton" reached his ears. That couldn't be good. Although he'd never met the man, he knew of Pinkerton's detective work before the war broke out. Why would Ladden and his three friends be discussing one of the nation's top detectives?

Ben paused to study them. They were clearly up to something.

THREE

VALERIE SPOTTED A FEW OPEN TABLES AND MADE her way through the ballroom, greeting friends and acquaintances as they passed. She paused once to converse with Mrs. Ethel Tyler, who'd been a dear friend of Mama. Then, of course, she had to exchange pleasantries with Mr. Grimshaw, one of Father's associates.

At long last Valerie arrived at a round table covered with a festive red cloth. An older gentleman in a gray uniform with gold braiding on the sleeves and a regal-looking woman who Valerie guessed to be his wife were seated at one side.

"Excuse me, but are these three seats taken?"

"Why, no, miss." The older soldier smiled from beneath a bushy gray mustache as he stood. "Please join us."

Valerie smiled. But before introductions could be made, Mr. McCabe showed up, balancing two plates of food and two glasses of punch.

"Allow me." Setting his load on the table, he held out the chair for her.

"Thank you."

"It appears Mr. Ladden got sidetracked," he explained, "so I took the liberty of selecting from the buffet for you."

"How kind of you."

Her mouth watered as the aroma of roasted pork, oyster dressing, and spicy ratatouille reached her nostrils.

"There's plenty more where that came from. I haven't seen such a hearty spread since the war began."

He silently prayed over his food, and Valerie watched him covertly as she did the same.

"You say you're from Missouri?" she asked after they'd finished saying grace.

Mr. McCabe nodded as he chewed his first bite. "Born and raised."

"And your father—what line of work is he in?"

"He's a preacher."

"And your mother?" She pressed her lips together, hoping she wasn't asking too many questions.

Mr. McCabe replied with a fond smile, then said, "Ma works around the clock trying to keep my brothers, sisters, and me in line."

"You're fortunate. I never had any siblings. I used to dream of having a sister." Valerie sipped her punch. "Never happened, though."

"Tell you the truth, there are times I wished I was an only child. My two brothers and two sisters sure could wear my patience as thin as onion skin, especially my baby sister, Sarah."

"Really? How so?"

Valerie leaned forward, intent on listening to him.

"One time," he began, "she wandered off and we all went searching for her. Looked for hours. Turns out she spent the afternoon in a neighbor's barn, playing with a litter of kittens. That was when she was only five years old. Her wanderings have gotten worse now that she's a young lady of sixteen."

Valerie couldn't suppress a grin as she enjoyed the image of the big, happy family. "I suppose you miss her and all your family terribly."

"That I do."

Hearing him speak about his family caused Valerie to feel drawn to Mr. Benjamin McCabe. He had what she'd always longed for: a family. She paused, considering her next question.

"So, if you don't mind my asking, why come here to New Orleans—why visit my father?"

He swallowed a bite of food. "A favor to my father. He's had a burden for your family ever since your mother died."

She tamped down her melancholy and focused on her present company. "So how exactly did your father meet mine anyway?"

"You don't know?"

Valerie shook her head.

"Do you know Maxwell Elliot?"

"Pastor Elliot? Of course. He's the pastor of the church I attend."

"He's also married to my mother's favorite second cousin. Growing up, Ma and my cousin Amanda were like sisters. So my folks visit the Elliots every so often."

Valerie suddenly made the connection with what her father had told her earlier in the evening. "And your father was in New Orleans when my mother took ill last June."

Mr. McCabe inclined his head, his expression somber. "I'm very sorry for your loss."

"Thank you." She managed a tiny but grateful grin. She sensed he understood how it felt to lose a loved one. "Will you tell me about your missing brother? He's a preacher, you said, like your father?"

"Luke's a chaplain. Last year when Clint and I headed out to document the war, he traveled with us to help those who needed it." He paused and seemed to select his next words with care. "That day, at Bull Run, there were so many—so many men who required my brother's services that we got separated." Mr. McCabe shook his head.

"That was months ago!"

"Five months and ten days, to be exact."

Valerie's heart ached for him. "Perhaps your brother got captured and is alive and well."

"Didn't get captured from what I've been able to find out, and I know he's not dead. I combed that entire battlefield."

That had to have been a gruesome task. She laid down her fork.

"Forgive me, Miss Fontaine."

She glanced up to see an expression of remorse on his face.

"I didn't mean to spoil your evening. You wanted to have fun tonight, and here I am talking of such things."

She gave him a reassuring smile. The subject of his missing brother obviously weighed heavily on his mind. A moment passed between them when their senses were filled with only each other. They no longer heard the din of laughter in the room, the orchestra, or the rustle of silk skirts as dancers twirled by their table. Valerie saw the moisture gathering in his eyes, and her heart went out to him. Reaching across the table, she gave his hand a squeeze, and he replied with an appreciative grin.

"So…" he said after a long moment, breaking the spell. He looked at his plate of food.

"So…" Valerie picked up the cue. "You mentioned you're a photographer. Tell me more about your work."

Mr. McCabe seemed grateful for the chance to continue their discussion, albeit on a more generic note. "As I said, I'm documenting the war with photographs. I've written a few articles that have appeared in several newspapers as well." A wry, almost shy smile played across his lips.

"How impressive." Valerie meant it sincerely.

"You're most gracious." His smile broadened. "There's a regiment in the area I'd like to photograph as I keep looking for

Luke. So I figured I'd check in on your family for Pa and accomplish a little work of my own in the process."

"We're glad you're here, Mr. McCabe."

"I appreciate the hospitality."

Their gazes met again, and Valerie's heart beat out the most unusual rhythm.

At that moment, the older gentleman at the table cleared his throat. "I beg your pardon, but I couldn't help overhearing...you say you're a photographer, son?"

Mr. McCabe gave a nod. "That's right."

The silver-haired gent in decorated uniform regarded him for several long moments. "And...are you for hire?"

"Well, that depends, sir." Mr. McCabe set down his fork.

The older man leaned forward and grinned. "Allow me to introduce myself. I'm Colonel William LaPorte."

"Benjamin McCabe." He stretched his arm across the table. "Glad to meet you."

The men shook hands, but Valerie was stunned by the revelation. Colonel LaPorte? Why, everyone knew the colonel was an important man with the Confederate Army!

Colonel LaPorte produced a *carte de visite* from the inside pocket of his uniform jacket. The small business card had the colonel's photograph on one side and his contact information on the other. "If you don't mind coming to my home tomorrow even though it's a holiday, let's meet at ten o'clock sharp. I have a business proposition for you."

Mr. McCabe seemed to think it over before replying with a nod. "I'll do that."

"Good." With that, the colonel returned his attention to his wife. "Shall we dance, Gertrude?"

"Oh, yes. Let's." The elegantly clad woman stood, and the couple waltzed off.

"Do you realize what has just happened?" Valerie leaned toward Mr. McCabe, smiling.

He shook his head, pocketing the visiting card.

"You were conversing with none other than *the* Colonel LaPorte. He has direct connections with Robert E. Lee. Why, it's even rumored that the LaPortes have entertained him in their home. Imagine it. Robert E. Lee!"

"Is that right?"

"Have you ever met him?"

"Can't say as I have." A lazy grin spread across Mr. McCabe's face. "But to tell you the truth, right now I'm more interested in the company I'm presently keeping. Somehow I've been doing all the talking. How 'bout telling me about Miss Valerie Fontaine?"

"Me?" She couldn't help the blush that flamed up her cheeks. "There isn't much to tell, I'm afraid."

"I don't believe it. I detect a spark of something...maybe adventure in your eyes."

"Perhaps." The blush remained. "Still, most men prefer to talk about the war or politics or...horses."

He chuckled. "Reckon I'm not 'most men.'"

Valerie found his manner quite beguiling. "All right, then." She wet her lips. "It's just my father and me. Most recently, I have returned home from finishing school, although my father isn't happy about it." The lack of welcome still hurt. "Unbeknownst to me, he wanted me to stay in Virginia. Too late now. Here I am."

"Why did you leave?"

Valerie took a few moments to think about the answer. "My reasons are somewhat complicated. Can I tell you about them another time?"

"Of course." Mr. McCabe mulled over what she'd told him. "But your father isn't happy to have you home? Hmm...maybe he wanted you to stay put for your own good. Skirmishes are breaking out all over Virginia."

"You might be right." Valerie sipped from the crystal punch glass. "Or maybe I remind him too much of Mama. We did look very much alike."

"She must've been very beautiful."

The compliment wasn't lost on Valerie. She brought her gaze up in time to see a light of sincerity glimmering in Mr. McCabe's golden brown eyes. "You're very kind to say so."

"Miss Fontaine, I know you don't know me—" His words were softly spoken, meant for her ears alone. "—but let's get something straight between us here and now: I never say anything I don't mean."

"All right." Valerie didn't quite know what to make of his candor. She stared into his handsome face, feeling overcome once more. "I guess that's good to know." Another waltz began to play, and James appeared out of nowhere. He grabbed Valerie's hand, causing her to gasp, and promptly whisked her onto the dance floor.

"James, really! I didn't even get a chance to excuse myself from the table."

"I don't like him." He deployed a scowl toward the table at which Mr. McCabe still sat. "I don't want you talking to him."

"Who are you to tell me who I can speak to?" When he didn't answer, Valerie said, "We were engaging in polite conversation, if you must know, and you can be polite too, if for nothing else than propriety's sake."

James ignored the reprimand. "He's not like us, Valerie. He's as unrefined as a stalk of sugarcane."

"But just as sweet."

James's dour expression said he didn't appreciate the retort. "Enough!"

Valerie pressed her lips together. She smelled the bourbon on

James's breath. If he behaved anything like Father did when he drank his scotch, Valerie saw no point in attempting meaningful conversation. If so many people weren't around, she'd end this dance with him right now. However, she'd hate to cause a scene.

A sudden smile stretched across his face. "Did I tell you how lovely you look tonight?" He tightened his hold around her waist.

She stepped back, seeking to put some distance between them.

"You've caught the eye of every man in this room, and—"

Glimpsing over his shoulder, Valerie hoped she'd catch Benjamin McCabe's gaze. But he no longer sat at the table. She wished he would cut in.

"—and you've won my heart."

"James, you shouldn't say such things." Valerie stepped back, surprised by his admission.

"Look at me." James halted right there in the middle of the dance floor. "Ever since you've come home from finishing school, I—"

"James, please, not here!" Her gaze darted around. Had anyone overheard?

"You're right. This is neither the time nor the place."

They began dancing again. Valerie wished the waltz would end. Then before she realized what he was doing, James whirled them to the doors that led out to the balcony. Pushing them open, he escorted her outside into the chilly night air.

"I'll catch my death out here."

"I'll keep you warm."

"James, really. I should go back inside." She inched away from him.

He ignored her request and moved toward her. "I'd like my New Year's Eve kiss early."

"You'll get no kiss from me." Valerie took another step back and bumped into the house. She could feel the cold brick of the house against her bare shoulders. "If I snag my gown because of your buffoonery, I'll—"

James lunged at her, cutting off further reply. Holding her head between his hands, he pressed his lips hard against hers. Repulsed, Valerie thrashed until she broke free. She raised her hand and the *crack* of her palm meeting his cheek sliced through the thick, night air.

Flabbergasted, James could only gape at her, but it was all the time she needed to make her escape. Flinging open the double French doors, Valerie lifted her skirts and fled across the ballroom's polished floor.

FOUR

ALERIE'S BODY TREMBLED AFTER THE INCIDENT outside. She leaned against the wall outside the ballroom and struggled to catch her breath. She'd never been so angry in all her life! Her jaw clenched. James and his insolence—just wait until Father heard about all this! He might be mourning Mama's death in a way she couldn't understand, but she was still his daughter. Father wouldn't stand for it when he learned of James's advances.

Across the foyer Valerie spotted her friend Caroline Bigby waving her into a small circle of women who were gathered in a whispering circle. She willed her shaky legs to move toward them.

"Why, Valerie, it's so good to have you back from school!" Caroline hugged her. "Have you seen Anna Joy Harrison?" Caroline brought a gloved hand to the side of her mouth and raised her tawny brows. "She's wearing a hideous creation."

"I–I haven't seen Anna Joy yet." Valerie glanced over her shoulder to make sure James wasn't on her heels. Reassured he was nowhere in sight, she willed her composure to return.

"Are you all right, Valerie? You look as though you've had a shock." Violet Drumming took her hand. "And you're positively pale."

"I–I'm fine." She smoothed the flounces on her skirt. "Everything's fine."

Awkward seconds ticked by, and then from the corner of her eye, Valerie spotted Benjamin McCabe. He stood near the ballroom's entryway watching her. She smiled and waved him over.

"Ladies, I want you all to meet my father's houseguest."

When he was beside her, he bowed in a mannerly way while Valerie made the introductions.

"You're a photographer?" Violet cooed.

"Yes, ma'am," Mr. McCabe replied easily.

"That's fascinating!"

"How very interesting!" Caroline added, touching a hand to his forearm lightly.

"I saw you talking to Colonel LaPorte," Cherie's dimples deepened with her coquettish smile. "Must've been something important."

Mr. McCabe loosened his tie and his face reddened.

Valerie found his reaction quite amusing. But she also found her friends' behavior rather simpering, and she realized she had very little in common with these young women anymore.

Before long, the other men noticed the way their escorts had flocked around Mr. McCabe. Within minutes they came, one by one, to claim their respective ladies for the next waltz.

Mr. McCabe turned to her. "I'm, um, not a dancer." He sounded apologetic.

"That's all right. I believe I've had my fill for the evening."

"Speaking of…where's your escort, Miss Fontaine?" His tone wasn't mocking but held a note of concern.

"I have no idea." If she never saw James again, it'd be too soon!

Mr. McCabe reached out and touched something on the back of her evening gown. "Your dress is torn."

"What?" Horrified, she strained to look over her shoulder and glimpse the damage. The satin trim had been pulled away from the silk bodice, no doubt a result of James's beastly behavior. "I'll fetch my shawl and perhaps no one will notice." She stared up into Mr. McCabe's face and saw the compassionate slant of his eyes.

"Back in Missouri we have names for men who manhandle ladies."

"I call them cads, plain and simple."

His sudden grin became a chuckle. "I reckon that's fitting enough."

"But…" She tipped her head and frowned. "How did you know?"

All traces of humor disappeared from his features. "I saw the two of you leave the ballroom through the balcony doors. When you came back in looking like a frightened doe, I knew something was wrong." Mr. McCabe raised his brows. "Next thing I see is Ladden sporting a fine red handprint on his face. It was rather obvious."

"I'm so embarrassed." Valerie could only imagine the sordid whispers making their rounds at this very moment.

"Wasn't your fault." He inclined his head gallantly.

A surge of relief coursed through her veins. "Thank you, Mr. McCabe."

"Please, call me by my given name."

"Benjamin." Valerie liked the way it sounded. Strong. Commanding. Her smile was unfettered now. "It's refreshing to be in the company of a true gentleman."

He extended his arm, and she threaded her hand around his elbow. He bent his head close to hers. "It's almost midnight," he said, "and I understand from Colonel LaPorte that the Donahues imported fireworks from China before the Union set up their blockades."

"Yes, the firecrackers are a tradition here on New Year's Eve."

They strolled into the ballroom, and Valerie collected her satin shawl, slipping it around her shoulders. Arm in arm they walked to the far side of the room where other guests had gathered. The heavy burgundy drapes had been pulled back, revealing the balcony. Beyond it, although unseen in the darkness, lay the terrace and the rest of the Donahues' acreage.

The rain had ceased for the time being, and those with sturdier dispositions stood outside, but Valerie and Benjamin chose to watch the fireworks in comfort from inside the house. Benjamin pulled over a couple of chairs, and together they oohed and aahed at the loud, spectacular, and sparkly display overhead.

James suddenly reappeared, and Valerie turned her back to him. She'd entertained the notion of asking the Donahues if she and Benjamin could borrow a conveyance so they wouldn't have to abide his company all the way home.

"The carriage is waiting for us." James took her gloved hand and bowed over it. "I promise to mind my manners."

She sent a questioning look to Benjamin.

"I'll make sure he behaves himself." He gave James a stern look, which was met with a glare.

James softened his features when he gazed back at Valerie. "You can't very well walk home."

"All right." It wasn't worth the argument and the effort it would take to procure another carriage.

Outside, a damp chill lingered in the night air as they climbed into the landau. James swung himself onto the padded bench beside her. Valerie cringed at his boorishness. Benjamin seated himself across from them, and while she would have preferred to sit next to him, Valerie decided from this vantage point she could study him undetected.

He lazed back on the leather upholstery. "Nice party."

James replied with a derisive snort.

Valerie ignored him. "We're glad you came, Mr. Mc—" She paused. "*Benjamin.*" James tensed at her side. She suppressed a grin. Served him right for being such a rake!

The carriage pulled up and parked in front of the Fontaines' townhouse. James jumped out and helped Valerie alight.

He held onto her hand longer than necessary. "Valerie, honey, how 'bout I come up and keep you company for a while?"

"I don't think so." She pulled free from his grasp and made her way to the front door. Behind her she heard the two men's voices, although she couldn't discern what they said. She hoped Benjamin was versing James on the basics of being a gentleman.

In the end, James went on his way.

Adalia greeted Valerie at the door, her green eyes wide with curiosity. "Did you have fun tonight?"

"Well, except for one, um, unfortunate incident—" Valerie pulled off her cape and placed it in the maid's waiting arms. "—I had a perfectly lovely time."

"What happened, dearie?"

"James behaved like his old self. Need I say more?" Valerie shook her head. "I thought he'd changed. He hasn't."

"The little monster," Adalia said. "Are you all right?"

"Yes. I'm fine now."

"That's a relief."

Benjamin entered the house.

"Good evening, sir. Did you enjoy yourself at the Donahues'?"

"Sure did." He closed the door behind him. "The company was unforgettable—" He inclined his head toward Valerie. His gaze locked on hers for several long moments before he looked back at Adalia. "And those firecrackers were something to behold."

"They were something to be heard as well." Adalia sent a glance upward. "Shook the whole house, they did!"

As they ambled toward the parlor, Adalia continued her tirade. "I'll never know why that Charles Donahue has to blast those things off every year."

"It's a tradition," Valerie said.

"Bah! It's a wonder those Yankee ships darkening our horizon didn't start firing back."

"Hmm, good point." Benjamin shrugged out of his dress coat.

"Well, Colonel LaPorte was in attendance." She removed her gloves. "He wouldn't have allowed any fireworks if there was a danger to the city."

"Another good point." Benjamin chuckled, folding his coat over his arm.

"If you say so, dearie, but those things nearly shattered y' mama's good crystal." Adalia lifted a brow and changed the subject. "Would y' like some of your special nighttime tea before retiring?"

Valerie nodded, and after Adalia sauntered off, she turned to explain to Benjamin. "The tea is a blend of herbs my mother grew in her garden and then dried. When brewed, they make for a very soothing mixture that helps a body relax and sleep."

"Thank you, but I won't need anything to help me sleep. In fact, I'd best say g'night right now."

Valerie felt a stab of disappointment.

He walked toward her and took her hand. For a good half minute he looked deeply into her eyes, and Valerie thought he intended to take her in his arms and kiss her. She wouldn't have minded it a bit either. But instead he brought her hand to his lips. "Miss Fontaine…" He placed a kiss on the backs of her fingers. "Thank you for a lovely evening."

"Y–you're very welcome." His touch sent tingles up her arm and straight to her heart.

"I'll look forward to seeing you in the morning."

He strode from the parlor just as Adalia returned with the polished silver tray and matching tea service. After setting it down, she regarded Valerie askance. "I'd say you've got 'smitten' written all over y' pretty face."

Valerie released an audible sigh. "There goes a gentleman of a most valiant kind."

"Mm-hm, I was right." The maid put her hands on her ample hips. "S.M.I.T.T.E.N."

Ben awakened to slivers of sunshine seeping through the wooden slats of the tall shuttered windows. A grin tugged at the corners of his mouth when he realized the rain had ceased.

1862. This year he would find Luke!

A knock sounded, and he pushed himself up on his elbows. "Yes?"

The door creaked open, and the slim, well-dressed man he'd met last evening entered the spacious room. "It's me, sir. Ephraim, the valet."

"Of course. Please, come in."

"I'm here to draw your bath."

"Appreciate it." Ben combed his fingers through his thick hair, thinking he hadn't experienced such lavish treatment since leaving Boston. He could sure get used to it, but as soon as he met his obligations here and at the Elliots', he'd visit that nearby regiment with Clint and Em and continue his search for Luke.

A good hour later, after he'd soaked in a tub of hot water, he felt like a new man as he dressed for the day. Since the War Between the States began, Ben, his partner, Clint Culver, and Luke had been living out of two wagons that doubled as portable darkrooms. They had taken many a cold bath along riverbanks and washed up with water heated over open campfires.

He smiled. Clint and Em were probably enjoying their time alone together at one of the local hotels. They'd been praying for time alone, so they decided to treat themselves to a stay at the St.

Charles Hotel. Pricey, but Clint and Em deserved it. Besides, it'd be two nights there tops.

Collecting the worn leather-covered Bible from the nightstand, Ben made his way to the dining room. During his growing-up years the day always began with a reading from the Scriptures. Sometimes duty or crisis only allowed for a few verses, but he knew from experience that God's Word held him firm—even kept him sane in these turbulent times.

"Good morning, sir." The plump maid straightened as he entered the dining room. "Miss Valerie will be down shortly."

Anticipation surged through him. He'd noticed something fragile and vulnerable about her. Those qualities drew upon his protective nature—of course, his protective instincts hadn't helped Luke any…

He shoved aside the guilt that seemed a constant companion ever since Luke's disappearance.

"Breakfast is at eight o'clock."

Ben checked his pocket watch and saw it was fifteen minutes past seven. "I don't mind the wait."

"I appreciate it, sir. In the meantime, might I fetch y' some coffee or tea?"

He pursed his lips in momentary thought. "Would that be *real* coffee?"

"All the way from South America." She winked at him. "Or so I'm told."

He grinned. "Is that right?" Ben thought of the troops he'd been traveling with. They typically used more chicory root than roasted coffee beans in order to stretch their supply. He had a hunch Sergeant Smith, the cook, often threw in a handful of dirt too. Tasted like it, anyhow. "I'd welcome a cup of good strong coffee. Thank you, ma'am."

She nodded and bustled from the room. Ben took a seat at one end of the long, white linen-covered table and turned his Bible to the Gospel of St. Matthew. Minutes later the maid appeared carrying a silver tray that held a polished coffeepot and porcelain cup and saucer. As she poured out some of the steaming brew, Ben savored its rich aroma.

"There y' be, sir," she said in her British clip.

"Again, my thanks." He sipped. "Mmm…I haven't tasted coffee of this quality in a long time."

"Oh, it'd be the best." Adalia pulled her thick shoulders back, a proud expression on her face. "The master of the house is quite selective. He personally oversees his incoming shipments."

"I'm glad to be the beneficiary of his diligence."

The maid's green eyes danced with amusement.

At the mention of his host's name, he couldn't help asking, "Will Mr. Fontaine be joining us for breakfast this morning? I'm looking forward to meeting him."

"Ah…" Humor fled her features. "Well, y' see, the master's a busy man, but he might drop in. There's no tellin' with him. Now if you'll excuse me, sir."

"Of course." Ben watched the woman scurry from the room then returned his attention to the Bible, turning to the New Testament to mark the New Year. He drank leisurely from his coffee cup and occasionally paused to pray.

By the time Valerie entered the dining room, he'd nearly finished the sixth chapter.

"Good morning." Her voice sounded as bright as the sunshine.

Ben stood. "Miss Fontaine." He couldn't help but notice that her less formal attire, a green and black plaid dress with a wide, ivory crocheted collar, was still far fancier than anything his sisters ever wore.

Her gaze fell to his Bible. "I hope I'm not interrupting."

"Not at all." Ben moved around the table and held out her chair.

She sat down and he caught a faint whiff of lavender...lavender and something else. Something both sweet and strong. Then her gaze caught his, and she gave him a smile. Just as last night, Ben felt intoxicated by her presence.

"You look lovely this morning."

A pretty pink hue appeared in her cheeks. "Why, thank you."

He reclaimed his own seat at the table.

"I trust you slept well."

"I did, indeed." Ben grinned and she returned the gesture.

Adalia appeared with another silver service, but this time it contained tea. She poured out, and as Valerie sipped from the cup, Ben took note of the way her slender fingers curled around the fragile dishware.

"Breakfast'll be a tad late, Miss," Adalia said. "Chastean's little boy took ill again and she had to leave for a bit, but she's back now."

"Quite all right. Please tell Chastean that I hope her son is feeling better soon."

After an efficient nod, the maid left the room once more.

Ben turned to Valerie again. "Your staff is hired."

"That's correct. My father doesn't own slaves. Adalia came from London, Ephraim from New York City. Chastean, our cook, and Willie, our head liveryman, are free blacks."

Ben respected Valerie's father already. He'd never got along with the idea that one man could own another.

Valerie's eyes roamed over the Bible again. "I wouldn't mind a bit if you read aloud while we're waiting for our meal."

Ben gladly acquiesced. "I was just finishing chapter six in the Book of Matthew." He found his place at verse twenty-six and read to the end. When he finished, he looked up and caught Valerie's gaze. Her expression seemed a mix of sadness and confusion.

"Anything wrong, Miss Fontaine?"

"Well, I...I..." She blinked and took to studying her teacup. "I wonder why God, who supposedly only wants what's best for me, allowed my mother to die and leave me all alone. I miss her terribly."

Ben stretched his arm across the table and placed his hand on the top of hers. "But you're not alone. You have your father—and your heavenly Father."

"Oh, please don't misunderstand. I love Jesus, and I trust Him with all of my soul. It's just...seeing how Mama's death has affected my father." She shook her dark head of curls. "I have a hard time understanding what good could come out of it."

"Your father is still taking your mother's death badly?"

Valerie nodded as her eyes brimmed with tears.

"Well, we'll keep praying for him," he said, wishing his brother Luke was here to offer his chaplain's wisdom.

Running one of her graceful fingers around the rim of her teacup, Valerie inclined her head. Her reflective, sad expression remained.

"I sense there's something else."

"Yes." Her small shoulders sagged as she exhaled. "Lately, my f–father has...well, Father is..."

"Miss Fontaine, has your father taken ill?"

"Not ill, exactly." She lifted her gaze and looked beyond him. Her eyes suddenly widened, and Ben turned to see the very topic of their conversation stroll into the dining room. The man was impeccably dressed in tan trousers, a matching waistcoat, and a starched white shirt.

"We were just talking about you, Father." Valerie's voice held a nervous lilt. "Our guest wondered how you fared."

"I've been better."

Ben stood and extended his right hand. "Benjamin McCabe, sir."

"Nice to meet you." With a quick handshake and a curt nod of his dark head, Mr. Fontaine moved to the far end of the table.

"Father, we had a marvelous time at the Donahues' last night," Valerie began as the maid brought in their meal. She set down a serving bowl filled with scrambled eggs, followed by a platter of meats and cheeses surrounded by a variety of sliced breads. "I wish you'd have been there."

Ben didn't miss the hooded glance of warning Mr. Fontaine sent his daughter.

She sipped her tea.

Ben surveyed the food around him. "My, but this would feed an entire regiment."

Valerie smiled. "I hope you're hungry."

"Sure am."

Fontaine stabbed his fork into a slice of ham.

"Shall I ask the blessing?" Ben offered. Valerie folded her hands, bowed her head, and Edward had the good grace to set aside his fork.

Once Ben gave thanks, the meal commenced in earnest. He put a bite of the fluffiest eggs he'd tasted into his mouth. Then he bit into a slice of sweet bread. "Delicious."

Valerie sent him a pleased smile. Then she glanced at her father. "Benjamin is a photographer. Isn't that interesting? He's been traveling with our brave men, documenting their progress. He's also looking for his brother Luke, who's been missing ever since the battle last July."

"How unfortunate about your brother. You have my sympathies, Mr. McCabe." Fontaine looked a tad wary as he drank his coffee. "Was your brother a Confederate soldier?"

"No, his views are neutral, as are mine, and Luke *is* a chaplain." Ben grinned. "I don't like referring to my brother in the past tense."

"Of course. Forgive me." Fontaine took another drink from his cup. "And why have you taken a neutral stance?"

"The journalist in me needs to be objective."

"Ah, of course." The silence that followed stretched into awkward discomfort.

Valerie spoke up again. "I must say, Colonel LaPorte was quite impressed with Benjamin's occupation, Father. In fact, the two are meeting this morning."

Fontaine stiffened. "Meeting with LaPorte, you say?" His dark gaze shifted from his daughter to Ben.

"Yes, the colonel seemed eager last night to speak to Benjamin about some possible work."

"I see." His gaze fixed on Ben. "About photographic work?"

"I'm assuming so." Ben shrugged. "I guess I'll find that out today."

Fontaine seemed to consider the information as he took another drink of coffee. "You'll have to let me know. I'd be interested to hear about this possible new opportunity of yours."

"Certainly. Do you know the colonel, sir?"

"I know of him. He commands about ten companies, all heavy artillery, and they're stationed at Forts Jackson and St. Phillip."

"The garrisons guarding the mouth of the Mississippi."

"Correct." He eyed him over the rim of his coffee cup. "You're very well informed, I see."

"An occupational must for me."

Fontaine grinned. "Then you'll understand that because I'm in the shipping business, I'm familiar with La Porte and his troops."

"Makes sense." Had he known that Edward Fontaine was in the shipping business? Pa must have said something to that effect. And speaking of Pa… "May I broach a different topic, Mr. Fontaine?"

"By all means."

"If you'll recall my telegraph, I'm here on behalf of my father. He's been concerned about you. What shall I tell him?"

He lifted one dark brow. "Judge for yourself. I'm living and breathing."

"A very good start, sir." Ben hoped to add a little levity to the conversation so Mr. Fontaine would relax in his company.

The man completely changed the subject. "I'm leaving. I have a meeting."

"On New Year's Day, Father?" A disappointed frown puckered Valerie's brows. "But I thought we'd—"

"It's business, *ma fille*. I'll have no arguments from you."

"Yes, Father."

Ben glimpsed the hurt expression on Valerie's face and wished he could do something to cheer her up again. She was even more beautiful when she smiled.

Mr. Fontaine stood and inclined his head toward Ben once again. "Perhaps we'll get a chance to talk later. Meanwhile, enjoy your stay. Now, if you'll excuse me." With that he strode from the room.

"But Father, you haven't touched your breakfast."

Ben heard the man pause somewhere behind him, then saw Valerie's look of chagrin.

A good minute later she said, "I must apologize for what just happened. As I stated before, my father's not been himself since Mama died, and I seem to be adding insult to injury."

"I can't imagine that. You obviously care deeply for your father. I'm sure he knows that."

Valerie rolled her shoulders.

"Last night you mentioned your father wasn't pleased that

you're home from boarding school. Would you mind sharing the reasons for your return with me now? If I'm being too forward, just say so."

"Not at all." Valerie lowered her teacup into its saucer and continued to stare at it. "When I received the news of my mother's death, everything in my life changed. Mama was my anchor. She was the one person in this world with whom I connected. I loved and trusted her. She was more than just my mother. She was my best friend."

Ben heard the little tremor in Valerie's voice, and his heart ached for her.

"Now that she's gone, I feel like a ship floating aimlessly out to sea. I'm at the mercy of every raging storm that comes along." Finally she looked at Ben. "I feel vulnerable, scared, and...alone." Embarrassment suddenly masked her features. "I imagine you might think I should add silly and childish to that list."

"I don't think you're either at all. Your pain is very obvious to me. But I don't agree that you're alone."

"I'm not speaking about my spiritual life."

"I understand. But from what I saw last night, you've got plenty of friends and even more acquaintances."

She fell silent for several seconds. "Benjamin, things aren't always as they appear."

And who would know that better than he? Reaching across the table once more, Ben set his palm on the top of her hand. "You're right."

At that moment Adalia burst into the room, and Ben straightened in his chair. "Your father just left the house, dearie."

"He said he had a meeting."

"He also said he won't be back for dinner."

"Nothing unusual about that, now, is there?" Valerie's expressive, beryl blue eyes grew misty, but she lifted her gaze and shrugged her shoulder as if she didn't care.

"I'll tell Chastean there'll only be you and Mr. McCabe for dinner tonight."

"Ah, well…" Ben halted the maid. "I've been invited to dine at the Elliots' home."

"Then it'll be one for supper, Adalia," Valerie said.

"Unless…" Ben caught her eye. "Unless Miss Fontaine will accompany me."

She blinked in surprise. "To the Elliots' home?"

Ben inclined his head. "I'll call on them to make sure it isn't an imposition."

"Well, if it's not…"

"Knowing Cousin Max and Cousin Amanda, it won't be."

Valerie thought it over for several moments before smiling. "Then I'd be honored."

FIVE

Y OUR OFFER IS QUITE TEMPTING, BUT I'M AFRAID I
can't accept it." Ben strode across Colonel LaPorte's darkly
paneled study and stared out a bank of windows that overlooked
the expanse of LaPorte's property. He recalled his conversation
with Edward Fontaine this morning and heard much the same
from the colonel just now by way of introduction. The colonel
oversaw a heavy artillery battalion and wanted particular photographs for the Confederate Navy. But it just wasn't possible. "It
would take Clint and me weeks to get you the sort of pictures
you're asking for, and I don't have that kind of time to spare. I've
got to find my brother Luke."

"You say he went missing in Virginia?"

"That's right."

"Any leads?"

"A few, but none panned out."

"Hmm…" The colonel fingered his silvery mustache while
a pensive frown knit his brows. "Tell you what." He leaned
forward. "If you'll take my offer, I'll call in a few favors and pull
some strings. Of course, there's no guarantee that any of my men
have seen him."

Ben pursed his lips and thought it over. The colonel might
be able to accomplish by telegraph to his commanders in the
field what would take him months to discover on the road.
"Why are you asking my partner and me to do this particular

assignment when there are photographers aplenty here in New Orleans?"

"Because none of them are...well, as objective as I'd like."

"Hmm..." Ben sensed there was something more but decided at this point it was none of his concern.

He rubbed his jaw, mulling it over. The assignment wouldn't be difficult, just time consuming. He walked to the padded leather armchair in front of the colonel's wide desk and sat down. "So let me get this straight. You want detailed pictures from Forts Jackson and St. Phillip along with photographs of the ports here in New Orleans and in Baton Rouge."

"Correct, and I'll pay you top dollar for them."

Ben didn't like the idea of taking sides, but if it would help him find Luke...

"And you'll put forth an earnest effort to help me find my brother?"

"Yes. You have my word."

Ben weighed the offer again. "Well, let me discuss the particulars with my partner, and I'll get back to you."

The colonel shifted in his seat. "Fine, but it's imperative that our conversation goes no further than your partner. No one else must know." He narrowed his gaze. "That includes your host and his lovely daughter."

The remark gave Ben pause, and his expression must have asked the obvious.

"I did some asking around," the colonel said, "last night at the Donahues' party."

"I see." Ben drew himself up. "All right. I'll hold this matter in the strictest confidence."

Cathedral bells marked high noon when Ben halted his horse and dismounted. He wrapped the reins around the hitching post in front of the Elliots' home. The quaint parsonage, situated on the east side of the unpaved road, looked just as he remembered from years ago when he'd last visited. He had to admit the simple red brick dwelling adjoining the church appeared inconsequential compared to the more ornately decorated structures that he remembered seeing in this city.

He knocked at the front door and, minutes later, it opened. He was greeted by a reed-thin woman about his age with nondescript brown hair and pale eyes that looked too large for her face.

Ben recognized her at once and removed his hat. "Hello, Catherine."

"Why, Ben McCabe!" A smile pushed up her hollow cheeks. "Is that really you?"

"In the flesh." He chuckled at her startled expression.

"Please come in." She opened the door wider to allow him room to step inside. "Mama, look who's here. Mama, it's Ben McCabe. All the way from Missouri!"

Once inside, Ben noticed her height rivaled his six feet, give or take an inch. She held out her hand.

He took it politely. "I've been to a lot of places, really. It's been over a year since I've been home." He released her hand.

"Well, it's so good to see you again." Her smile faded. "Any word from Luke?"

Ben shook his head. "But I'm not giving up."

"Such a shame."

"I'll find him."

Catherine looked doubtful.

He looked past her then, as Cousin Amanda swept into the

room. "Ben! How marvelous to see you!" Tall and lean like her daughter, she didn't appear to have aged a bit, although wisps of gray graced her narrow face. "I hope you'll stay with us while you're in New Orleans."

"And hopefully it'll be a good long while," Catherine added.

"Thank you, but that won't be necessary. I know you don't have extra room here."

"We'd make room," Amanda insisted.

Ben smiled. "I appreciate the offer, but I'm staying at the home of Edward Fontaine and his daughter, Valerie."

"The Fontaines?" Catherine's jaw slacked, and she looked at her mother with skepticism creasing her brows.

"Pa asked me to check on Mr. Fontaine," Ben explained. "When I wired to say I was coming, Mr. Fontaine asked me to stay as his guest. Thought I would—as a favor to Pa. I hope you understand."

"Of course." Amanda gave him a motherly hug. "Disappointed, perhaps…"

"I promise to stay another time."

"I'll take you up on that." She looked him over, as if checking to be sure he was in good health. Satisfied, Cousin Amanda stepped back. "So how is Mr. Fontaine?" Her voice held its usual gentle and caring tone.

"Struggling at best."

"I'm sorry to hear it. Max has tried to follow up after Marguerite's death, but he never finds the man at home."

"But, as you know, Valerie is there now." Catherine shook her mousy-brown head. "I heard she left boarding school without her father's permission…just in time for all of New Orleans's balls." Her brow furrowed and a stern glint entered her eyes. "She's a rebellious one, that Valerie. I know. My classroom is filled with the same such disobedient imps."

"Forgive me, but I believe there's more to Valerie's homecoming story." Ben found himself bristling at Catherine's remark.

"Hmm, well, I suppose there always two sides to everything." Catherine's schoolmarm expression softened, but in a way that made Ben wonder if she was really contrite.

He shifted his stance. "Actually, Miss Fontaine is the reason for my visit this afternoon."

Catherine stepped forward. "Don't tell me you're not planning to eat New Year's Day dinner with us tonight." She seemed alarmed.

"Oh, I'm coming back for dinner," Ben assured her. "But I asked Miss Fontaine to join us, and I wanted to make sure I didn't speak out of turn."

"Valerie? Coming here?" Catherine said as if not comprehending. "*Here?*"

"I hope it's all right." He frowned. Maybe he shouldn't have been so quick to extend the invitation without checking first.

"And she accepted?" Catherine couldn't seem to get over it. "Our modest home can hardly compare with the regal estates she frequents."

"She said she'd be honored."

"Oh, Catherine—" Cousin Amanda laughed off her daughter's reaction and peered at Ben through eyes as pale blue as her daughter's. "We're the ones honored to have Valerie as another dinner guest. We'll set two extra places at the table instead of one."

"Thank you." He inclined his head politely, although Catherine's reaction puzzled him greatly. "Pardon my curiosity, but has Miss Fontaine turned down your invitations in the past?"

"Not to my knowledge." Cousin Amanda folded her hands primly.

Ben felt confused.

Finally Catherine explained. "The Fontaines move in different social circles than we do." She seemed troubled. "I just wondered if Valerie would feel uncomfortable here. That's all. She doesn't know us well…"

"I understand." Ben thought he did anyway. "She seemed at ease when I mentioned the possibility to her this morning."

"Again, we'd be honored to have her," Cousin Amanda put in with a smile.

Ben tipped his head. "Meanwhile, I need to take my leave. I have to speak with my partner, Clint, before I head back to the Fontaines'."

"Please extend the dinner invitation to your friend." Amanda stepped forward. "You said his name is Clint?"

"Clint Culver." Ben grinned. "I'll inform him of your offer, Cousin Amanda, but I expect he and his wife, Emily, have other plans."

"Well, I do hope that you and I will have time to catch up, Ben." Catherine took his arm. "It's been a long time since our last correspondence. I'm waiting patiently for a teaching position to open up in Jericho Junction's school."

A frown creased his brow. "I didn't realize that."

"Didn't you get my letters? I asked your mother to forward them to Boston."

Ben hid a wince. He'd received them, all right. But with school and his preoccupation with Gwyneth Merriweather, he hadn't kept up on correspondence. "I'm not much of a letter writer, Catherine." It's all he could think of to say.

"I wondered why you never replied."

Ben felt doubly guilty.

"When I heard you were engaged to be married," she went on, "I stopped writing. But then, last year, Cousin Rebecca wrote to say the weddings plans were called off."

Ben grimaced. He had no defense. Gwyneth had broken

their engagement a year ago last November, just as the wedding date neared. Finally Ben realized she was merely stringing him along—like she did to a whole lot of other men.

"Any chance you and Miss Merriweather will reconcile?" Cousin Amanda asked.

"None. I've learned once and for all that Gwyneth's not the woman for me."

"At last." Catherine smiled into his face and hugged his arm. Ben found it both odd and amusing that she seemed so pleased. "I knew it all along."

"Oh?" Stepping closer to the doorway, Ben politely pulled free of her hold on his arm. "Then I admire your perception. Wish I'd had it." But, he reminded himself, he hadn't consulted the Lord about his relationship with Gwyneth. Since his mentor, Ivan Axelrod, had been for it, Ben figured God was too. However, he'd been very, very wrong.

"You're still planning to settle in Jericho Junction, aren't you?" Catherine asked.

"Yes, ma'am."

"I'd love to move out there and teach. I believe it's a calling." Her cheeks pinked at the admission.

"There's surely a need for teachers out West."

"I know. I've been studying up on it and receiving letters from other women who have made the trek into Missouri."

Seeing her dreamy expression, Ben affixed his wide brim hat onto his head. "We can talk more later. For now I'll say good-bye." He peered around Catherine, which didn't take much doing considering her slight frame. "Good-bye to you too, Cousin Amanda."

He left the house. Walking to his roan, he mounted up into the saddle. The leather creaked beneath his weight. As he urged the animal into the mud-caked street, he thought over the conversation he'd just had with Catherine. He had a strange feeling he missed some valuable information somewhere along the line.

Maybe he should have taken the few extra minutes to read those letters from Catherine that his mother had sent.

"Unless y' be needing anything else, dearie, I've dinner plans of my own. My friend Lavina invited me and some others to her home to celebrate New Year's Day and all. Cleared it with y' father months ago."

"Of course." Valerie set aside the journal in which she'd been penning. "How selfish of me to forget."

"Bah!" Adalia lifted her shoulders, and a faint blush crept onto her doughy face. "I don't mind assisting you even on my afternoon off. I've helped raise you since y' were a tot."

Unable to help herself, Valerie stood, crossed the music room, and pulled Adalia into a firm embrace. "I don't know what I would have done without you this last week."

"Now, now, I'll have none of this blubbering." She gently pushed Valerie back, then looked hard into her eyes. "I don't mind telling you that the world is changing, dearie. Y' mama is gone now, and I think y' father wants you to marry Mr. Ladden and be happy."

"He said that?" A chill ran through her. "He wants me to marry James?"

"Well, he didn't say those words exactly."

"But I don't want to marry him!"

"Could be worse fates for a woman than gettin' wed to the likes of him, y' know?"

"Like what? Being burned at the stake?" Valerie arched a brow.

"Now, now, just because he stole a kiss doesn't mean he

won't make a good husband. Why, you and Mr. Ladden used to climb trees and chase each other around the gardens until y' mama warned you to stop for fear you'd behead all her precious blooms."

"We were children then, Adalia."

"Yes, but I think Mr. Ladden has loved you since then. It explains all his pranks and naughtiness—he wanted you to notice him."

"How could I not notice when he sat up in Mama's pear tree and threw fruit at me?"

"You threw a few pears back as I recall."

Valerie lifted a shoulder. "Self-defense." She strolled to the pianoforte and, thinking it all over, glided her forefinger down its ivory keys. "The point is, I don't love James."

"Ah, romantic love." Adalia shook her head, and several grayish-blonde strands slipped from beneath her white crocheted hair covering. "It's nothing like *true* love."

Valerie regarded her askance. "And what do you know about 'true love'? You've never been married."

"That's where you err, blessed one. I've been in love, and I've been married too." She dropped her arms to her side.

"You have?" Valerie's mouth dropped open in surprise. "Why didn't I know this?"

She shrugged. "I was from a good family in London. My parents arranged a marriage for me—to a decent fellow. But I was in love with Dalbert Dempsey, a handsome rake who traveled with a theater group in London." Adalia smiled wistfully. "He could charm a rose into blossoming in the dead o' winter, that one."

Valerie sat back down to listen to the tale.

"Anyway, my folks allowed me to follow m' heart. I went away with Dalbert. Then one day I woke up to the fact that m' true love was nothing more than a selfish black-heart who'd left me miserable and penniless."

Valerie gasped, stunned by the revelation. "What did you do?"

"Since my folks had both passed, God rest them, I ran to m' brother, and he put me in touch with your father, bless him. I left England and came to America, where I've been content ever since. So y' see? Romantic love doesn't have anything to do with true happiness."

"But—"

"It's mere fairy tales."

"But James is—"

"—that proverbial boy next door you might read about in a penny novel."

"Hmm..." Valerie folded her hands, resting them on top of the polished table. "Romantic fiction aside, I think James has more in common with your Dalbert."

Adalia clucked her tongue. "James Ladden comes from money—same money you do—and he obviously has feelings for you. Why not marry him?"

Valerie tensed. "Well, he hasn't officially asked for my hand in marriage."

"Ah, but the proposal is coming. And stop frowning so hard. You're liable to give yourself a permanent wrinkle!"

On a tiny gasp, Valerie ran her fingertips along her forehead, hoping to thwart off the prediction, when she spied Benjamin standing outside the doorway. Their gazes met, and he quietly entered the room, causing Valerie to wonder if he'd overheard any of her conversation with Adalia.

"I hope I'm not interrupting."

"Not a'tall, sir. I was just leaving." Adalia lifted the tea service off the table and cast a quick glance at Valerie. "Willie said he'll bring the buggy around and drive you to the Elliots' when you're ready."

"Thank you." Valerie peered at Benjamin. She couldn't help noticing the way his broad shoulders filled the expanse of his black frock. "I had thought, if there's time, that you might enjoy a tour of our fine city before we go to the Elliots'."

He pulled out his pocket watch and glanced at the hour. "I think we'll have plenty of time. I'm ready whenever you are." Meanwhile, his gaze swept the circumference of the music room.

Valerie followed his line of vision as it roamed over the peach-colored wallpaper. In the center of the room stood the round cherry tea table and its two matching chairs. A settee, upholstered in multicolored silk, had been placed between the two floor-to-ceiling windows that were graced with delicate white sheers. Mama's rocker and spinning wheel were at one end of the room and the pianoforte at the other.

"Beautiful room," he said.

"This has always been my favorite part of the house—our music room. I enjoy taking my afternoon teas in here."

"Very nice indeed." He walked to where Valerie's violin was stowed in the nook above the piano. "Do you play?" He lifted it for closer inspection.

"Yes, but not since Mama died."

He gave an understanding nod before gently setting the instrument aside. Then he turned toward Valerie.

She flushed beneath his gaze. "I thought, perhaps, you might like to see Jackson Square," she said, mostly to get her mind on something besides him, "and the shops in the *Vieux Carre*, the theater, and Antoine's—one of New Orleans's finest restaurants."

"That'd be fine."

She extracted her gaze from his, hoping she'd think more clearly if she didn't see him looking back so intensely. "I might show you my father's business near the docks." Valerie paused. "But perhaps we should stay away from the docks. No telling what sort of riffraff may be lurking about once it's dark."

"Sounds awfully wise."

She glanced back in time to see his crooked smile.

"Did I say something amusing?"

"No, I—" He chuckled. "Miss Fontaine, I must confess. You've enchanted me."

"I have? Oh, well…" She knew her tone sounded tentative, but she'd never had anyone say such a thing to her before. *Enchanted?*

Benjamin laughed. "I meant it as a compliment."

She felt her blush grow to her hairline. "Why, then, I do thank you." With a smile, she added, "Shall we go?"

SIX

AS THE HORSES *CLIP-CLOPPED* THEIR WAY AROUND the city's unevenly paved streets, Valerie pointed out the various sites of interest. Jackson Square. The four-story brick building that housed William Washburn's studio on Canal Street. Prince's Photographic Studio on the opposite corner.

"I'd surely like to speak with those men. I wonder if they've photographed troops in the area."

Valerie noted his hopefulness. Perhaps he thought he might learn something about his brother's disappearance. "I'm positive an interview can be arranged."

The buggy rolled on and the tour continued.

"Where I come from," Benjamin said, "there aren't any theaters, no fancy shops. Just Taylor's General Store."

"Yes, I've read several articles about those frontier towns." She shifted in her seat. "Are there really savages running loose, kidnapping women and scalping men?"

"You mean Indians?" Ben nodded. "Yes, we see our share. But ours is a fairly peaceful town, and the Indians we've dealt with have been reasonable souls. We trade with them, often our more modern conveniences for their animal hides and furs. And Jericho Junction is hardly the frontier. The train that stops in town runs from St. Louis and goes clear through to Jefferson City. There's a small hotel and eatery, a bank, livery, and blacksmiths and the like. But to say Jericho Junction is anywhere near being a full-fledged city like New York, Atlanta, New Orleans, or Chicago is just plain wrong. Still, it's not like the territories either."

Valerie imagined what the town looked like. "Jericho Junction sounds charming."

The carriage leaned sharply as they rounded a corner. Valerie found herself pressed up against Benjamin and made a mental note to remind Willie to slow down before he took one of those turns again. Righting herself, she touched a hand to her hair to make sure her pins were still in place. Glancing at Benjamin she wondered why he looked so amused. "As you were saying?"

"Oh, right. Well, it's taken me a long time to realize Jericho Junction is home and that's where I want to settle down when the time comes."

Valerie mulled over his statement. "I don't know where I'll settle down."

"You don't think you'll stay in New Orleans? I thought you said this was home."

"Exactly. It *was*."

"You know, there's an old saying about time healing all wounds."

She turned to gaze out the carriage window.

"God knows how much you miss your mother. Jesus Himself wept when Lazarus died."

It meant a lot to her that Benjamin tried to console her when she knew his own heart was breaking over the disappearance of his brother. Looking back at him, she pushed out a smile. "Thank you."

"Feeling better, Miss Fontaine?"

"Please, call me Valerie."

"Valerie."

She liked the way he pronounced her name in his smooth, country drawl. But it reminded her of something that nagged her ever since she'd met this handsome photographer. She decided to bring it up. "While you claim to be a country boy, I detect more education and social refinement—and practiced charm—than your description of Jericho Junction would afford."

"You're very astute."

The compliment made her smile.

"I was actually educated in Boston from the time I was seventeen. Before that, I was the preacher's son and the town rabble-rouser."

"No!" She had to laugh when the boyish image of Benjamin with a blackened eye flitted through her mind. "I would have guessed you to have been something of a bookworm. A lover of poetry."

"Not hardly." He chuckled. "I just barely made it through school. Of course, I did have something of a distraction. But getting back to when I was a kid. Yep, I used to fight all the time. Seemed I was in one scrape or another, trying to prove I wasn't some sissy just because I was a preacher's son. My father was at his wits' end with me."

Valerie picked up on the "distraction," but since he didn't explain, she let it go.

"Finally a wealthy philanthropist named Ivan Axelrod came to town. He was a staunch supporter of my father's ministry, built us a church. But he didn't stop there. He built a fine home for my family with enough room to host visiting missionaries— or big-hearted philanthropists." A wide smile stretched across his clean-shaven face and admiration darkened his amber eyes. "Well, ol' Ivan took me under his wing and set out to cure me of my fistfighting."

"How did he manage that?"

"By taking me to Boston and showing me that there was a whole world of reasons not to spend my time brawling. He stressed to me the needs of others, and I got the message. I lent my time to different charities in the community. When I finished college, I eventually decided to pursue my lifelong interest in photography."

"Where is Mr. Axelrod now?"

"Back in Boston, living with his granddaughter, Gwyneth. I write every so often and let him know what I'm up to."

"Gwyneth?" The way he said her name gave Valerie the impression that there might be more to this story, yet she dared not pry.

But then he explained. "Yes, Gwyneth Merriweather." A faraway look entered his eyes.

"And do you write to her too?"

His chuckle beheld a note of disbelief. He shook his head. "Gwyneth would rather hear news of my drowning in the Mississippi River than get a letter from me."

Valerie leaned back, squelching a gasp. What could Benjamin have possibly done?

And then it occurred to her: He broke her heart. Of course. What else?

"My apologies, Valerie." He took her hand. "I've marred our conversation."

"Think nothing of it. May I be so bold as to ask what happened between you and Miss Merriweather?"

"You may." He sat back and met her gaze. "Gwyneth and I were engaged to be married—a number of times. She'd get mad at me, call off the wedding, then she'd change her mind and I'd forgive and take her back. It'd go on and on like that. It wasn't healthy for either one of us. I know that now. But the last time we argued was over a year ago. I told her I wanted to settle down in Jericho Junction, and at first she agreed. But after stepping one foot off the train, she decided the place was a boring little nothing town. She thought I misled her. Made the town sound like more than it was. Within two days she insisted I take her back to Boston. On the way there, she blamed me for everything from her mud-splattered gowns to her ruined dainty kid slippers. When I wouldn't change my mind and stay in Boston with her, she said she hated me. I knew that was the end." Benjamin's voice had gotten quieter and more somber.

"If she had truly loved you, she'd have followed you to the ends of the earth." Valerie allowed her hand to remain in his. "I know I would have…that is, I'd follow the man I love…when I find him, of course." Oh, how embarrassing to stammer like some besotted schoolgirl!

His eyes seemed to assess her every feature, and when they paused at her mouth, she quickly glanced out the window. "Oh, look at the decorations in that store window." Had he been thinking of kissing her? She wouldn't have minded, but here inside the carriage wouldn't have been an appropriate place.

He sat forward and leaned over to glimpse the shop as the carriage rolled past.

"So what's your next step in finding your brother?" Valerie changed subjects.

"Funny you should ask." Sitting back again, he released her hand. "My strategy might be changing some. I might stay in New Orleans awhile."

Valerie wasn't at all disappointed to hear it.

The carriage rolled to a halt in front of the Elliots' red brick house.

Benjamin jumped down and helped Valerie alight. He removed his gold pocket watch from inside his waistcoat, opened it, and peered at its face before replacing it. "Looks like we've arrived at our destination right on time."

"Perfect." Valerie smoothed her skirts and adjusted her cloak.

"The tour of New Orleans was most…informative. I enjoyed it." He extended his arm, and Valerie placed her hand around his elbow. Together they strolled to the house.

~~℮℮⅋℮℮~~

A Christmas tree stood in the corner of the Elliots' cozy living room. Valerie paused to admire the homemade decorations that hung from its branches. She noticed too the little red bows tied here and there.

"I'm sure our tree is quite pitiful compared to the one at your house," Catherine said.

"No, on the contrary, your tree is lovely." Valerie fingered a tiny replica of a gingerbread man cookie. "This ornament is adorable."

"I made it and others with my students."

"How ingenious of you."

When Valerie turned, Catherine followed. "What kind of ornaments do you hang on your Christmas tree? I imagine they're frosted glass and quite costly."

"Some are, yes, but this year I arrived home too late to decorate." She didn't mention that Father refused to allow her to dig out the holiday decorations.

"Oh, that's right. You were away at boarding school." Catherine bent to speak softly into Valerie's ear. "Mama told me you left school without permission."

"No, that's not true." Despite the soft reply, discomfort beat loudly in her ears. "I wired my father when I left Virginia, but the message never reached him." They stepped nearer to where Benjamin talked with Pastor Elliot and Robert, Catherine's younger brother.

"So next thing I know, Luke's gone. Clint had left to get his wife out of harm's way when the pandemonium broke out."

Pastor Elliot shook his head, but his young son looked at Benjamin with wide, curious eyes.

Benjamin added explanation for the boy's benefit. "You see,

carriages filled with spectators had been lined up to see what was supposed to be a huge Confederate defeat. A lot of civilians were hurt."

"I wish I could've been there to see it," Robert said. "Better, I would have liked to fight with the Rebs."

"Robert, honestly!" Catherine was aghast.

Benjamin did his best to quell a small grin. "Well, in the midst of it, Luke disappeared."

Valerie saw the angst that now shadowed Benjamin's face, and sorrow filled her own heart. *Lord, please let him find his brother…*

Mrs. Elliot suddenly entered the room. She wore a black and white ensemble that was simple yet elegant. "Dinner's ready."

Valerie followed Catherine. In the dining room, the small table had been covered with a white linen cloth and set for six. Candlelight flickered from the tall white tapers in the middle of the centerpiece created from evergreen boughs.

"Valerie, you'll sit here. Beside Robert." Catherine nodded to the place.

Benjamin came up behind her and held the chair for Valerie. She smiled her gratitude, then watched as he did the same for Catherine. Finally he took his own seat opposite Valerie. When their gazes met, he gave her a quick wink.

Pastor Elliot seated Mrs. Elliot, then took his place at the head of the table. "Let's pray, shall we?" All heads bowed. Once the blessing was asked, bowls and platters of food were passed.

"Mm-mmm…roast goose with all the trimmings." Benjamin helped himself to a good-sized portion.

"With mashed potato stuffing. Your favorite."

"Well, now, Catherine Elliot, how would you know a thing like that?" Benjamin wanted to know.

"You made mention of it the last time you visited."

He paused to consider the reply. "That was a long time ago." He passed the platter to Mrs. Elliot. "You have a mighty good memory."

"Well, yes, I do—especially when it's of you and your family."

Valerie arched her brows and looked from Catherine to Benjamin. She couldn't see his expression as he ladled several spoonfuls of rich brown sauce onto his meat before passing on the porcelain gravy boat. But Valerie had quickly drawn her own conclusions.

"What's your favorite food, Miss Fontaine?" twelve-year-old Robert asked.

She looked at the boy. "My favorite meal…hmm…well, I must admit, this one is certainly up there in the top three." She peered over her lashes, first at Mrs. Elliot and then at Catherine. They gazed back at her expectantly. "It smells delicious. I can't wait to try a few bites."

"Thank you, my dear." Mrs. Elliot handed her the bowl of sliced beets, and Valerie helped herself to a spoonful.

"I'm sure you're accustomed to more elegant fare," Catherine said on an apologetic note.

"Accustomed? No, not really. This meal is one of the nicest I've had in a long while. At school we ate very simply, and since I've been home, our cook Chastean goes home to her family in the evenings." She looked at Benjamin. "Unless there's a guest, of course."

He grinned politely.

"Tell me more about Bull Run, Cousin Ben," Robert said, changing the subject. "I want to hear all about the fighting."

"Robert, dear…" His mother shook her head at him. "Let's remember our manners, shall we?" She turned to Benjamin. "Have you heard from your mother recently?"

"Not for a while. I'm assuming she's just fine."

"And how's Jacob?" Mrs. Elliot leaned forward, an earnest expression on her face.

"Well, as you might know, Jake enlisted with the Confederacy under General McCulloch and served with his army of the West. Last August he was wounded at Wilson's Creek near Springfield. He returned home with a permanent leg injury. Foiled his plans to be a lawman." He drew in a heavy breath. "He's disappointed, to say the least, but God has other plans for him."

Catherine placed her long fingers on Benjamin's wide wrist. "What a shame."

"Jake is alive. We're all grateful for that." He politely removed his arm from beneath her hand and lifted his fork.

Valerie felt every bit the outsider, so she said, "Where does Jacob fall into line in the McCabe family?"

"Second oldest," Catherine replied before Benjamin could answer. "Just a year younger than Ben and myself. Jacob comes next, followed by Leah, then Luke, and Sarah's the youngest."

"I see." Valerie chanced a look across the table. Benjamin sent her a grin before forking a bite of food into his mouth.

"We remember Jacob and Luke in our prayers every evening." Pastor Elliot dabbed the sides of his mouth with his linen napkin. "Just as we remember every one of your family members." He cleared his throat and peered at Valerie. "We pray for our congregational members too, of course."

"I'm sure you do." Valerine didn't doubt it. She'd always known the wiry, energetic pastor to be sincere and very sacrificial with his time.

"And the girls? How are they?" Mrs. Elliot asked.

"They're well," Catherine interjected. "No wire has come through yet, announcing the birth of Leah's baby."

Benjamin gave her such a surprised look that Valerie found

the woman's behavior quite funny. She bit one side of her mouth to keep from smiling.

"Cousin Rebecca said she'd send off a wire to you, Ben, in care of our name and address. I've been watching for it," she went on to explain.

"Well, thank you kindly, Catherine. I'd forgotten that Ma had told me of the plan." His gaze captured Valerie's, and he shrugged as if he didn't know whether to be amused or irritated by Catherine's behavior.

"And Sarah's still—?"

"—as sassy as ever." Benjamin quickly put in. He glanced at Catherine and grinned. "Did I take the words right out of your mouth?"

"Well, not exactly." She pulled her chin back in surprise.

Laughter flitted around the table, and at last Valerie rid herself of the mirth she'd been holding in check.

SEVEN

BEN SAUNTERED AWAY FROM THE DINNER TABLE WITH a full and satisfied feeling. "A marvelous dinner, Cousin Amanda."

"Thank you, but Catherine did most of the cooking."

"My compliments." He turned to Catherine with a small bow of appreciation.

She smiled and latched on to his right arm. Ben glanced at Valerie, who was deep in conversation with Robert, and for a moment he wished she was the one holding his arm. They moved into the parlor.

"Catherine can cook and bake practically anything."

"Good for you." He pulled his arm free when they reached the red-upholstered settee.

Catherine blushed.

"She's a musician too."

"Oh, Mama—" Catherine gestured with her hand.

Ben grinned. "You'll have to play something for us."

"She'd love to!" Cousin Amanda wore a broad smile. "Why, she makes up melodies and writes poetry to go along with them. Plays for church and her students mostly."

"I'm impressed. Let's hear something from your repertoire."

Catherine fingered the tiny embroidered bow on her high neckline. "Well, I don't know…"

"C'mon, Sissy," Robert said, coming up behind them with Valerie. "You've been practicing for hours every day since you learned Cousin Ben was coming to New Orleans."

"Robert!" Cousin Amanda clucked her tongue.

Ben suppressed a smile. Typical little brother...

Luke came to mind—as a kid he could be was just as irksome when he'd been the same age as Robert. "Now, Catherine, we'd all like to hear you play."

Catherine ran her long hands down the folds of her green and white striped skirt. "I...well, I..."

Seeing as Cousin Amanda had seated herself in one of the two printed armchairs, Ben sat down on the settee. "Don't be shy, Catherine. Play a song for us."

"All right, if you insist."

Robert plopped down beside him, causing Ben a measure of disappointment. He'd been hoping Valerie would sit next to him. Instead she lowered herself into the second armchair while Cousin Max dragged in a dining room chair for himself.

Across the room, Catherine took the piano bench. Her frame was so thin that her shoulder blades looked like clipped wings poking out of the back of her dress. Once more Ben hoped she wasn't ill. Her countenance appeared healthy enough. Seconds later, she began to plunk out a simple tune before singing.

It was all Ben could do not to wince at each flat note she hit, but he noticed that Valerie sat quietly, attentively, with her delicate hands folded in her lap.

> Our needs are met.
> Our God is great.

"Hey, that doesn't rhyme!" Robert shouted.

Catherine struck an errant key and glared at her brother.

"Robert, don't interrupt your sister," Cousin Max said.

"But the words *met* and *great* don't rhyme," he argued.

"Let's not be so critical." Cousin Amanda sent her son a stern look before her gaze returned to Catherine. "Please continue, dear."

Robert groaned and Ben winked at the boy. His family members were all musically inclined, so he knew a little bit about making "a joyful noise unto the Lord," and he appreciated Catherine's efforts.

The recital finally ended, and everyone applauded, Ben included. Catherine lowered her gaze and smiled, blushing.

Her mother looked pleased and swung her gaze to Valerie. "Do you play a musical instrument?"

"Yes." She shifted in her chair. "I'm trained on the violin and piano."

Ben didn't detect an air of haughtiness, but he sure could feel the sudden tension crackling in the air.

"Oh, yes, now I remember." Cousin Amanda looked as though she wished she hadn't asked. "Your mother told me about your lessons a while back."

Valerie merely smiled.

"Then you must play the piano for us too!" Robert exclaimed. "Please. I want to hear you play!"

"Um…" Her questioning gaze flew to Ben. "I haven't played in months."

"You're under no obligation."

"Perhaps I'll fetch the coffee and dessert," Cousin Amanda said.

But the suggestion came too late. Robert was already out of his seat and tugging on Valerie's elbow. "Oh, come on. Please. Play a song for us."

"Well, I suppose I could play just a little something."

Valerie moved to the piano and Robert reclaimed his seat, forcing Catherine to seek refuge in the now-vacated armchair.

Meanwhile Valerie gathered her hoop skirts and made herself comfortable on the wooden bench. "After I received news of Mama's death, it was hard to practice at school," Valerie said. "That was last June."

"We understand if you're a tad rusty." Cousin Max had straddled a wooden chair and rested his arms along the top of its slatted backrest.

Valerie began to play, and Ben stole the moment to admire her from afar—her beauty awed him. The soft curls in her dark hair that hung to her shoulders, her flawless, pale complexion, and pert nose. While petite, she still possessed an attractive, curvy figure. It was little wonder that he'd overheard several men comment about her beauty at last night's gala.

Her delicate fingers cavorted across the piano's ivory keys. He recognized the melody she'd selected as an Irish folk song.

Then she began to sing:

> The water is wide,
> I cannot get o'er.
> Neither have I the wings to fly.
> Give me a boat that can carry two,
> And both shall row, my love and I.

Valerie's wispy soprano coupled with the heartfelt melody stirred up something deep inside of Ben. But that was no surprise—so far he was enamored by everything about her.

The shaking of Catherine's head caught his eye, and he glanced her way. "It's one of those insipid ballads," he heard her mumble to her mother, who had the good grace to ignore her.

Ben wondered. She almost seemed...jealous.

The notion brought him up short. Surely Catherine didn't think...no, it wasn't possible...she couldn't be entertaining the idea that he'd come to New Orleans for the purpose of courting her! Could she?

He closed his eyes. *Oh, Lord, I should have read those letters she wrote me.*

Valerie finished the song, and again, everyone applauded. Her cheeks turned a striking strawberry pink.

Cousin Amanda stood, and Ben noted the frown lines on her forehead. "I think it's time for our dessert. Catherine made her specialty—coconut custard."

"Can I have an extra helping?" Robert lifted his tawny brows in hopefulness.

Catherine flung a warning look at him. "Perhaps you ought to help Mama in the kitchen, darling brother." The words came out through a clenched jaw.

Robert looked doomed. But he stood and, without complaint, followed his mother out of the parlor.

Still near the pianoforte, Valerie smiled after the boy before walking over to the vacated place beside Ben. Gathering her skirts, she sat down. The scent of lavender and spice wafted to his nostrils, and Ben fought the urge to lean closer and inhale deeply of the sweet scent.

"Well, now, Valerie dear," Cousin Max began, turning his chair around and seating himself, "you must play for us at church. I had no idea of your musical talent. Why didn't your mother tell us? You could be playing in church on Sundays."

"Perhaps because Catherine plays so nicely week after week."

Cousin Max jutted out his bottom lip in momentary thought. "Even Catherine needs a day of rest." He smiled at his daughter. "Sometimes I think she's wearing herself too thin."

"Oh, Daddy, I'm fine." Catherine shifted uncomfortably. "A picture of health. Besides, I read that women who are more slender have less difficulty living on the prair—"

Ben saw her eyes dart in his direction before she turned her gaze to the braided rug on the wooden floor. He had a sinking feeling his earlier hunch was correct. He prayed he'd done nothing in the past to give her false hopes.

"My daughter has a bit of wanderlust." Cousin Max sounded amused. "She fancies herself a prairie bride."

"Daddy, please!" Catherine looked mortified.

"There are plenty of good men in our congregation who would make fine husbands, and they live right here in New Orleans."

Catherine pressed her lips together.

"And if you never marry, my dear, you'll always have your teaching."

"Yes, Daddy." She was clearly trying her best to be patient with him.

Obviously Valerie took note of it too. "Pardon my saying so, Pastor Elliot, but my friend Elicia Donahue has a cousin who met her husband through correspondence. She became a mail-order bride, moving out to the territories. She's quite content."

"Well, I...well..." Cousin Max cleared his throat. "We'll not encourage this talk of mail-order brides and prairies."

"Yes, sir." Valerie folded her hands in her lap.

"I personally don't like the idea of young ladies traveling long distances," Cousin Max said, "especially now while there's a war going on. Although I'm aware our Valerie, here, made the trek from Virginia in one piece."

Ben felt Valerie tense at his side.

"Thank God for her safe arrival," he said.

"Yes, sir, and I do," Valerie replied.

"But the war will be over in just a month or so, Daddy." Catherine's huge eyes rested on Ben. "People will begin traveling out West again. Isn't that so, Ben?"

"One can only pray the fighting will end soon," he said with a long sigh.

"Son, you'll find him." Cousin Max had about read his next thoughts.

Ben shook his head, amazed that his emotions had been so transparent. He noticed the compassionate stares from the three people surrounding him. "I'm sorry."

"Let's all pray," Cousin Max suggested. Catherine came over to sit on the floor near Ben's knee, and the four of them clasped hands. Ben couldn't help feeling the difference between the two women, Catherine's hand long and cold, and Valerie's warm, soft, small, and fragile.

"Heavenly Father, we come boldly before Your throne of grace and ask after Luke McCabe. We pray for his protection. Lord, please send Your angels concerning him to guide him home. Give Ben Your peace that passeth all understanding as he searches for his younger brother. May Thy will be done, Lord God, and may we have the courage to accept it. In Jesus's name, amen."

"Amen." The word tumbled from Ben's lips as doubts filled him. What if God's will had been to take Luke home to heaven?

He squeezed his eyes closed against the very idea. And in that split second, he realized he didn't possess the mettle to accept that possibility. *God, help me!*

Valerie tugged on his hand, and her sapphire eyes snared his gaze.

"You'll find him." She spoke the words in whispered reverence. "Somehow I know...I can *feel* it."

"Can you?" Ben wanted to latch on to that nugget of hope and never let go.

A smile inched its way across her lovely face, and he knew right there that Miss Valerie Fontaine had not only encouraged his soul, but she had also captured his heart.

~~⚭✆⚭~~

Around ten o'clock Valerie and Benjamin bade the Elliots good-bye. She hugged her woolen cape more tightly around her shoulders as she stepped from the parsonage. The night air felt thick, damp, and cold. A dense fog had rolled in from the gulf, impairing visibility. But Valerie managed to see Willie waiting by the buggy. The brown-faced man helped her climb in, and Benjamin soon followed suit. Within minutes the vehicle lurched forward.

For several long seconds neither of them spoke. Finally Benjamin broke the awkward silence. "I hope you had a nice time, Valerie." An apologetic note lingered on his words. "I have a feeling there's been a terrible misunderstanding between Catherine and me."

"I have a feeling you're right. She's in love with you."

"What?" Benjamin jerked his body back. "I wouldn't go so far as to say that."

"But it's true. I saw it in her eyes each time she looked at you."

"We haven't seen each other in years!"

"Perhaps she's in love with the last memory she has of you."

"Well, maybe…" Benjamin cleared his throat, clearly uncomfortable with the notion.

"Did you correspond with her from time to time?"

"No. I mean, she wrote to me, but I was too busy to answer."

Valerie folded her gloved hands. "Perhaps your parents encouraged a match between the two of you."

"I highly doubt it." He shook his head. "We've never spoken of such a thing."

Valerie recalled how Mama used to tell her that when she met the man with whom she was to spend the rest of her life, she'd know it. He would encourage her in her faith and she in his.

"Valerie, I want you to know that I never intentionally gave Catherine false hope."

"Well, you are charming to a fault."

Benjamin chuckled. "I'll try to act less chivalrous in the future."

She smiled at his jest. A minute later, however, she grew solemn. "I do feel sorry for Catherine though. How dreadful if she's brokenhearted."

"Hmm…and here I thought you viewed Catherine as some sort of musical rival."

"I wanted to impress you. After all, you brought me as your guest to my pastor's home."

"I was very proud to escort you tonight."

"Mama would be pleased if she could hear the compliment. She spent hours cajoling me into practicing despite all my sour chords."

"Yes, I'm all too familiar with those 'sour chords.' I've hit many wrong notes playing my bugle."

"You play?"

"Yes, and once I took quite the ribbing after a certain Christmas program."

"Poor boy," she teased.

He shrugged his broad shoulders.

The conveyance slowed to a halt in front of the Fontaines' townhouse. Benjamin jumped down and then assisted Valerie. After thanking Willie for his service, she took Benjamin's proffered arm, and they strolled together up the walkway.

Adalia opened the door before they even reached it. "What perfect timing. I just got home myself."

Once inside, Valerie removed her woolen cape and hung it up while Adalia dutifully saw to Benjamin's overcoat. Leaning close, the maid whispered, "Y' father's home. Had a fit that the house was dark and the hearth cold when he walked in. Now he's sitting in the library, nursing a bottle o' scotch."

Valerie gasped, drawing a concerned look from Benjamin.

"Everything all right?" he asked

She forced a smile to say it was nothing and proceeded to untie and remove her velvet hat.

"Might I suggest you say good night," Adalia whispered, "and encourage your houseguest to retire for the evening?"

"Good idea." Valerie pulled off her gloves.

Meanwhile Benjamin moved toward the parlor's entrance.

She stepped toward him. "Well, I'm quite tired, so I think I'll—"

A shadow down the hall caught her eye, and before she could say more, her father appeared in the foyer.

"Where have you been, *ma fille*?" He moved next to her.

"I dined with our houseguest, Mr. McCabe, at the Elliots' tonight. You remember Pastor Elliot, don't you, Father?"

"Of course." He nodded a greeting to Benjamin. "Shall we sit down?" Father inclined his head in the direction of the parlor, and with his palm at Valerie's low back, he guided her forward.

She wondered at the wisdom of conversing with Father when he'd been imbibing; however, his words didn't sound slurred and he seemed steady on his feet.

"Would you like a drink, Mr. McCabe? A bit of scotch, perhaps? Otherwise I've got some of the finest bourbon in all of New Orleans."

"No, thank you, sir. I don't partake, but I appreciate the offer just the same."

Father regarded him for a long moment before nodding to Adalia. "Bring in my scotch, please. I believe I left it in the library."

The maid left the room to do his bidding while Valerie sat

down on the settee and began to fret. It wouldn't do if Benjamin saw her father in one of his pathetic, inebriated states.

Father claimed his usual armchair, and as there was nowhere else around the fireplace to sit, Benjamin planted himself next to her on the settee.

She pushed out a weak smile.

His understanding expression let her know she needn't worry.

"I saw James Ladden at the club tonight." Father pulled out a fat cigar from its ornately carved box. He struck a match and lit the tobacco, then held out the cigar box.

Benjamin politely declined.

"James told me he enjoyed the Donahues' gala last night, and he hoped he didn't offend either of you with his, um, *enthusiasm*."

Valerie tossed a gaze upward. The last person she wanted to discuss was James Ladden!

"All's forgiven on my end." Benjamin leaned back and casually brought his left booted ankle up to rest on his right knee, bumping against Valerie's leg. "Pardon me."

"Quite all right." Valerie couldn't say she minded sitting so close to him. Father cleared his throat, and she realized she'd been staring. "Well, I..." She blinked and looked over at her father. "I'd say James owes us an apology."

"He told me that he expressed his regrets more than once to you last night, but you were being stubborn about accepting his apology."

She didn't know what to say. Had he apologized? She couldn't recall.

"Well?"

"I suppose I am being stubborn." Valerie lifted her chin. "But James wasn't much of a gentleman. He tricked me into going outside with him, kissed me, and made me tear my gown."

Beside her, Benjamin tensed.

Just as Valerie suspected, her father did not look pleased by the news. A frown creased his forehead as he puffed on his cigar. "I'll talk to James."

"Thank you." Valerie waved away a cloud of smoke. "And could you please extinguish that dreadful thing?"

Father scooted to the edge of his seat. "This is my house, and I shall smoke wherever I wish."

Valerie pressed her lips together. There was no use getting Father all lathered up. But Mama wouldn't allow smoking in the parlor. In front of a guest, no less! Mama always insisted that he smoke in his library or out in the solarium.

Adalia entered the room, carrying a large silver tray. On it stood Father's crystal decanter and matching tumbler, a teapot, and two cups and saucers. She poured the scotch first and handed it to Father. Then she set the tea service in front of Valerie and Benjamin. "None for me, thanks," he said as Adalia poured out.

Valerie welcomed a cup of the steaming brew.

"Mr. McCabe," Father began, "how did your interview with Colonel LaPorte go this morning?"

"Fine."

Father squinted his eyes to study him as he took another puff on his cigar. "Well, you're welcome to stay here as long as you'd like."

"I appreciate the offer, Mr. Fontaine. As of now, I'm not sure how long I'll be in New Orleans."

Valerie hoped it would be a good while longer.

"But on that note, I think I'll say good night. I hope you'll excuse me. The last forty-eight hours have been exhausting."

"Of course." Father waved a dismissive hand in the air. "I certainly understand."

Benjamin stood and turned to Valerie, lifting her hand and bringing it to his lips. "Good night, Miss Fontaine." His warm, golden gaze seemed to fasten onto hers, and he lingered a moment longer than necessary. "See you in the morning."

"Good night. Sleep well." Valerie couldn't keep her eyes from following his long-legged, broad-shouldered frame out the door.

"So you like our houseguest, do you?"

"Hmm?" She looked back at her father.

"Mr. McCabe? You enjoy his company?"

"Oh, yes, Father. He's very nice."

Father sat back, pursing his lips, looking thoughtful.

Valerie smoothed out her skirt. "I think Mama would have liked him."

Strained moments of silence passed during which she regretted mentioning Mama. At long last, he replied, "Your mother was glad to have both Pastor Elliot and Reverend McCabe nearby during her darkest hour."

Valerie felt a surge of anticipation. She'd yearned to talk about Mama. He drained his glass in a single swallow. "I didn't meet Reverend McCabe until..." He shook his head and rose from his chair, heading for the decanter on the polished sideboard. "Enough of this talk." He sighed and lifted a hand as if to brush the conversation away.

"No, Father, please..." Valerie stood and strode toward him. "I have to know. I want to hear how it happened...from you."

He cursed, causing her to jump back. "I wasn't there."

"What?" Valerie's mind raced to understand. "Where were you?"

"I have a business to run, you know!"

"Yes..."

"I had no idea your mother had taken ill."

"Didn't she send for you?"

"I couldn't receive messages, and a terrible storm kept me from getting home. She sent for Pastor Elliot and his wife. Not wanting to bring a woman out in the bad weather, the pastor brought his friend Daniel McCabe instead."

"Benjamin's father." Valerie gave a quick nod of understanding, hoping to encourage him to go on.

"*Benjamin?* That's twice now." His dark brows furrowed. "You're on a first-name basis with the young man, and he kissed your hand before he left the room."

"He's very polite."

"Indeed."

Valerie wished the subject would return to her mother. "Father, please, let's talk about Mama."

"The more pressing matter is you and our houseguest—and the fact you're not speaking to James Ladden."

Valerie whirled away from him. "Oh, James and all his buffoonery. I'm tired of him." She strolled to the hearth where the fire crackled behind the brass-trimmed screen.

"I said I'll speak to him about his behavior last night, and I will. Nonetheless, I think he'd be a good match for you."

Valerie suddenly felt as though she couldn't breathe. "I refuse to marry him. I don't love James. I never will."

"What do you know about love?" Father guffawed. "You're so young, not even nineteen years old. What could you possibly know of the subject of love?"

"Enough to know I don't want to marry James."

Folding her arms obstinately across her chest, Valerie turned away from him, but she could hear her father emptying his tumbler. His silence sent an eerie message that she might not have a choice in this matter.

EIGHT

BEN BARRELED DOWN THE STEPS, HIS BIBLE CLUTCHED tightly in one hand. Landing at the bottom of the stairwell, he swung around in the direction of the dining room when he collided headlong into the lovely Miss Valerie Fontaine. He heard her tiny cry of alarm when they hit, his chest sending her careening backward.

He quickly wrapped his right arm around her slender waist to keep her from falling while his left hand came to rest on her delicate shoulder. "I beg your pardon. I hope I didn't hurt you."

"I–I think I'm unharmed." She stared up at him with those azure eyes while her pretty pink mouth beckoned to be kissed.

Ben wanted to oblige in the worst way, but he forced himself to step back a pace. He steadied her on her feet before letting her go. "I'm afraid I overslept."

"I'm sure you needed the extra rest." She ran her hands down the skirt of her simple dark brown dress with its cream-colored lace cape. He couldn't help but notice how nicely she filled out the gown's shapely bodice.

He cast off the thought and forced a polite grin. "You're an understanding hostess." He glanced at the Bible he still clutched in spite of their collision.

"There's plenty of breakfast left," she said. "In fact, I was just going to fetch more tea. Shall I have Adalia bring you some coffee?"

"I'd be grateful." Ben's smile grew.

She returned the gesture. "Well, then, make yourself comfortable in the dining room. I'll be along in a minute or two."

After a nod of affirmation, he continued on and, reaching the long, polished oak table, pulled out a chair and sat down. He turned his Bible to Matthew chapter seven, where he'd left off in his reading yesterday. After a few minutes Ben paused to mull over the words of Jesus Christ when Valerie entered the room.

"Adalia will be in soon with your coffee," she said.

"Perfect." Ben stood and pulled out the adjacent chair for her. An idea formed. "May I be so bold to inquire about your plans for today?"

"I haven't any really. And you?"

"I'm meeting my partner, Clint, and his wife a few miles outside of the city at a Confederate camp. We'll see what we can gather about Luke there and photograph some officers."

"Sounds intriguing—at least to me who's never been around officers and photographers."

With a smile, Ben sat back down on his chair. "Would you like to come along? It wouldn't be dangerous or anything."

Her countenance brightened, and her eyes seemed all the more blue. "I'd like that."

It was the response for which Ben had hoped—but now dreaded. He wanted to get to know Valerie better, and what better way to accomplish that feat than to spend more time with her. And yet, he must be stark raving mad to think he had time for a woman in his life. First and foremost, he had to find Luke.

Adalia came in and set the silver coffee service in front of Ben. She poured out his first cup.

He inhaled deeply of the rising steam. "Now this is some kind of good coffee."

Valerie smiled while Adalia poured a fresh cup of tea for her. "I'm going with Benjamin to a Confederate camp today," she told the maid. Then, looking at Ben, she added, "To look for his brother and take photographs. But I suppose I shall require a chaperone for propriety's sake." She folded her arms and a pensive frown creased her forehead. "It'll take too much time to send a message to Elicia, and chances are she couldn't come anyway with her cousins in town."

Adalia cleared her throat loudly.

"Same with Violet."

Again Adalia cleared her throat, but this time she added a hacking cough.

Valerie whirled around to face the plump maid. "Good heavens! Are you all right?"

"I'm fine, miss. It's just that you mentioned you needed a chaperone today, and well, I believe I'm available."

Valerie inhaled sharply. "You?" She thought it over, then a smile inched its way across her lovely face. "That would be marvelous!"

"I can be ready to leave right away," Adalia added.

"You don't suppose my father will mind?" Valerie pressed her pink lips together in thought.

"Oh, I imagine he won't be bothered one bit. He left early again and said he wouldn't be returning for another day or two." The maid shrugged. "Some sort of important meeting. Meanwhile, Chastean is here and can cover for me, should something arise." Arching a brow, she added, "Besides, I think y' father would be more vexed if you went off without a proper chaperone."

"You've got a point there." Valerie folded her hands. "Then it's settled." She looked at Ben and smiled.

"There will be other women at the campsite too," he said. "Some are visiting their husbands, and others cook, sew, and write letters for the men before they leave for battle."

"I could write some letters," Adalia offered.

"So could I." Valerie's sunny disposition shone all the brighter.

He grinned, hardly able to take his gaze off the younger woman. "Good."

"Will the soldiers need food?" Adalia wanted to know. "Chastean made a pot of soup we could take along."

"I can secure the pot in the back of my wagon." Ben forced his attention to the maid. "I haven't met a soldier yet who turned away a home-cooked meal." Anticipation swelled inside of him. This day was shaping up better than he'd imagined.

Around midmorning, Ben began to prepare his wagon for the short journey to the campsite. He hitched up his two horses and checked his equipment, the glass plates that were loaded into his camera, the chemicals he used to sensitize their surfaces, and more chemicals that he used in developing the pictures. Everything appeared to be in its rightful place.

Typically he and Clint developed their photographs right there on the campsite or, in the case of the battle at Bull Run, right there on the battlefield. It wasn't a comfortable job, and the smell of ether was sometimes overwhelming. But when the nearest photographist's studio was fifty, sometimes a hundred miles away, developing their own pictures was a necessity. However, today might prove a different story as Clint had mentioned wanting to check in with the photographer here in New Orleans. For a small fee, the man might allow them to use his developing studio.

"I believe I'm finally ready."

Hearing her honeyed statement, Ben smiled. But when he pivoted and saw her walking toward him carrying a kettle and a small wicker basket, he rushed to relieve her of the load. The aroma of chicken broth and a mix of spices filled his senses. "I presume this is the soup Adalia spoke of earlier." He lifted the pot and basket into his arms.

"Your presumption is quite correct, Mr. McCabe." She feigned a lofty look before adjusting her woolen wrap. "And actually—" She opened the basket that he now held. "I believe there are a few jars of preserves in here as well."

"This food will not go unappreciated. I can guarantee it." He gently placed the kettle into the back of the wagon, then put the basket in beside it. They were each quite heavy. "Did you carry these items all the way from the kitchen?" Turning, he faced her once more.

She nodded and retied her bonnet so a large velvet bow now rested beneath her chin. "I'm really quite strong for a woman."

Ben fought to conceal his grin. The words *delicate* and *demure*, even *fragile* seemed to more accurately describe Valerie Fontaine. Never *strong*, although she was full of surprises.

"Mama used to say we hail from sturdy stock."

Ben gave in to a chuckle. "Is that right?"

Valerie bobbed her head before her attention turned to his unusual wagon. "My, my, this is quite the conveyance. I didn't see it the night you came in, and then yesterday Willie brought around the buggy for us."

"Yes, this is it. My home away from home and a portable darkroom." Ben gave it a quick once-over. The vehicle had four wheels and a hitch, and its base was made of hardwood, just like most other wagons. Its only oddity was that the upper portion had extremely high wooden supports that were covered by a thick black drape, like a macabre covered wagon.

"I gather I am to ride on this contraption of yours."

Ben laughed aloud at her tentative expression before nodding. "Sturdy stock and all."

Valerie lifted one of her dark, shapely brows. "I sincerely hope you were referring to the soup."

"Oh, yes, ma'am!" He swallowed another laugh.

She placed one hand on her hip. "Hmm…"

Taking her hand, Ben helped her aboard the wagon, and once Adalia emerged a few minutes later, he assisted her up also. Finally he climbed up onto the long bench as well and collected the reins. A slap of the leather straps against the horses' rumps, and they started off for the campsite.

"So tell me why your wagon is designed in such a peculiar fashion. Do people on the street stop to gawk as you pass by?"

"In answer to the first part of your question…" Ben glanced at Valerie, enjoying her close proximity. "The back of my wagon serves as a portable darkroom. When I'm in the middle of nowhere and in need of a place to develop my pictures, this setup does a fine job."

She glanced at a boy on the street who pointed at his odd vehicle. He saw her face flame. "I hope neither my wagon nor I are a source of embarrassment for you."

She looked his way and her features softened. "I'm never ashamed to be in your company, Benjamin McCabe. Your wagon, on the other hand—" She momentarily peered over her shoulder at the boy who was now behind them. "—it does take a bit of getting used to."

Adalia's chortles reached his ears.

"Fair enough." Ben too chuckled at her honesty.

"Imagine it. We were in Manassas at the same time," Valerie said. "We might have passed each other on the road and never known it." She paused. "On second thought, I'm sure I'd have remembered your wagon."

Ben smiled. "I reckon you're right about that."

She grew quiet for several long minutes. Ben thought he could actually feel her heavy thoughts. "What are you thinking about so hard right now?"

"Well, to be perfectly honest, I was remembering how terribly afraid I felt after that first battle."

Ben thought it over. "If it helps any, I learned you've got to talk through those bad times, sometimes more than once, or else that wily devil will haunt you with 'em. So feel free to talk away." He didn't mind listening.

From the corner of his eye, he saw Adalia reach over and pat the back of Valerie's hand.

"I remember on that day in July, everyone was abuzz about the battle. It was supposed to be a quick victory for the Union; however, the battle seemed to drag on forever." Valerie's shoulder bumped against his when the wagon wheel rolled over a particularly large rut in the street. "Miss Hollingsworth kept us girls indoors, and we had a lengthy prayer time in the chapel. Later the newspapers were filled with stories about the hundreds of unknown dead buried in mass graves. I'd hoped they were gross exaggerations."

"They weren't." He would never forget the sight of all those men's bodies littered across the countryside. His camera recorded the scene forever.

"So it's all true then?" There was no mistaking the tremor in Valerie's voice.

Ben drew in a deep breath. "I'm afraid so."

"All that killin'. It's dreadful. Simply dreadful!" Adalia exclaimed from her place on the other side of Valerie. "May God rest those poor boys' souls. The way they must have suffered…"

"Unimaginable!" Valerie held her gloved hands to her heart.

"Their mothers must be devastated," Adalia said.

"Ladies, ladies…I think it's time to change the subject." He figured his female companions would be sobbing in another minute, and he couldn't console the two of them and try to steer his team safely into camp at the same time. "I've got good news for you."

They both regarded him with expectancy.

"The troops we're visiting today are very much alive."

Benjamin's odd-looking wagon rolled into the Confederate campsite, garnering stares from everyone they passed. Valerie tamped down her embarrassment long enough to take in her surroundings. Several men clad in gray hustled along the muddy pathway that ran up the middle of the camp. A couple of them led horses, while others walked alone but with purposeful strides. Clusters of soldiers could be seen here and there, and more still sat outside of their tents, smoking, drinking coffee. And, just as Benjamin said, there were women too. Dozens of them. Valerie couldn't quite believe her eyes. They were dressed in formal attire and strolled along, many arm in arm with their uniformed escorts.

"It's not unusual for women to visit their husbands," Benjamin explained, "especially since the ladies may not see them for months once this camp breaks up and the soldiers head for the front."

Valerie thought those ladies must be quite brave to carry on with their lives after the men they loved went marching off, some never to be seen again.

"You're frowning, Miss Fontaine." She didn't miss his teasing tone. "I've heard the habit leaves permanent winkles."

"Very funny."

He laughed. Then, helping her alight from the wagon, Benjamin introduced her and Adalia to his partner, Clint Culver, and his wife, Emily, who were setting up the photographic equipment. They'd obviously arrived sometime before and were situated in a wagon similar to Benjamin's. The first two things Valerie noticed about Mr. Culver were his dark brown whiskers and eyes that possessed an enormous amount of energy as he darted around the wagon. She noticed too his wife's slower movements as she assisted him.

Standing by, Valerie watched Benjamin pull equipment from his wagon. "What can I do to help you?" she asked when he came within earshot.

"Nothing right now." He sent her one of his easy smiles. "I'm going to ask around about Luke, and then, later on, I'll be grateful for your assistance as we begin taking photographs."

"All right. Perhaps I'll see if Adalia needs help with the food."

"I'll come along," Emily offered. She tugged her wool coat around herself while wisps of cinnamon-colored hair slipped from the clip at her nape.

Together they headed toward where Valerie had last seen her trusted maid. She felt awed by the goings on around her—the din of voices, an occasional laugh. The entire base was a tent city, and beneath one of the larger canvas shelters a number of crude wooden tables had been erected—a makeshift dining hall. Nearby, kettles hung over open flames and bubbled with interesting brews.

"Ben didn't tell us he'd have company today," Emily said.

"Oh?" Valerie turned and regarded Emily Culver's sweet-looking face. From the manner in which she spoke, Valerie guessed the woman wasn't a Southerner. "Well, it was a last-minute decision."

"I'm glad you're here."

"You are?" The wind blew at their backs.

"Now I'll have someone special to talk to. You must be special if Ben brought you along."

Valerie didn't know what to make of the remark. She felt flattered and, yes, *special*. However, her growing feelings for the handsome photographer had her mind in a whir. "Benjamin's a guest in my father's home. He simply extended an invitation to join him."

"An invitation to work your fingers to the bone?" Emily laughed. "No, my dear, he only makes that sort of offer to people he cares about."

"Excuse me?" Confused, Valerie halted in mid-stride and regarded Emily.

She stopped too. "I'm being facetious. Please forgive my sarcasm. I've grown accustomed to being around men like Ben…and Luke before last July." For a second a sad shadow crossed her face. "All I meant to say is that it's nice to have a female companion, even if it's just for a day."

A smile came easily to Valerie's lips. In that moment she decided she liked Emily Culver—and her candor. It was a rare but precious trait in women.

"I hope we can be friends."

"I'm sure we will be."

Linking her arm with Valerie's, Emily gave her a tug toward the mess tent.

"So," Valerie said, "you're not from the South, are you?"

Emily shook her head. "I'm from Boston. Clint and I met there. We met Ben there as well. New Orleans almost feels like the other end of the world."

"I'm sure it does." Valerie smiled. "So, Clint is from the South?"

"His family's originally from Charleston, but they have relatives in Boston. An opportunity presented itself there, and so when Clint was sixteen years old, his father moved them to Massachusetts. Papa Culver is a merchant commissioner."

"Really? My father's in the shipping business too."

"See? We have something in common already."

They caught up to Adalia, who stirred the soup pot over an open fire in the outdoor kitchen area. Within minutes, the overseeing cook, a burly sergeant with a laugh as big as his paunch, put both Valerie and Emily to work, dishing out rations of stew to the men who came and stood in line with their tin cups in hand. Adalia too busied herself, doling out bread and serving soup. Before long Chastean's expertly made food had been devoured.

"I could have brought five more pots of that soup." Adalia's voice sounded both pleased and perplexed. "These boys are so hungry I'm lucky they didn't chew off m' arm while I ladled out their helpings."

Valerie felt glad to help their young men in gray, even in some small way.

Benjamin sat down for a quick bite to eat as well.

"Did you find out anything about your brother?" Valerie asked.

"Nothing." His expression was downcast.

She touched his sleeve. "You'll find him."

He gave her a doubtful look.

"Don't get discouraged." She tipped her head, watching him swirl the coffee in his cup. "Perhaps this is a silly question, but why do you think Confederates might know where Luke is? You said your brother was—make that *is*—politically neutral."

"We were closer to the Confederate lines when the army swept by us. I figure Luke got caught up with passing soldiers. Everything happened so fast."

Valerie mulled it over, wishing there was something she could do.

"Well, I'd best get to work," he said, changing the subject. "How 'bout helping me with the photographing process?"

"I'd be honored." Valerie followed him back over to where his large, black, boxlike camera sat upon its tripod.

"Several officers have requested photographs of themselves and their wives. What I'd like for you to do is collect the money and write down the name of each man, the post office where his photograph can be sent, and the amount paid so I have a record in my logbook."

"All right."

He handed Valerie a ledger, a quill, and ink, and she set to the task. In between her documenting, she observed the photographic process.

Mr. Culver busied himself with the glass plates. He coated each with something called collodion.

Em sat beside her, on a chair that one of the soldiers brought over. "The whole procedure is tricky business even in a studio setting," she explained to Valerie. "Clint sensitizes the plates for several minutes and...see him now?"

Valerie watched as Mr. Culver pulled his wagon's drape around himself. "What is he doing in there?" She craned her neck to see.

"Clint works beneath a reddish glow that's filtered through special windows that won't harm the plates like daylight will. He immerses each one in a silver nitrate bath. Once he blots away the excess chemical, he secures the plate in a wooden holder before taking to Ben, who operates the camera. It's quite a science."

"It seems so."

At that precise moment, Mr. Culver reappeared from under the wagon's tarp and rushed toward the camera, where he inserted the plate.

Benjamin had already pointed the instrument in the direction of the subject matter, in this case Captain Frederick Banks. Benjamin bent inside the camera. Its dark cloth covered his head. "Hold very still," he told the captain.

Valerie found herself holding her breath as if her own movement would mar the photograph. Almost fifteen seconds later,

Benjamin replaced the lens caps and the plate holder's front cover. Valerie inhaled and watched as the protected plate came out of the camera and he ran it over to the wagon.

"Clint will store the exposed plates in a chemical mixture for the time being," Emily said, as she leaned her head closer to Valerie. "The actual printing of the photographs onto albumin paper will be done later."

"I'm positively amazed by all this." Valerie tugged her woolen cape more closely around her shoulders. The photographic session continued, and Valerie decided she enjoyed conversing with Emily. Later, they walked to the mess tent to retrieve some hot coffee for Benjamin and Clint. Mud caked the hems of their gowns, but Valerie didn't mind. She couldn't imagine any of her friends—Elicia, Cherie, or Violet—ever stepping into an army camp and getting dirty. They'd likely be appalled if they saw her now.

Valerie handed Benjamin the cup of hot coffee. "Thank you kindly."

"You're welcome." She watched him take a sip of the hot liquid, noticing how the January wind had reddened his face. And his eyes—

Suddenly she noticed him studying her. Valerie quickly lowered her gaze.

"May I be so bold as to ask to take a photograph of you?"

"Now?"

"Right now. We're done with all the paying customers." He smiled and took another drink from the tin cup.

"But I look completely disheveled." Valerie shook her head. "Look at my skirt!"

"I'll make sure my camera only captures you from the waist on up."

Valerie managed a little nod. What could it hurt?

He grinned. "Is that a yes?"

"Yes."

Benjamin moved the chair nearer to his wagon. "Sit here." Placing his strong hands on her shoulders, he gently turned her just so. "I'll try to capture my wagon in the background so this photograph will serve as a reminder of your outing today. Something to show your grandchildren one day."

"Grandchildren!" Valerie blinked.

Emily raised a gloved hand to her mouth and laughed. "Mercy, Ben!"

"Now, Em, don't go twisting things." He set his hands on his hips and narrowed his gaze at her. "I only meant the photograph will be a keepsake for future generations, that's all."

Valerie hid the smile that touched her lips.

Benjamin turned back to her. "Now, you're going to have to stay still."

"I'll do my best."

"I need Valerie to hold still, Em, so stop your giggling."

"I can't help it, Ben."

Valerie smoothed her skirts, adjusted her woolen cape, and straightened her bonnet. She tried to summon her most serious expression, but it wasn't easy with Em laughing nearby.

Meanwhile, Benjamin repositioned his camera. "Don't move."

Valerie held her breath and willed every muscle not to quiver.

Half a minute later, he appeared from beneath his camera's black drape. "Got it." He handed the plate to Mr. Culver, who ran it over to the other wagon for the developing process.

"Well, I guess that's it. Let's get things put away and head back."

Emily glanced at her husband as he collected his equipment. "Ben, Clint and I are staying in our wagon tonight. Clint said we'll just stay here at the camp."

He paused, looking from her to his partner. "Why's that?"

Clint sent him a quick look. "We just decided it'd be best."

Benjamin didn't reply but stood there with hands on hips in tentative thought.

Valerie sensed the reason for the Culvers' camping in their wagon had something to do with limited resources.

"You're welcome to stay at my home." She blurted out the offer before thinking better of it, although she doubted her father would mind. And there was another spare bedroom. "We have plenty of room." Valerie glanced at Adalia, who replied with an enthused nod. Then she peered at her new friend and finally at Mr. Culver. "So, will you be my guests?"

A long moment of consideration passed before Emily crossed the short distance between them and placed her arm around Valerie's shoulders. "Thank you for your kind offer. We'd be honored." Looking back, she added, "Right, Clint?"

He replied with a half bow. Gratitude shone in his dark eyes. "Yes, thank you, Miss Fontaine."

"Good. Then it's settled." She smiled and turned her gaze to Benjamin, noticing his expression of appreciation for her offer.

Once the gear was packed, they headed for their wagons. "I enjoyed m'self today," Adalia said as Benjamin helped her up onto the bench.

Valerie had already climbed aboard with his assistance and noticed Adalia's cheeks were as pink as raspberries from the sun and crisp, winter air.

"I must have written ten letters to fathers, mothers, and sweethearts for our brave soldiers." She adjusted her skirts.

Benjamin swung himself up onto the bench and picked up the reins. "Clint and Em are going to stop at a photographer's in the city and drop off the plates. The proprietor has agreed to rent a corner of his studio to us. But after that, the Culvers will be along."

"In time for supper, I hope," Adalia said.

"Yes, ma'am." He gave a slap of the reins and they started off, jostling along the dirt pathway that led in and out of camp. "Thank you for coming along today. I know you ladies were a blessing to the soldiers."

"Perhaps, but 'twas us who got blessed," Adalia said.

Valerie agreed but noted Benjamin's somber expression.

"I just pray the Confederate Army realizes what it's up against. The North is developing its weaponry and increasing the size of its navy. The South sadly lags behind. I fear the worst is yet to come."

Hearing the news, Valerie began to tremble as a dark apprehension threatened to sweep her away. She'd had a similar feeling back at school—was it fear or just the realization that she had no control over many of life's circumstances?

"Are you cold, Valerie?" Benjamin asked.

"I–I'm all r–right."

"Why, you're shaking, dearie. Y' must have caught a chill." Adalia pressed in Valerie's cape so it fit more snugly. "These wraps might be the height of fashion, but they sure can't keep a girl warm like a thick wool coat."

Benjamin shrugged out of his overcoat. "Here, take mine." He set the horses' reins under one boot momentarily as he blanketed Valerie.

"But then y–you'll be c–cold."

"I'm used to a lot colder. Boston is freezing this time of year, and back home in Missouri, this weather would be considered downright balmy for January."

"Th–thank you." A musky, manly scent filled her nostrils, and the heat from his body still lingered in the wool, warming her at once.

"You mentioned Missouri. Tell me more about Jericho Junction."

Benjamin chuckled. "Not much more to tell."

"What does your home look like? How many rooms?"

"Hmm, let's see…" He seemed to do a quick mental inventory. "Drawing room, kitchen, dining room downstairs, three bedrooms upstairs. My parents in one, us boys in another, and Sarah and Leah in the last but biggest bedroom." There was a smile in his voice when he added, "My sisters were always favored over us boys. But now, since Leah got married and moved out, Sarah has that nice, big bedroom all to herself, the spoiled little thing."

"And Leah's the sister who's expecting a baby any day now?" Valerie recalled hearing the fact last night at the Elliots'. "How exciting for your family."

"I think it's going to be a boy. Just a hunch, though."

Valerie watched him, noting the smile that touched his eyes at the mention of a nephew. "What does Leah's husband do for a living?"

"Blacksmithing, although Jonathan enlisted and went off to fight with the same regiment as Jake."

"But Jake was wounded and returned home."

"That's right." Benjamin chuckled.

Valerie grinned, glad she'd remembered correctly. "Is Jericho Junction part of the Union or Confederate States?"

"Union, although not officially. There are still a lot of staunch Confederates in the state. Our town and my family are true representations of that political split in philosophies—just like Missouri itself. My parents are Union supporters. Jake is a Confederate. Luke and I, however, tend to waver in our views because of our professions. In fact, I photographed Federal soldiers the night Luke held a big camp revival meeting—that was before he went missing."

Valerie tipped her head. She couldn't resist teasing him. "Does Colonel LaPorte know of your, um, wavering?"

"Can't say as I know whether he's aware of it or not." Benjamin said with an easy chuckle. "No doubt, if he found out, he'd intend to convert me."

"I'm sure. What about the Culvers?" Valerie continued. "I don't get the feeling they lean toward one side or the other."

"We're all of the view that God handmade each human soul regardless of whether they wear blue or gray."

"Hmm…" Valerie realized that she belonged somewhere in the middle too. "Mr. Culver seems quite refined," she observed absently.

"And I'm not?" Benjamin acted insulted. "For your information, little lady, I'm just as refined as Clint."

"I suppose that's debatable." Valerie enjoyed ribbing him.

"I beg your pardon?" A note of mock defense entered his voice.

"Beg all you want, but I suspect you're more country boy than you know."

"Listen here, *Miss Refinement*, you've got mud caked on your dress clear up to your knees."

Valerie peered around his overcoat at her poor skirts. "I do, don't I?" She shared a laugh with both Benjamin and Adalia.

"Mud or no mud, I'm proud of you for what y' did today, dearie. And I'm equally as proud of you, Mr. McCabe, and y' friends Mr. and Mrs. Culver. You did a fine thing for The Cause by taking photographs of those men today. Pleased as punch, they were, to get their pictures took."

Valerie voiced her agreement and then wondered how long Benjamin would stay in New Orleans. His search for Luke and his quest to photograph the war would surely take him away soon. The thought of his leaving saddened her. She felt safe whenever he was near—and she felt something else too.

She only hoped she'd have a chance to fully discover what that *something* could be.

NINE

NIGHT HAD FALLEN BY THE TIME THEY RETURNED to the city. As they neared the house, Adalia insisted on being let off at the servants' door since not a single light shone from any of the windows.

"It looks so desolate," Valerie remarked, thinking their home never appeared empty when Mama was alive. Even if they were gone for the day, Mama somehow made sure the home fires always burned brightly when they arrived home.

"Oh, that Chastean," the maid grumbled. "She should have lit the lamps. What will the neighbors say, our residence being all cold and dark this way?"

Benjamin jumped down and helped Adalia from the wagon. "Can I be of some assistance?"

"No, sir. There's just some things a good housekeeper has to do herself. Give me a few minutes before you come in."

"Of course."

Valerie pressed her gloved hand over her lips to keep from smiling as Adalia muttered all the way to the side door.

Benjamin climbed back up into the wagon. "Should we wait here?"

Valerie pondered his question but decided against taking a houseguest through the servants' entrance. "May I ride with you as far as the stables? Willie can see to your horses and wagon, and then you and I can use the garden entrance."

"I won't argue that idea."

A light drizzle began to fall, growing steadier by the second. Benjamin steered his team around the brick house. As he pulled up to the stables, the huge, wooden door slid open and Willie stepped out. He held a lantern in his hand and lifted it high, illuminating the horses and wagon.

"Miz Valerie! Missah McCabe! I been waitin' on you." Hanging his lamp on a nail, the loyal attendant rushed over to take the horses' reins.

Benjamin hopped down and helped Valerie from the wagon. She handed him his overcoat, deciding she didn't need it anymore, as Willie led the team into the barn. She gathered her cloak more tightly around her neck just as a sudden, hard rain began to fall.

Grabbing hold of her elbow, Benjamin propelled her toward the shelter of the overhang. Warm air emanated from the barn's entrance, mixing the pungent odors of straw, wet animals, musty wood, and leather.

"So, how soaked would you like to get?" Humor filled his voice. "We could make a run for it, or we could stay here for a few minutes and see if this downpour abates."

"This is New Orleans in January. It might be days before the rain abates."

"We'll make a run for it, then?"

Valerie nodded. "Yes, I think so."

Benjamin put his overcoat around her again.

"What about you?" she said. "You'll be soaked to the skin."

"I won't melt." Wearing a grin, Benjamin held out his hand.

She took it, feeling his fingers curl around hers protectively. And in that moment, Valerie imagined that this was how it felt to be loved and cherished.

"Ready?"

"Ready."

Together they dashed through the yard, past the fruit trees, and one hundred feet beyond. They ran alongside Mama's flower-beds and favorite herb garden, and Valerie squealed when her foot landed in a rapidly growing puddle between two of the walk stones. Then they reached the solarium, pushing open the French doors and hurrying inside.

"Oh, my goodness!" The sprint left Valerie breathless. "I believe those were the largest raindrops I've ever encountered." She removed her bonnet and peeled off her wraps, shaking them off onto the tiled floor before slinging them over a wrought-iron plant rack. "Are you all right?"

"No worse for wear." Benjamin raked his hand through his wet blond hair before removing his frock. After giving it a good shake, he reached around Valerie and set it alongside the others.

In that very moment, she realized his close proximity and how dwarfed she felt beneath the long shadow of his muscular frame. She could smell the wet linen of his shirt, the soaked wool of his gray waistcoat and trousers. She felt paralyzed, yet all she could do was stare up into his face. Its angles and planes were barely visible beneath the faraway glow of the gas street lamp.

Suddenly Benjamin reached out and traced the side of her face with the back of his fingers, but he said not a word. The intense expression on his face, the look in his eyes, let Valerie know his intentions. Her heart beat hard in her chest.

In one fluid move, he gathered her in his arms and lowered his mouth to hers. Unhurriedly, his lips moved across hers, and his embrace pressed her closer to his body. She responded to the passion building between them. Her arms slipped around his waist, and she kissed him with a fervor she'd never realized she possessed.

He pulled away slightly. "Do you believe in love at first sight?" He whispered the words against her mouth.

"I–I don't know." Did he really expect an intelligent reply? She couldn't think straight at the moment.

He kissed her once again. But then all too soon, he gently pushed her away. "Valerie, no more. We have to stop."

"But why?"

With a soft chuckle, he allowed her to sag against him as he rested his jaw against her temple.

"I know better, that's why. I shouldn't have taken such liberties, and I apologize."

"Please don't. It wasn't as if you stole a kiss. I freely gave it." She peered up into his face. "And please don't think badly of me, but I–I rather enjoyed it."

"Yes, I gathered as much." He sounded amused. "Regardless, it's not right."

Valerie laid her head against his shoulder. She watched the rain stream down the windows of the solarium. "I've had beaus before, but I never felt for them what I feel for you right now...and I've only known you two days."

Stepping back, Benjamin took both of her hands in his. He wore a soft expression as he reached one hand up and caressed her cheek. "But the truth of the matter is we both need to pray about this, about us. I made a mistake once before because I didn't seek God's wisdom and plan for my life. I'd hate for us to make the same mistake."

"It certainly didn't feel like it was a mistake."

"No, it didn't." His voice sounded heavy. "But let's give things between us a chance so we can find out for sure. Let's follow the Lord and do this the right way, so we have His blessing. And so we'll always know deep down that we made the right choice."

"You're right, and I agree."

"Good, 'cause I wouldn't want to hurt you for the world."

Valerie lifted her gaze to his, thinking Benjamin McCabe had to be the most tender and sincere man she'd ever met. "That Gwyneth Merriweather is awfully dim-witted to let you escape."

His grin said he found the remark amusing. "Let's see if you feel that way after some time passes."

Valerie wasn't daunted by the challenge. But before she could say anything more, an acrid wisp of cigar smoke tickled her nostrils. A chill crept over her when she sensed another presence. Was it her father?

She felt Benjamin tense, and he slowly released her. Then, looking toward the doorway, Valerie spied the shadowy figure of a man stepping into the solarium.

"Well, well, if it isn't my dear Valerie and the transient photographer, having a tryst out here in the dark."

"James!" Insult coupled with humiliation heated her blood. "What—! Did you—?"

"Oh, yes, Valerie honey." He produced a wicked-sounding chuckle. "I heard you throw yourself at this man in the most shameful way." Stuffing the cigar into his mouth, he gave it a puff, and the tobacco's tip glowed fiery red. "But don't worry...I won't tell your father."

Valerie shook with anger. "How dare you enter my home uninvited. Get out!"

"Not before I give this miscreant a piece of my mind." He turned to Benjamin. "This photographer, as he refers to himself, rolls into town and takes advantage of my intended. I'll not stand for it."

"I am not your intended, and the only *miscreant* in this room is you, James Ladden." Valerie's body shook with anger. "Now, leave here at once!"

Benjamin set a placating hand on her shoulder. But it did little good to quell her anger.

She lifted her chin. "You're just jealous, James, because I didn't welcome your advances."

James lunged at her so suddenly that Benjamin barely had time to shove Valerie behind him. "Don't you dare raise a hand to her, Ladden!" A razor-sharp warning edged his tone.

James slowly lowered his arm. "I'll not stand for such insults!" His voice increased in decibels with each word.

Holding on to Benjamin's sleeve, Valerie trembled in a rage tinged with fear.

"Listen, Ladden, you're the one who snuck in here. I suggest you leave immediately."

"You *suggest*?" James let out a curse such as Valerie had never heard before. Her ears burned and her face flamed.

"Ladden, need I remind you that there is a lady present?"

"Bah!" James threw his cigar onto the tiled floor and extinguished it with the toe of his boot. "Come on, McCabe, you can't be that big a fool. Can't you see she's just trying to make me jealous?" Quite abruptly, James turned calm and collected. "You see, we're engaged to be married. We had a little spat, and—"

"Liar!" Valerie attempted to come around Benjamin, her fists clenched at her side, but he stepped in front of her. Benjamin's human barricade, however, didn't stop her mouth from shouting what was on her mind. "Get out of my house, James! Get out now or I'll summon the authorities!"

Adalia suddenly hurried into the room with a lamp in her hand. Its glass shade rattled precariously with her every hurried step. "What in the queen mother's name is goin' on in here?" She stopped short and surveyed the trio. A knowing look darkened her gaze. "Oh, dear…"

"Send Ephraim for the authorities, Adalia," Valerie said. "James stole into our home like some petty thief."

"Don't bother; I'm leaving." He pointed a finger at Valerie. "Don't think this matter is settled."

"Don't you think it's settled either." She lifted her chin. "When my father comes home, I intend to tell him all about this."

James doubled over in laughter. "And what will he do to me in his usual inebriated state, hmm?"

Valerie was horrified.

Shame roiled deep inside of her until she thought she might be sick. Covering her mouth with her gloved hand, she bolted from the room, through the dining room and kitchen, and up the back servants' stairwell, not even daring to breathe until she reached the sanctity of her bedroom.

Closing the door, she sagged against it. Only then did she let go of the first of many gut-wrenching sobs.

The Culvers arrived, and Ben followed them upstairs as Adalia led the way. But as they turned one way down the hallway, heading for their guest room, Ben stepped around the other way and paused in front of Valerie's doorway. He couldn't hear anything. He knocked.

"Valerie, it's Ben. Are you all right?"

A long moment past before she answered. "I–I'm fine." Her voice sounded weak, and Ben figured she'd been crying. He winced.

"The Culvers have arrived."

"Thank you. I'll be down for supper in a bit."

Not wanting to push her, he let the conversation go at that. He felt terrible about the way James humiliated her, although he'd also been impressed by her tenacity. There were moments during her confrontation that Ben wasn't sure whom he tried to protect, her or Ladden. But in the end he was sorry he hadn't shielded Valerie more. Ladden was a true rapscallion.

He also regretted giving in to his desires and kissing her. *Lord, forgive me. It won't happen again.* Ironically, he couldn't help but remember how Gwyneth hadn't allowed more than a pristine kiss on her cheek in all the time they'd been engaged. Even then, she seemed to only endure it while Valerie said she enjoyed their kiss. *But I know I overstepped my bounds this evening, Lord.* Reaching his own room, located down the dimly lit hallway and across from the Culvers', he decided to get into some dry clothes.

"This is lovely. Thank you." Emily's voice reached his ears, and gratefulness filled Ben. His friends would sleep far better here at the Fontaines' home than in the back of their wagon, that's for sure. It was nice of Valerie to offer.

"Supper will be served at seven," Adalia told them. "When you're rested, you can go downstairs to the parlor. I imagine Miss Valerie'll be there by then."

The maid hurried into the hallway, and Ben inclined his head politely as she passed.

"And I'll be needin' those wet clothes of yours, Mr. McCabe."

"Yes, ma'am." Her tone left no room for argument.

"Did you hear me say that supper's at seven?"

"I did." He grinned at her bossiness. "And I'll be punctual."

Valerie changed her clothes and repinned her hair. Glancing at her reflection, she determined her eyes weren't nearly as puffy as they'd been an hour ago. The cloth that Adalia had soaked in salt water and brought to her had done wonders. As for James, Valerie hoped to never see the scoundrel again. She would, of course, inform her father of the incident. This time James had disgraced not only her but Father as well—and in front of a guest, no less.

Valerie's mind drifted to Benjamin. He hadn't been far from her thoughts since she'd left the solarium. She kept remembering his gentle voice talking about love at first sight. Could that be possible? She felt an unusual draw to him. Was it love? *Lord, please tell me...show me.*

With one last glance at her appearance and the dark brown checked gown she wore, she left her bedroom. In the parlor, she found Benjamin and the Culvers sitting near the hearth, chatting.

"Good evening." She stepped farther into the room.

Benjamin came toward her. "Are you all right?" He whispered the question.

She gave him a brief nod. He offered his arm and she took it.

Clint Culver rose to his feet as well. "Miss Fontaine—"

"Please call me Valerie."

"Valerie." A smile inched across his whiskered face. "Em and I can't thank you enough for inviting us to stay here."

"Much more comfortable than our wagon," Emily added, smoothing the skirt of her slate-colored gown. "Your home is beautiful, Valerie."

"And you can't beat the company," Benjamin jested with a chuckle.

Ephraim strode in on Valerie's heels. "Excuse me, but if you'll all be seated in the dining room, dinner will be served."

She turned and gave her father's valet a quizzical look. Why had he stepped into Adalia's role?

As if reading her thoughts, he said, "Chastean went home, so Adalia's in the kitchen."

Before she could reply, Benjamin led her through the parlor. The table had been set with a white linen cloth, two places on one side and two on the other. Benjamin helped Valerie into a chair before taking the seat beside her. Opposite them, Clint and Emily did the same.

After Adalia brought in bowls of steaming seafood chowder, Benjamin asked the blessing before they ate.

"How long do you anticipate staying in New Orleans?" Valerie hoped it would be a good long while. "Of course," she quickly added, "you're all welcome to stay here as long as you wish."

"Thanks, Valerie," Em said, smiling at her from across the table. "I guess it all depends on whether the boys accept Colonel LaPorte's offer."

Benjamin and Clint paused in their eating while Valerie sat by, feeling confused. She thought Benjamin had told her and Father that nothing came of the colonel's offer.

Emily inhaled sharply. "Oh, I'm sorry."

The apology furthered Valerie's puzzlement.

Benjamin rose and shut the doors of the dining room. When he returned to his seat, he leaned in close. "Valerie, please don't breathe a word of this—even to your father. Colonel LaPorte has asked us to stay in New Orleans and do some photographic work for the military. But it's a covert assignment, and no one other than Clint was supposed to know."

"I had to tell Em," Clint said in his own defense.

She appeared chagrined. "Forgive me, Ben."

Valerie gave Emily a sympathetic glance before looking back at Benjamin. "I won't tell a soul. I promise."

"We haven't yet accepted the colonel's offer. If we do, Clint and I will be gone during the day and, maybe, a few days on end."

"Emily and I will bide our time." Valerie sensed what he hinted at. "We can go to the theater, shop—"

"What will your father have to say about it, Valerie?" Benjamin continued his close proximity and hushed tone of voice.

"To tell you the truth, I think he'll say it's all just fine. Father has seemed less reticent since you arrived, Benjamin, and he told you to stay as long as you liked. I don't believe he'll mind that your partner and his wife are here too."

"If that changes," Emily said, "let us know, and we'll leave at once."

"I'll be absolutely honest with all of you." Valerie looked from Emily to Clint and then finally at Benjamin. "I promise."

TEN

"I CAN'T BELIEVE IT!"

"Well, it's true." Sitting in an upholstered armchair, Valerie's gaze wandered as her father angrily paced his study. Books lined three of the walls of the spacious room, and a brick fireplace occupied the fourth. Heavy emerald-green drapes hung alongside each of the floor-to-ceiling windows, and beyond them, the late afternoon sun fought to shine through gray clouds. Benjamin and Clint had been gone since breakfast, and Emily rested upstairs. The house was quiet. So when her father arrived home, Valerie chose this time to inform him of yesterday's events.

"I simply cannot believe it. James's behavior is despicable." Father seemed to be raging aloud more than assuaging her doubts and fears. "Arnold Ladden will hear about this, that's for sure." Father shook his head. "And he has a lot of nerve, entering my house like a common thief!"

"Does that mean you no longer think James is a good match for me?"

Father stopped and flicked a glance over her. He clasped his hands behind his back. "You have someone else in mind?"

Valerie blushed at her father's retort. "To be honest, Benjamin and I have both agreed we would like to get to know each other better." She shifted, averting her gaze and adjusting her hoop-skirt.

"Hmm…"

"Is it all right if he and the Culvers stay with us awhile? Emily Culver and I have become good friends."

He thought it over. "Yes, I suppose it's fine." Father moved to his large mahogany desk. "I imagine Mr. McCabe and Mr. Culver have business here in New Orleans, hmm?"

"I imagine so." Valerie knew she couldn't divulge any details.

"Did they mention if they're working for Colonel LaPorte?"

"No." She wasn't lying. How could she know whether Benjamin and Clint accepted the colonel's offer?

"They're not intending to sit around my home all day doing nothing, I hope."

"Of course not."

Father's dark gaze settled on her.

Valerie shrugged, hating that awkward middle ground between keeping her promise to Benjamin and lying to her father.

"I'll ask them myself."

"Yes, do." She sighed with relief. "And do I have your solemn promise that you'll speak with Mr. Ladden and James about yesterday? I hope never to see James again."

Father pursed his lips as something akin to contempt mixed with disappointment wafted across his features. "Yes, I'll take care of the matter. But I would suggest that you forgive and forget. James has always been a prankster, right?"

"Father, I don't want anything to do with James."

"He'd make a fine husband. He'll provide for you. I won't be here and—"

"Where will you be?"

"I, um...well, I'm speaking hypothetically."

Valerie tipped her head, regarding him.

"Then, again, I might like another trip to France. You know how much I travel."

She did. He'd been away much of her childhood. She only had bits and pieces of recollections of him.

"So you will be taken care of if you marry James."

"No!" Valerie stood, her arms at her sides, her fists clenched. "Father, please don't make me marry him. Please!"

His expression was unreadable. "We'll discuss this another time. Now, why don't you run along?"

Valerie bristled. "Please don't speak to me as though I'm a child."

"Forgive me, *ma fille*." Father closed his eyes, looking suddenly weary. She wondered what sort of business had been keeping him away from home so often these past weeks. "I'll do my best to remember you're a young lady. Seems like just yesterday you were a little girl, sitting on my knee, and your mother was—" He choked on unshed emotion.

"Oh, Father..." Valerie stepped toward him and reached for his hands.

He stiffened and turned away.

A wave of hurt crashed over her. Why did she ever think this man, who'd always been a distant figure, could ever play a major role in her life? She watched as he strode to the shelf behind his desk on which his bottle of scotch stood. "You can't drink away your sorrow over Mama's death."

"And you, *ma fille*, can't run from it," he shot right back. "Is your pain any less here than it was at school?"

"No. In truth, I've found little comfort in this house." She glanced around the study before looking directly at her father again. "Or with you," she added softly.

He paused in filling his crystal tumbler and eyed her speculatively. Then shrugged.

It was then that Valerie realized her terrible mistake. She'd run to him, her earthly father, when instead she should have sought the arms of God, her heavenly Father. "Looks like you were right all along—I should have stayed at school."

"A lesson that's come too late for us both." He muttered the reply.

Valerie didn't quite hear the reply. "What?"

Father gupled down his scotch. "Nothing, *ma fille*. Nothing."

Ben noticed that Valerie seemed unusually quiet throughout dinner. Her actions as she ate appeared mechanical. Her replies were polite; however, she said nothing to contribute to the small talk flittering around the table. It bothered Ben to see her troubled, so when Valerie disappeared while they transitioned to the parlor, he went looking for her.

He found her standing outside the solarium and purposely let the door creak open then slam behind him so he wouldn't give her a start.

"Kind of chilly out here—" He stepped toward her. "—but warmer than last night."

"Yes…"

"Everything all right?"

Valerie sighed audibly and crossed her arms. "I just needed some air."

Ben half sat on the nearby wrought iron railing. "I hope whatever's bothering you doesn't have to do with your present company."

"You? No, of course it doesn't." A smile laced her tone as she turned to face him. "I'm sorry I gave you that impression. It's…well, my father…" Her voice trailed off.

"You're concerned about his drinking?"

Valerie's nod seemed timid at best.

"I can assure you that neither the Culvers nor I stand in judgment. Instead you can count on us to pray."

"Thank you."

"If it's any consolation, your father has been nothing but cordial tonight. I know I speak for all of us when I say we're mighty grateful for the hospitality." In the darkness, he saw her smile, and, not for the first time, he noticed how soft her hair looked as it framed her face.

His eyes melded with her gaze, and he longed to hold her in his arms and kiss her again.

He turned away and cleared his throat along with his thoughts.

A few moments laden with silence passed. Finally Valerie spoke again. "Mama and I were so close. She's the one who made this house a home. She loved and respected my father even though he was hardly ever here. But Mama somehow made me feel like he was, so when I returned from boarding school I naturally assumed I had a relationship with him. But the sad truth is I don't. It's all very disappointing."

"I'm sure." Ben took Valerie's hand. It felt soft and fragile. "And I'm sorry this is happening between you and your father."

"Thank you, Benjamin."

"Well, look on the bright side. He seems to have a protective nature. He approached me before dinner and said he planned to talk with James about yesterday's incident. He seemed quite indignant about it."

"Of course he is, but it has nothing to do with me." Again Valerie sighed. "Oh, perhaps I am making too much of the situation and my expectations of Father far exceed his capabilities."

Ben pushed out a rueful grin. "I know all about those far-exceeding expectations."

"You do?" She searched his face in the darkness. "You're

thinking of your brother right now, aren't you?" Valerie moved closer to him until they were only inches apart. "You have high expectations of finding him."

"Yes, I do. But is that so wrong? To have high expectations and believe God will do above and beyond what I think is possible?"

"Of course not." She shivered. "Perhaps my faith is weak."

"I don't know about that." Ben touched silky strands of her hair, then caressed the side of her face. She leaned into his palm and, a heartbeat later, stepped into his arms. Her fragrance filled his senses, and he wanted to say something consoling, but all he could think of was how good—and yes, how right—it felt to hold her. *Lord, she's the one, isn't she?*

Then Valerie placed a kiss on his jaw. Ben knew they trod on dangerous ground. "You must be freezing." Even though it took every ounce of his will, he pushed her gently back. "I think we best go inside." When she nodded, he stood and wrapped his arm around her shoulders. "I don't want you catching your death out here. Besides, your father and the Culvers are probably wondering where we are."

"You're right on all accounts."

Together they walked into the house. Ben released her as they made their way to the parlor. He realized his feelings for Valerie surpassed anything he ever felt for Gwyneth, and they went beyond mere physical attraction. A friendship had formed, a kindred spirit existed, and Valerie respected his work and him. *And she loves You, Lord.*

They reached the parlor, and Clint stood when Valerie entered the room first.

Edward Fontaine got to his feet also, but only so he could walk to where his scotch stood on the polished sideboard. "Would you like a drink, Mr. McCabe?"

"No, thank you."

Clint caught his eye. "Mr. Fontaine asked about our work and how it's keeping us in New Orleans. I told him we've rented space in Washburn's studio."

"Yes," Fontaine said, "and I replied that one would have to be taking pictures in order to need space in Washburn's." He pivoted, his refilled crystal tumbler in hand. "And isn't the rent costly? Unless you're both independently wealthy, of course."

"Don't I wish," Ben joked while he pulled up a side chair and sat down. "Seriously, though, rent's not too bad." He chose his next words carefully, knowing he couldn't say anything about Colonel LaPort's assignment that he and Clint had accepted earlier in the day. "We're freelancers, Mr. Fontaine, and commissioned to document the war in photographs."

"Commissioned by whom?" Fontaine took a seat. "And there's no war in New Orleans."

"Thank God for that!" Valerie interjected. She'd taken the chair beside Emily.

Ben sent her a quick smile before looking back at her father. "About our commission, Clint and I secured a government grant." It was true, although those funds had been expended long ago. "As for the war itself, you're aware of the Union's blockades."

"Of course." Fontaine rolled a shoulder. "I'm in the shipping business."

"Well…" Ben gazed at Clint, who seemed as poised and ready to hear his explanation as Mr. Fontaine. "Clint and I would like to get pictures of the warships." He eyed Fontaine. "Maybe even travel down the river to Fort St. Phillip." Ben waved his hand in the air. "I realize it's a long shot. We might be a couple of dreamers, or worse, fools to think it's possible, but we'd like to try."

Clint spoke up then. "Those gunners would make for some dynamic photographs."

"You'd like to capture Union gunboats with your camera, eh?" Mr. Fontaine pursed his lips.

Ben steeled himself. He expected a guffaw.

But instead Fontaine drained his glass, stared at it, and worked his lips together. "You know, gentlemen—" He tossed a glance at Clint then Ben. "—I just might be the man to make that happen for you."

ELEVEN

VALERIE LISTENED TO THE INCESSANT CLICKING OF Emily's knitting needles and glanced up from her own sewing. For the past week she and Emily had retired here to the music room during the afternoons for tea and to sketch, practice the piano, or work on their needlework. Meanwhile Benjamin and Clint occupied themselves during the day with the various stages of photography. Today they'd gone down to the docks for another photographic session and then over to Washburn's. Father had gone along with them. It was amazing how well the men were getting along.

"What are you making?" Valerie had noted her friend's diligence on this particular project over the last few days.

"Pardon?" Emily glanced up, then realized the question. "I'm sorry. My thoughts have been elsewhere." She smiled and set the yarn in her lap. "I'm knitting a sweater."

"Quite a small one from the looks of it. Is it for a child?"

Emily nodded, and the blush that crept over her face next told the rest of the story.

"Emily?" Valerie rose and strode to where her friend sat in an upholstered armchair. "Are you—?"

Again a nod.

"—expecting?"

"I believe so." Emily clasped onto Valerie's wrist. "Please don't tell anyone just yet."

"All right. I promise." She tamped down her enthusiasm. "Does Clint know?"

"Yes." Something akin to sadness entered her hazel eyes. A moment of silence descended. "A baby will change everything, Valerie. I won't be able to travel with Clint anymore."

She understood the dilemma. "What are you going to do?"

"Pray and pray hard. Having a child means Clint and I will need a home, not a portable darkroom in which we camp out as we roam the country."

"You're thinking of returning to Boston then?"

A hard knock sounded at the front door. Valerie heard Adalia's swishing skirts as she hurried to answer it.

But in answer to the question, Emily shook her head. Strands of her reddish-brown hair pulled loose from their pins, and she tucked them back in. "There's nothing in Boston for me anymore."

Women's voices filled the foyer, and before Valerie could ask Emily anything further, Adalia bustled into the music room.

"It's Mrs. Elliot and her daughter, Catherine," she stated in a discreet tone. "Are you receivin' company today?"

An odd mix of hope and dread sliced through Valerie—hope that she and the Elliots could be friends and dread that it'd never happen with Catherine's obvious disdain. Nevertheless, Mrs. Elliot had been Mama's special confidante. It would be rude to refuse their visit. "Yes, of course, I'll receive them. Please show the ladies into the parlor."

"All right, dearie." Adalia smiled. "And I'm assuming you'll be wantin' some tea while you visit?"

"That'd be lovely." Valerie glanced at Emily, who nodded.

After packing away their sewing and knitting, they strode down the hall to the parlor. Mrs. Elliot and Catherine had seated themselves in a couple of armchairs. They both wore somber attire, Catherine in a plain brown dress and her mother wearing charcoal.

"What a lovely surprise," Valerie said as she entered the room.

"Our visit is quite tardy, I must say." Mrs. Elliot stood and placed a perfunctory kiss on Valerie's cheek. "Even though Catherine and I saw you just a little over a week ago, we never got a chance to find out how you're adjusting to life without your mother." Her eyes moved to Emily. "Oh, I'm sorry. I see we're interrupting..."

"Not at all." Valerie made the introductions.

"Oh, yes." Recognition lit Mrs. Elliot's gaze. "We met at church last Sunday."

"Emily's husband is Benjamin's partner," Valerie further explained. "They're all staying with Father and me."

"Of course. I remember hearing that too."

"I imagine Ben's still staying here too," Catherine said.

"Yes."

She nodded. "That's good, because it would be quite inappropriate for him to stay with us, given the situation that arose."

A curious frown grew heavy on Valerie's brow, but she decided not to ask about it. Instead she stepped over to Catherine and offered a greeting but didn't get past a smile. The woman's pinched features and icy-blue eyes said she wasn't pleased to be here with her mother. Valerie felt mildly offended, but with a knowing sense, she continued on her way to the settee where she claimed the place next to Emily.

"Is your father home?" Mrs. Elliot asked.

Valerie shook her head. "He's with Benjamin and Clint today. I expect they'll all be home in time for dinner."

"What a shame he's not here," the older woman said. "We'd hoped to visit with him. But you'll let him know we came by and that he's in our prayers, won't you?"

"Yes, of course."

"And you all will be at church tomorrow?"

Valerie nodded. "I'll be sitting in Mama's favorite pew, just like last week."

"I'm so glad." Mrs. Elliot sent her a pleased grin that slowly slipped into a sad-looking smile. "I so miss seeing your mother, sitting there in the third pew from the front."

Valerie bobbed her head. "So do I."

Adalia walked in, carrying the silver tea service. Setting it down on the low-standing table in front of the settee, she poured out. "How do you prefer your tea, Mrs. Elliot? Miss Elliot? One lump or two? Cream or sugar?"

"Plain for me," Mrs. Elliot replied, "but Catherine likes two sugar cubes and just a dribble of cream."

"How nice for you to have a maid." Catherine watched Adalia's preparations.

"Adalia's more than a maid. She's a part of the family."

"Bless you, dearie." Adalia gave her a wink.

"Nonetheless…" Catherine took the proffered cup of tea. Her dusty-brown hair had been parted in the middle and tightly rolled around the sides of her face, further constrained by a drab, beige net. "With her around you needn't ever exert yourself."

"Someone should have explained that to me." Emily grinned as she accepted a teacup from Adalia. "I'm exhausted."

Valerie had a hunch as to why. The growing babe inside of her. And given Emily's delicate condition, she probably shouldn't have helped wash and hang clothes this morning. When Mama was alive, Valerie always assisted with the wash and housekeeping. The job was simply too big for Adalia to do on her own. Since she'd been home from boarding school, Valerie resumed her old duties, and this past week Emily had insisted upon helping.

Mrs. Elliot sipped her tea. "So tell us what has been keeping

Ben and his partner…" she inclined her head toward Emily, "…here in New Orleans."

"The boys have got some unfinished business here," Emily replied.

"Unfinished business?" Catherine scooted forward. "I knew it!" Dullness fled from her sallow-blue eyes, and her features brightened. She turned to her mother. "Didn't I tell you I had a feeling about this? Ever since last Sunday after service when Ben came over and talked to me. I'm sure he'll speak with Daddy about courtship soon."

Valerie glimpsed the incredulous look on Adalia's face and realized it matched her own reaction.

"Will there be anything else, dearie?" She faced Valerie and rolled her eyes so no one else could see.

"No, that'll be all. Thank you." She hid her grin.

Emily leaned closer to her. "Did I miss something?" she whispered. "What courtship?"

"I have no idea." Valerie sunk her gaze into her teacup. *Courtship!*

The sound of men's voices and hard footfalls on the foyer's tiled floor signaled additional company. Moments later, Benjamin and Clint entered the room. Valerie thought perhaps Benjamin might clear up any speculation.

"Well, look who's here." Benjamin wore a wide smile. "My favorite cousins." He bent to kiss Mrs. Elliot's cheek then walked over and bestowed the same greeting on Catherine.

Straightening his waistcoat, Benjamin strode toward Valerie and reached for her hand. He gave it a gentle squeeze.

"I trust you've had a good day." She gazed up at him.

"I did."

"Any new leads on Luke?"

Benjamin shook his head. "None."

Clint pulled up a chair and sat beside Emily. "Valerie, your father insisted upon taking Ben and me to lunch at his club. He introduced us to a blockade runner who shared some of his experiences with us."

"I took pages of notes." Benjamin brought over a side chair and parked it next to Valerie. He sat down. "The man was most informative, and I hope to get a full article out of it."

"I'd love to read it." Her eyes met his, and as always that special caress of a feeling enveloped her. *Lord, I'm falling in love with him.*

"I'll make sure you get a copy." A grin tugged at the corners of his mouth.

Valerie blinked, breaking that mystical aura between them.

"And I'm mighty grateful for your father's assistance today."

Valerie folded her hands, proud of her father. He'd gone to great lengths to see that Benjamin and Clint got the photographs they sought.

"A blockade runner?" Mrs. Elliot fingered the broach at the base of her dress's neckline. "What would the South do without those men?"

"Starve to death most likely," Clint said.

As he continued to converse with Mrs. Elliot, Benjamin bent his head close to Valerie's. "Your father said not to wait dinner for him. He's staying at the club."

Valerie's heart sank. She knew what that meant. Father would spend the night imbibing again. She looked into Benjamin's face and met his compassionate stare. "I guess I should tell Adalia to set the table for four instead of five." She stood and regarded her company. "Please excuse me for a few minutes."

Mrs. Elliot gave her a gracious smile. "Of course,"

It didn't take long to locate Adalia. She was upstairs, folding linens in the long dusky hallway.

"I just learned that Father won't be home tonight. It'll just be the Culvers, Benjamin, and me for dinner."

"I'll tell Chastean. But to tell you the truth, I expected as much seeing as it's Saturday night."

Valerie expelled a disappointed sigh. She'd thought Father had been doing better this past week.

Well, apparently not.

"Don't worry, dearie, I'll set the table for four tonight."

"Thank you, Adalia." Gathering her teal hoopskirt, Valerie made her way back to the first floor and her guests in the parlor. But as she descended the stairs, she spied first Catherine then Benjamin standing in the foyer. Her hands were on his broad shoulders, his hands on her waist, and they were…kissing!

Valerie gasped.

Benjamin pushed Catherine away and did a double take when he saw Valerie. "This isn't what it appears." His tone was almost pleading. Then his jaw hardened as his gaze returned to Catherine. "And you, young lady, had best behave yourself."

"Oh, Ben." She giggled before dropping her gaze. "Go ahead. Blame me. But the truth is—"

"Stop it, Catherine." His voice sounded like a low, angry growl.

She pressed her lips together.

Speechless as well, Valerie could only gape at the pair.

Benjamin stepped toward her. "Valerie, if you'll let me explain—"

What was to explain? She knew what she saw. "There's no need." Descending the last stair, she strode back into the parlor where her guests awaited her.

Swirling the warm, white liquid in his cup, Ben poised himself and then swigged it down in a single gulp. He grimaced. Warm milk. He hated it. But if it would help him sleep...

Pushing the cup aside, he tried to see the paperwork spread out in front of him, but the lamplight wasn't strong enough.

His concentration was just as weak. Valerie consumed his thoughts. He knew she was hurt, but she was being downright unreasonable now! He had tried to explain numerous times that Catherine had followed him out of the parlor and caught him off guard. The fact she stood nearly as tall as he did somehow made him an easy target.

Ben cringed inwardly. He never saw the kiss coming. But it didn't last long. At the precise moment of contact, he'd pushed Catherine away—unfortunately Valerie had happened upon them right then too.

Should he tell Cousin Max or just talk to Catherine? Ben hadn't decided yet.

As for Valerie...his heart crimped painfully. Just tonight her father had mentioned their upcoming voyage to France. He'd been shocked. Still was. Why hadn't Valerie said something about it? Wouldn't setting sail be dangerous with the Union's blockades? He feared for their lives. Yet Fontaine seemed convinced it would be safe enough. While part of Ben wanted to state his intentions, he didn't because he had nothing to offer her. Not yet anyway.

Lord, I thought Valerie was the one. Would their paths somehow cross again? Was it right to ask her to wait for him?

Sitting in the kitchen, the lamp flickering on the long table, Ben tried to push her from his mind for now and focus on plotting out next week's expedition. He and Clint would be gone at least five days. So far the colonel had been satisfied with the photographs they'd given him. What's more, he encouraged Ben and Clint to forge a relationship with Fontaine. Except Mr. Fontaine's political sympathies clearly lay with the North. He didn't hide his viewpoints. They aligned with those of many New Orleans residents. And after what happened last week, Ben thought maybe he was more Yankee than Reb himself.

Days ago he and Clint had been down at the docks when a ship carrying human cargo was being unloaded. Men, women, and children, captured in Africa, were roughly reloaded by the dozens into boxcars. He'd learned the train was headed to Atlanta, where the poor souls would be sold like cattle. Ben still recalled the fury that had welled within him at the sight, yet he had been helpless to do anything about it. He could only watch the travesty unfold. Ben wondered if Fontaine had allowed them to see the slave ship come in so he could hammer in his views. "Isn't war worth fighting if it means freeing these people?"

Ben thought it surely was.

His brother Jake, on the other hand, didn't believe in slave ownership but still saw things quite differently. He had volunteered to fight Federal policies, specifically the tariffs Washington imposed on the importing and exporting of goods. It was no secret that for years Southerners had to pay higher taxes and interest rates that, in turn, had been handed down to farmers and small Southern businessmen, like his brother-in-law Jonathan's blacksmithing business. And why? Jake blamed greed on the Northern banking industry.

Ben shook his head, still thinking back on the past several days of discussion with Fontaine. The controversy over the war had made for some excellent debates. The man enjoyed a lively conversation, that's for sure. However, something didn't feel right when it came to the colonel and Fontaine. Either the two men had personal vendettas against each other, or there was something else going on—something Ben couldn't quite put his finger on.

A sudden rustling behind him caught his attention. He swiveled himself around on the wooden stool in time to see Valerie enter the kitchen. The satin trim of her quilted robe shimmered in the light of the lamp she carried. She must not have seen him sitting there, even with his tiny flame on the tabletop. He reached for the lamp so it wouldn't crash onto the stone floor when he startled her—which seemed inevitable.

"Valerie?"

He heard her inhale with a start, although she'd hung tightly to the lamp. She clutched the neckline of her robe. "Benjamin? What are you doing down here?"

He indicated his paperwork and the dwindling candlelight. "Adalia warmed some milk for me before she went to bed. I'm having trouble sleeping."

"Me too." There was a note of resignation in her voice that gave him hope.

Leaning forward, Ben took the lamp from her and set it on the table behind him. Then he faced her again. Her dark hair hung loosely around her face and brushed the tops of her slender shoulders. Her blue eyes were wide, perhaps from embarrassment, although the robe she wore was adequately modest. He'd seen his mother and sisters in their nightclothes often enough.

Slowly he reached out for her hand. When she allowed him to hold it, he pulled her closer to him. Suddenly they were eye to eye.

"I thought about what you said earlier," Valerie whispered.

"What was that?" He felt captivated, even though he knew he might be left with a broken heart to nurse—as well as a missing brother to find when all was said and done.

"About Catherine. It's just hard for me to believe a pastor's daughter would do such a brazen thing. And yet, I can't blame her."

"No?" That was surprising.

"I guess it just confirms our New Year's Day suspicions."

He remembered them.

"She loves you."

Ben shook his head. "I don't know why."

Valerie arched a brow. "It's the McCabe charm."

"Oh, right." He grinned. "So you're not miffed with me anymore?"

Her features softened. "I had no right to be miffed in the first place. It was just such a shock to see the two of you—"

"It was a shock for me too."

Valerie gave in to a light laugh. "So you have no plans to court Catherine like she said?"

"The notion never entered my head, but I reckon I'd best talk to her and clear things up between us."

"Good." She glanced around the kitchen. "I came down for a bite to eat. Can I fix you a little something also?"

"I'd appreciate that. Thanks."

Valerie disappeared into the pantry and returned with a long loaf of bread and something round wrapped in cloth. "*Le pain*," she said in French. "And *au fromage*."

"Bread and cheese," he guessed.

"*Oui, monsieur.*" Valerie smiled, then turned wistful. "Whenever I couldn't sleep, Mama always brought out the bread and cheese and prepared a cup of herbal tea for me. So that's what I'm serving up."

"Fine by me." He found it ironic that she spoke French to him tonight. Obviously she knew she'd soon embark on an overseas voyage with her father. Once more he hoped she would be safe, getting around the Union's gunners once they set out to sea. Ben couldn't stand the thought of her ship being fired upon, and yet that would likely happen unless—

Unless the Union allowed that particular ship to pass.

Ben thought it over. Fontaine Shipping. Edward Fontaine's Federalist ideas. Colonel LaPorte's animosity…

He kneaded his stubbly jaw, deliberating.

Valerie put the kettle on to boil and, finding a sharp blade, sliced the bread. The mound of cheese she placed on a small platter. Then she handed him a plate and a spreading knife. "Help yourself."

Ben smoothed the soft cheese onto a piece of bread. "You know, Valerie, it really saddens me that you'll be leaving soon."

"What are you talking about?"

"Your trip to France. Your father told me about it after dinner." Ben took a bite of his bread. The cheese had a distinct flavor, and at first he wasn't sure he liked it.

"France?" Valerie shook her head. "Father never said anything to me."

Ben couldn't figure out why she didn't know, but that explained the reason she hadn't spoken of the trip earlier. For a long moment he didn't say anything. "You don't know about the trip to France?"

"No, I don't, so perhaps you'd better tell me."

Ben figured there was no turning back now. "After you excused yourself from the dinner table, your father mentioned that he'd booked passage to France. He cited the obvious—that the shipping business has dwindled in the South because of the Union's blockades. He said he plans to start a new company in France."

Valerie paled beneath the lamplight, and her breathing became more pronounced. She looked stunned, frightened, and hurt all at the same time. "Did my father specifically mention me?"

"No, but—"

"I knew it!" She set down the silver spreader harder than necessary.

"Valerie…" Ben reached for her, but she moved away.

"I knew my father still harbored the idea of marrying me off to James. I could just tell."

"You're jumping to conclusions." Ben prayed he was wrong. "When I spoke to your father today, I had the impression you were going to France with him."

She shook her head. "He doesn't want me. He had hoped I'd marry someone and stay in Virginia. Now he wants me to marry James so I'll be out of his hair. He's always been a distant figure in my life. Why would that suddenly change?"

Ben finally caught a hold of her wrist and pulled her closer to him. "Valerie, that can't be true." He thought of Pa and his protectiveness over Leah and Sarah. "I'm sure your father loves you."

She didn't reply. She didn't have to. The little jut of her chin that was supposed to offset the anguish in her eyes said it all.

"Well, I'd rather die than marry James."

"Don't say such things." Ben set his hands on her shoulders and gave her a mild shake.

Her palms covered his wrists. "I don't love James. I never will."

The whistle on the kettle screeched, and she whirled out of his grasp. Ben wished there was something he could say to assuage her fears—especially the part of marrying Ladden. *God, don't let it be so.* Ben hated the thought of Ladden touching Valerie in any way.

And yet, Ben knew he couldn't make her any promises.

She carried over the teapot, followed by two cups and saucers, and set a cup and saucer in front of him. "It's my mother's special blend of herbs. Try it. It'll help you sleep."

"Thanks." A war of his own raged deep within his heart. He believed he loved Valerie, and somehow even the idea of her going to France hadn't deterred him completely. But marriage to Ladden…

"I've enjoyed your company this week." The corners of

Valerie's mouth moved upward, although the gesture didn't reach her eyes. "It was fun to watch you and Clint play checkers the night before last."

"He cheats," Ben teased.

"He won fair and square." Her smile was full on her face now. "I've enjoyed my stay here."

She fiddled with her teacup and grew serious again. "You once asked me if I believed in love at first sight." She looked into his eyes. "Do you remember?"

"I'll never forget." The evening he'd kissed her in the solarium. He had a sense of where she was going with this conversation. "Valerie, please don't say anything you might regret later."

"I'll never regret it. I love you, Benjamin. I've known it from the first night we met."

And he loved her. He'd known it from the start. But he also knew he carried a great amount of responsibility in saying those three little words. He'd nearly murmured them once before, and he wouldn't mind declaring them now. But he wasn't in a position to ask for her hand in marriage. He was committed to finding Luke. Photographing the war. "Valerie…"

She stretched her arm across the short distance between them and touched his lips with her fingertips. "You're not obligated to reply. I just felt the need to tell you."

Holding her wrist, he moved aside her hand. "Valerie—"

She moved around the table and slipped her arms around his neck. She touched her lips to his, and her sweet scent assailed him. He couldn't help but gather her into his arms. Her kiss was fervent, letting him know she meant what she'd said.

But then he gently pushed her away. "Don't. We can't do this. I told the Lord I wouldn't let this happen again and—"

"It's my fault. I love you, Benjamin."

"I know." He loved her too. "Valerie, if there was any way—"

"I understand." She lowered her gaze and took a step backward.

"No, I don't think you do."

"You have to find your brother."

He nodded. "That's part of it—most of it."

"And the other part...I think I know that also."

"Valerie—" He cupped her chin, urging her eyes to his. "—I keep trying to see how it'd work between us now, and I can't." How could he ever afford to give her the lifestyle she was accustomed to here? Every stick of polished furniture in this house mocked him. His future lay in Jericho Junction. He almost laughed. An observer might say Valerie was more suited to James and Catherine to him. But even if Valerie agreed to live in Missouri, he wasn't in a position to get married. "It's all in God's timing, and this isn't it."

She replied with a few little nods. "Please forgive my shameful actions just now." She moved farther away, averting her gaze.

"Sweetheart, I understand. It's natural to act on your feelings. I'm sorry for defying propriety and giving in to mine too."

"You're the only man I've ever thrown myself at."

"Don't be so hard on yourself."

Collecting her teacup, she sent him a shattered look that splintered his heart. "I guess I should say good night."

Ben wanted to stop her. But with what? Promises he couldn't keep? He expelled a disappointed sigh. "Good night."

TWELVE

W HAT PERFECT WEATHER WE'RE HAVING TODAY," Emily said as they rode to church in the buggy.

"Beautiful," Clint agreed. "Don't you agree, Ben?"

"Yes. Nice day."

Valerie hated the way his shoulders were turned slightly away from her, but she understood why he tried to put distance between them. It wasn't meant to be.

"Valerie, that blue dress you're wearing looks lovely on you."

"Thank you." She sent Emily a smile.

Benjamin seemed lost in his thoughts, and Valerie knew she wasn't doing a good job disguising her clamoring emotions. Her heart was broken—

And then came the shock and the shame.

She'd waited up until the wee hours of the morning for Father to arrive home from the club. Finally he stumbled in, and despite his inebriated state Valerie insisted he answer her questions. Alone in his study with the door closed so as not to wake the household, she pressed him until he admitted that, yes, he'd booked passage to France—for himself. He planned to leave on the twenty-seventh of this month. Valerie, on the other hand, would marry James Ladden—just as she feared. He'd arranged it all. When she refused, Father became angry. Valerie had never seen him in such a state. It frightened her.

But then an odd calm came over him, and he explained, almost soberly, that he owed Arnold Ladden money from an investment gone wrong. Valerie's dowry would nearly cover it. Her marriage to James would clinch the deal. Father would be free and clear of the debt, and in anticipation of it, he'd purchased passage back to his ancestral home country, France.

"You're trading me off like some piece of property?" The words had rammed through her disbelief.

Father's face flamed with another onset of rage. "This is your fault. You should have stayed at school!"

Her heart dropped. Two rejections from two men she loved in one single night.

"Valerie, your expression seems so troubled," Emily said, bringing her back to the present. "Are you all right?"

"Yes," she fibbed. "I'm fine."

Benjamin turned toward her, and she glanced up into his face. The remorse in his eyes only increased her feelings of humiliation. Twice she'd thrown herself at him. How could she criticize Catherine for being so bold?

She looked away. It didn't matter anyway. Benjamin didn't love her and had no desire to marry her. He'd said as much last night.

As for James, she wasn't about to pledge herself to the likes of him!

The carriage halted in front of the church, and Valerie remembered more of her conversation with her father. She looked at the Culvers, then at Benjamin. "There is something you all probably should know right away." Valerie hated to say it.

All eyes regarded her expectantly.

"My father has asked that you find other housing accommodations." Valerie looked at Emily and ached at the thought of losing her sweet friend. "I don't want you to leave, but Father's insisting…because of the circumstances." Her gaze slid to Benjamin, but she couldn't seem to form the words to tell him that her worst fears had been realized.

The driver appeared at the side of the buggy and Valerie stepped out. After Benjamin debarked, he offered his arm. Valerie shook her head. It was no longer appropriate.

"Valerie, I think we need to talk." Benjamin leaned close to her ear. "I'm sure we can find a private spot to—"

"I'm afraid it's too late."

She quickened her pace when he reached for her elbow. Entering the vestibule, she pasted a smile on her face and greeted several acquaintances. Benjamin was just behind her, and the Culvers followed him. As they all approached the sanctuary, a gentleman dressed in a light gray tweed suit stepped into their path. Valerie's gaze traveled upward, and she took in the man's auburn hair and green eyes.

"James!" She couldn't quite believe it. The Laddens weren't churchgoers. He seemed somehow out of place. "What are you doing here?"

Ignoring the question, he gave Benjamin a condescending grin. "McCabe." He offered his right hand. "Ever so nice to see you again." His eyes moved to Clint and Emily. Valerie noticed both the strain in Benjamin's voice as he made the introductions and the arrogance in James's tone as he greeted them.

"Your father told me where I could find you, honey." James's gaze flitted to Valerie. Then he sported a triumphant grin as he turned to Benjamin. "And I thought this might be the perfect place and time—" He looked at Valerie again. "—to announce our wedding engagement."

Sitting at the end of the long pew, Ben cast a glance at Valerie. The Culvers sat between them and Ladden on the other side of her. She wore a miserable expression on her face.

Lord, You know me through and through, and You know I can't let this happen.

"Love covers a multitude of sins," Cousin Max preached from the pulpit. His voice echoed through the vaulted sanctuary, and Ben forced himself to pay attention. "Jesus Christ is that 'love'—the love of God the Father, sent to Earth, born of a virgin. Why, less than a month ago, we finished celebrating Christ's birth—Christmas."

Hearing Valerie's delicate cough—or was it a sob?—Ben sat forward to check. Her sad eyes met his gaze until James leaned close and whispered something in her ear. She turned away, looking straight ahead.

Ben sat back, frustrated. Her proclamation last night that she'd rather die than marry Ladden rang loudly in his memory. While he didn't think she'd purposely hurt herself, she might be willing to risk her life in order to avoid the marriage.

What is Fontaine thinking? Money had to be the motive. As he prepared to leave for France, he wanted his daughter to marry a man with means. The Laddens were certainly wealthy judging by their stately manse. Contrarily, Ben was a freelance photographer without a permanent business. Fontaine knew he hailed from Jericho Junction. He probably figured it was no kind of place for his bright, talented, and beautiful daughter.

Sorrow washed over him. Yes, he loved Valerie. But it was just like he'd told her last night. He couldn't settle down now. Finding Luke took precedence.

"God's greatest gift to mankind is His only begotten Son, Jesus Christ," Cousin Max said. "Our greatest gift to God is giving Him our souls—our lives."

Ben forced his tense muscles to relax as he focused on the sermon. He listened to Cousin Max deliver the good news and, amazingly, found it within himself to pray for James Ladden. He had no idea where the man stood in his spiritual life, but the Lord knew of all his needs.

Ben realized then that God was bigger than his worst problem. The Lord knew where Luke was, and He only wanted the best for Valerie.

Ben bowed his head. *Lord, help me to trust You more.*

After the service ended, Ben hung back, waiting for Cousin Max. His hat in hand, he wandered up and down the aisles while the pastor stood at the entryway, greeting each member of his congregation.

"What exciting news."

Ben pivoted around to find Catherine nearby.

She smiled and walked toward him. "I just heard Valerie Fontaine and James Ladden are going to be married."

Not if I can help it. Ben pushed out a polite grin.

"They look so perfect together."

"Well, you know that old saying, looks can be deceiving." He set his jaw and held the rim of his hat in both of his hands.

"Why, Ben McCabe," she drawled, "you're acting as if you have feelings for that girl. She's not your type."

"Oh?" He noted Catherine's rusty-brown dress with its ivory collar. Even though she was reed-thin, Ben had to admit she made a comely sight this morning. With the stained glass window at her side, she almost seemed to have a heavenly aura about her. "And just what sort of woman is *my type*?"

She glanced around the emptying church. No one else was within earshot. "Your type of woman is one who has a yearning for life west of the Mississippi, where the land is plentiful. Someone who's read all about milking cows and plucking chickens. One who can plant gardens, harvest, can, and preserve the fruits and vegetables of her labors." Catherine inched closer. "You need a woman who wouldn't mind wearing homespun dresses and who sews her own wardrobe—and yours too." A blush crept into her face. "You need a sensible woman, and one who understands what it's like to grow up in the midst of sacrificial ministry with a father who's a pastor."

"A woman like you?" Ben hid his amusement but couldn't help admiring Catherine's list of abilities. On the other hand, he disliked the fact that her words hit their mark—and that her accurate assessment of what he needed in a wife didn't exactly describe Valerie. How had he ever thought a woman like Valerie Fontaine would ever be content in Jericho Junction?

Gwyneth had certainly hated it.

"I'd make you a good wife, Ben." Catherine's voice was but a whisper and her face flamed with innocence. "God told me long ago that I would marry a McCabe."

"Well, that might be, but it's not me, Catherine." He hated to hurt her. "I'm sorry."

"You're just too stubborn to know it yet." A sudden angry glint in her eyes stole whatever prettiness he'd seen in her face before.

Deciding it was time to go, he quickly stepped around her. He'd talk to Cousin Max another time. He donned his hat. "Have yourself a good afternoon, Catherine."

Walking outside, he squinted as his eyes adjusted to being out in the bright sunshine. He spotted Clint and Em waiting for him at the street.

"Valerie left with Mr. Ladden." Emily tipped her head, and Ben looked away so he wouldn't see her wounded expression. "I'm confused. When did she get engaged?"

"Not sure. I reckon her father made the arrangements."

"Who is that fellow?" Clint wanted to know. "Seems I've heard his name before. Ladden?"

"A neighbor. He escorted Valerie to the party on New Year's Eve." Ben took off his hat and ran a hand through his hair. He felt downright hot standing in the sun.

"Is it just me," Em asked, "or did anyone else notice that the bride-to-be looks extremely unhappy?"

Clint lowered his gaze and kicked a stone with the toe of his leather boot. "I'd say 'unhappy' doesn't even begin to describe it." He glanced at Ben. "What are you going to do?"

"Don't know." He shoved his hat back on his head when a movement off to the side caught his attention. He looked over and saw Catherine standing on top of the steps, near the entrance of the church. A slight wind blew across her skirts as she lifted her gloved hand. Ben inclined his head out of politeness.

"Miss Elliot obviously thinks of herself as more than your friend," Clint remarked.

"I explained to her that the feeling is not mutual."

"So now what happens?" Em asked. "We're suddenly thrown out of the Fontaines' home and I'm never going to see my dear friend again?"

Clint placed a comforting arm around his wife and sent Ben a helpless stare.

He understood. They needed a plan. This mess was all his fault anyway. "How 'bout we get in the buggy and you both leave me off at the Fontaines'? I'd like to have a word with Mr. Fontaine— hopefully he's home. Meanwhile, you two enjoy some lunch. When you're finished, come on back, seeing as we might have to pack up the wagons." Ben hoped he could talk the man into allowing at least Emily to stay on. If nothing else, Valerie could use a friend right now.

"And then what?" Clint asked. "You know we've got that big assignment this week. Em can't come along."

"I know." Along with learning about the voyage to France, he'd found out that Em was expecting. That pretty much changed everything. She figured the baby would come in July. Getting jostled around in a wagon for days on end wouldn't do her a bit of good. That included this upcoming week.

He cast a quick glance Catherine's way. She still stood there, watching them, looking subdued. He always remembered her as a good person, kind…and he loved Cousins Max and Amanda.

"Hey, Clint…if my discussion with Mr. Fontaine doesn't go the way I hope, could Em stay with the Elliots this week?"

Both Ben and Clint looked at Emily. She rolled a shoulder, but then nodded.

"Cousin Amanda extended an invite to all of us last week," Ben went on to explain. "I'll make sure it still stands. I'm sure it does. But—" He nodded toward the buggy. "—first things first."

They boarded the conveyance, and on the way to the Fontaines' home, Ben silently prayed. For the right words. For wisdom.

When the carriage stopped at the Fontaines', Ben climbed out. He didn't see another buggy parked nearby and figured Valerie was somewhere with Ladden. He tamped down the infuriating thought. "I'll see you back here in a couple of hours."

Clint replied with a nod.

Walking to the front entrance, Ben was taken by surprise when Adalia pulled open the door even before he reached it. The maid's eyes were wide and curious—or did she look frightened?

"Good afternoon, Mr. McCabe. Won't you come in?"

"Yes, thank you. I'm here to collect my things."

"I know, sir."

Ben moved into the house. "Is Mr. Fontaine here?"

"In his study."

He gave Adalia a grateful half bow and then made his way down the hallway. He found Fontaine sitting at his desk, although he didn't appear to be busy.

"Mr. Fontaine?"

"Come in. I've been expecting you."

"Valerie told Clint, Em, and me that you requested we leave today. We'll comply with your wishes, of course, but I wondered if Emily could stay. I believe Clint mentioned their surprising news, and he and I have some business that'll keep us away this week."

"A week?"

"That's it."

Fontaine pursed his lips as he gave it some thought. "I'm sorry, but that won't be possible. It's best you all take your leave now."

Disappointment enveloped him, but he ventured farther into the stately room. "I also learned this morning that Valerie is marrying Ladden. You're not taking her with you to France."

"No. What would I do with her in France? Whether I marry her off here or there, what does it matter?"

Ben felt a bit taken aback by the man's insensitivity. He narrowed his gaze, curious. Fontaine hadn't ever behaved that way before. He took a seat in one of the handsome leather chairs in front of the large desk. "Both risky choices."

"Risky?" Fontaine chuckled. "Hardly."

"How do you expect to get around the Union's blockades once your ship is out to sea? Aren't you the least bit worried they'll blow you right out of the water?"

"I'll get around the blockades."

Ben admired the man's confidence. "I'm assuming you have contacts...I mean, being in the shipping business."

Fontaine stared at him. "Do you think I'm fool enough to tell you if I did?"

Ben wasn't sure he really cared. "Back to Valerie...she told me she'd rather die than marry Ladden. What does that sound like to you?"

"Sounds like a spoiled young lady who's determined to have her way." Fontaine stood. Attired in brown trousers, a matching waistcoat, and a freshly starched white shirt, he looked as impeccably dressed as always. "But she won't. Not this time." He stared at some volumes neatly lined on a shelf.

"So marrying Ladden is her punishment of sorts?"

He whirled around. "She came home from school without my permission, and it's made life rather difficult."

"Difficult?" Ben couldn't imagine a father not welcoming his daughter home. "In what way?"

"More ways than you could possibly guess."

"Well, I'm concerned." Ben sat forward, his elbows on his knees. "Do you think she would risk her life to flee this situation?"

"She'd better not. She'll ruin everything—"

Ben sat upright.

Chagrin flashed in Fontaine's eyes. "I've said far too much." He all but muttered the reply. His gaze darted around the study before settling on Ben. "I shall be eternally grateful to your father. He was at my beloved wife's side when she died. So for that reason alone, I invited you into my home. Since then I've come to respect you, and I know my daughter has feelings for you—and from what I gather, you have feelings for her too."

Ben couldn't deny it.

Fontaine looked away. "That's why I've asked you to leave. She's engaged to James now. It's unfortunate that things couldn't have worked out differently."

"Yes, it is." Ben stood. "And it's a crying shame when money wins over respect."

Fontaine raised his chin. "I didn't have a choice."

"You always have a choice."

Hardness stole over his features. His eyes narrowed. "If you'll excuse me, Mr. McCabe," he said in strained formality, "there are pressing matters that require my attention."

At the dismissal Ben gave him a parting nod. What could he say? He had no jurisdiction here. But he was suddenly determined to find out what was going on.

His jaw set, he headed upstairs to pack his belongings.

THIRTEEN

"Y**OU'VE GOT TO TALK WITH YOUR FATHER, VALERIE.**"

She sent a glance Emily's way as they strolled down the block. "I've tried. Many times. He refuses to change his mind."

"So you've resigned yourself to marrying James at the end of the month?"

Valerie hesitated.

"Or do you have something else in mind?"

"In mind? Oh, I have plenty of ideas. But nothing realistic." A buggy rolled past and Valerie half-expected James to be in it. He watched her every move. She was surprised when he allowed Emily to visit. And taking a walk without him? Valerie savored every second.

"Have you been all right? I mean, James seems to be quite the authoritarian."

"I'd like to say he's just protective of me. But that's not true." The past few nights sprang into mind. During the last three parties that she'd been dragged off to, James parked her in a corner with his mother while he enjoyed himself with friends. Valerie had nothing against Mrs. Ladden at all; the woman was quite pleasant. But James's actions were less than chivalrous as he waltzed with other ladies and drank his bourbon. Valerie never felt jealous. James could only wish. But worse, there was no rapport between them. Not a single spark. He wasn't even a friend as far as Valerie was concerned. "He's quite controlling.

His mother is at his beck and call. All James's brothers are the same way—demanding."

Emily linked arms with her. "Valerie, I noticed your...well, your bottom lip looks a bit swollen."

She brought a gloved hand up to the sore spot on her mouth. "That happened by accident. James's elbow bumped my lip." She didn't add that it happened while she fought off his advances in the carriage the night before last. At least she'd won the battle—this time. "I didn't think it showed."

"It shows." Emily's tone hardened. "Oooh, what I wouldn't like to do to that man!"

"James really didn't intentionally hurt me."

Emily narrowed her gaze as if she didn't believe it.

They rounded the corner, and Valerie took a moment to admire Mrs. Saunders's window box full of colorful blooms.

"Emily, my trunk is nearly packed. Adalia's been helping me. She has a friend whose son lives in Savannah. He and his wife mentioned in a recent letter that they might like a housekeeper. Adalia thinks they'd pay my way if I agreed to work for them for a year or so."

"No, Valerie." Em stopped short and peered hard into her face. "You can't do that. You don't know what you'll be walking into. What if the situation there proves worse than this one? And I'm sure it could be worse."

"Not much more."

They continued walking.

"I haven't committed to anything. It's just one of my many notions for escape."

"Good. Keep thinking."

She did, and she recalled her recent conversation with James's mother. "Mrs. Ladden talked to me about what she termed as 'wifely duties.' Her husband and James both insisted we have that discussion so I'd know what's expected of becoming a Ladden." Valerie felt almost sorry for the older woman as she described her life. "Mrs. Ladden made marriage sound like sheer drudgery. No voicing of opinions. No discussions. Just fetching, cooking, and altogether submitting like a hound, not a wife. I could hardly sleep last night just thinking about it." Valerie didn't add that Benjamin had constantly crept into her thoughts too. She had to get him off her mind—

Except not a day went by that James didn't bring up the solarium incident. He used it as a form of manipulation, but it only made Valerie recall Benjamin's kiss all over again.

"Valerie, keep trying to get through to your father."

So they were back to that again. "I'm telling you, Emily, it's no use." She couldn't bear to tell her friend about the debt Father owed and how her marriage to James would cancel it. James said Father had ruined the Fontaine name in New Orleans. He'd shown up drunk at business meetings. He'd embarrassed friends with outbursts. He'd all but lost Fontaine Shipping. That explained why he chose to take off for his ancestral country where he hoped to start a new life from the place where Grandpapa began. Forget the pain of losing Mama. Forget her…

Valerie thought it so sad that her father wanted to run from his memories, from responsibilities.

But wasn't she just as pitiful, running from her circumstances? The notion had crept into her thoughts more than once.

"You know, Emily, perhaps I'm going about things all wrong. What if I don't run away?" The thought terrified her. But she had nowhere to run. So, what if…

"This morning Pastor Elliot read from the Bible. Afterwards he talked about handing over our troubles to God, as well as our hopes and dreams and our plans."

"Casting your burdens on the Lord..." Valerie was reminded of her mother's favorite verse. "Psalm 55."

Emily smiled. "Mm, yes. And Pastor Elliot emphasized that the key to having a sense of peace, even in a time of war, is not to take back our burdens once we've surrendered them. His advice has stayed with me all day."

"Why, thank you for passing it along." Immediately Valerie thought of the fishermen near the docks she'd seen many times as a child. They cast their lines out into the sea. But if they continually pulled them back in, they'd never catch anything. They had to cast, wait, trust... and pray.

Hoofbeats sounded from behind, and then a rider reined in beside them. Valerie looked up and saw James in the saddle. "I think you ladies have traversed far enough." He stared down into Valerie's eyes. Emily hugged her arm. "Time to turn around and head for home."

Raindrops drummed an anxious beat on the carriage's hood. Valerie trained her gaze straight ahead as she wondered at James's mood. It was a miracle that he'd allowed her to accept the Elliots' dinner offer this evening. Knowing Benjamin was still away, Valerie thought it'd be a good excuse to see Emily again.

Suddenly she felt James shift his weight next to her. His arm snaked across the back of her shoulders. Valerie tried not to squirm.

"Kiss me." His husky whisper sounded close to her ear.

"Not now, James, stop it." She was forever fending off his advances.

"We're engaged."

"Yes, but there's just one problem." She hesitated. "I don't love you." She turned slightly. "I'm sorry, James, but I never will."

The weight of his anger filled the carriage, but he didn't act on it.

Silence followed; however, Valerie's senses remained on high alert. With James, she never knew what might happen next. How could she possibly live like this day in and day out?

"You know," James said, "I've always admired your willfulness—your determination." His voice resounded on a sensible note.

Valerie stared at her gloved hands.

"You're a challenge for a man like me. Every reply you give me is another dare that I can't refuse."

She wisely kept her mouth shut.

They arrived at the Elliots' without another incident. Once inside their cozy home, Valerie sensed God's presence and began to relax.

Emily gave her a knowing look and then a hug. Catherine came forward and sent a brief smile before she collected her and James's outer wraps.

Pastor Elliot welcomed him with an enthusiastic handshake. "I met you Sunday. It's a pleasure to see you again. Come in."

James hung back and grasped Valerie's elbow. He bent close to her. "You said the invitation was from the Elliots."

"Indeed it was. You met Pastor and Mrs. Elliot last Sunday. This is their home."

"These aren't the same Elliots I had in mind." He spoke out of the corner of his mouth.

"Hm, well, I must admit I was surprised when you agreed to come tonight. The activities will be quite different from the parties we've attended this week." One part amusement and three parts gratitude swelled inside Valerie. She'd grown weary of being tucked into a corner while James lived it up.

Valerie claimed an armchair, and Pastor Elliot engaged him in conversation. Then dinner was served. James picked at his beef stew. He shifted in his chair from time to time, but the dinner topics weren't anything uncomfortable or vexing. What's more, no one brought up the subject of their engagement, much to Valerie's relief.

At last they retired to the parlor. James made his excuses and started for the small entryway.

"Come along, Valerie."

She had just seated herself opposite Emily on the settee and started to rise when Catherine got to her feet. She walked toward James with an air of confidence and stood a good deal taller. "Go about your business, and we'll see to it that Valerie arrives home safely." Her tone left no room for argument while Catherine stared him down like a stern schoolmarm.

"I imagine that'll be all right." James took a step back. Glancing at Valerie, he added, "But I want you home by midnight."

Once he'd gone, Emily clucked her tongue. "Ooh, that man and his condescending ways!"

Relief that he'd gone peaceably washed over Valerie. She loathed what seemed her lot in life, and it certainly didn't feel like God's will. But what could she do about it? Their wedding was in a week. Her heart sank like a lead ball.

"Well, he couldn't argue with me, could he?" Catherine looked proud of herself as she sat down in an armchair.

"Thank you for standing up for me, Catherine." Words couldn't describe Valerie's appreciation.

"Well, now you know, I do carry some sway. I'm just as important as anyone else."

"Of course you are." Valerie pulled in her chin, somewhat taken aback by the response.

Just then Robert traipsed in with a wooden game board in his hands. One side was peppered with holes. "This is a game I invented." He set it down on the coffee table. Next he removed some pegs and a set of dice from one pocket and a small square of paper from the other. He explained the rules. "Who wants to play?"

"I will," Valerie said. Feeling more lighthearted than she had in some time, she was up for having a bit of fun.

Everyone else said they'd give it a try as well, and soon they traded laughs and giggles as they answered history questions and inched their pegs toward the goal line.

Then suddenly a ruckus at the back of the house caught their attention.

"It's Clint." Emily stood and picked her way around Robert and Catherine, who sat on the floor. Pastor Elliot was already on his way to see about the commotion. Mrs. Elliot followed both of them.

Valerie waited, trying to act calm and natural, but inside her heart raced. If Clint just came home, then Benjamin wasn't too far away.

Emily's delighted squeals wafted into the parlor, causing Valerie to wish that she could greet Benjamin the same way.

Someday. The word came from deep inside, and yet she didn't trust its source. Her emotions were in such a tangle, loving one man but being forced to marry another, trusting God or fleeing New Orleans for a housekeeper position.

Emily and Clint walked in. "We're going upstairs to deposit Clint's things."

Smiling a hello, Clint carried the baggage and followed Emily up the steps.

"I don't suppose she's going to play anymore." Disappointed, Robert pulled out Emily's peg.

Valerie grinned at the child. And then Benjamin entered the room. A week's growth of whiskers covered his jaw, increasing his rugged good looks. Catherine walked over and gave him a friendly hug that he seemed to tolerate, although his gaze stayed on Valerie.

Catherine followed his line of vision. "The future Mrs. James Ladden."

Valerie couldn't completely subdue her wince.

"We invited the couple for dinner tonight. A pity Valerie's fiancé left early."

"A real shame." Sarcasm weighed on Benjamin's words. He sent her a nod. "Valerie."

"Hello, Benjamin."

He set down his bags, and Catherine helped him shrug out of his coat.

"How was your trip?" Valerie asked.

"Very productive."

"Any leads on finding Luke?"

He shook his head. "None."

Valerie felt his disappointment.

"Did you see any fighting?" Robert wanted to know.

"No." Benjamin's smile worked its way through his beard. "But I've put together a photograph book. Would you like to see it?"

"Sure!" The boy shot up off the floor."

"You ladies are invited to look too."

"We'd love to." Catherine caught his arm. "Oh, and Cousin Rebecca sent a telegram saying Leah gave birth to a baby boy. Mother and child are doing fine."

Benjamin let the news digest. "I guess that makes me an uncle." A slow smile spread across his face before he let out a joyous whoop.

His reaction tickled Valerie, and she laughed. Then he smiled into her eyes. She stared up into his.

"About those photographs?" Catherine's voice sliced between them.

"Right." Benjamin bent over and took a bound volume out of one of his bags. He carried it over to the dining room table, where he opened it and sat down. Robert was quick to pull a chair in beside him and Catherine claimed the other seat next to Benjamin, so Valerie peered over his shoulder.

"I worked on this all week."

She began wondering. Was it part of his assignment for the colonel? If so, how could he be showing it off?

"This is a personal project." He answered her musing. "Many of these pictures I took when Valerie's father gave us a tour of New Orleans's port."

Page after page, Benjamin told stories behind the photographs. Pastor and Mrs. Elliot came in and sat down, and then Emily and Clint joined them around the table. One picture in particular caught her eye.

"May I see that one on the left?"

"You may." He handed it to her.

Valerie recognized her father and the man with whom he stood. The pair obviously didn't know their picture was being taken because the camera only captured a side view of each man.

"That's a ship your father commissioned some time back," Benjamin said. "It's being retired soon, but the vessel's said to have run the Union's blockades dozens of times in the last year."

"Oh, I didn't notice the ship. I was looking at my father and Captain DeMere. He's a Frenchman." Valerie searched her memory, as it'd been awhile since she'd seen or heard of him. "I believe he's an important naval officer now that the war's begun."

"DeMere?" Clint held out his hand in a nonverbal request to see the picture.

Valerie gave it to him, and he studied it.

"Do you know the captain's first name?"

Valerie gave it a moment's thought. "No. I can't remember."

Clint slid the photograph across the table to Benjamin. "There's a man named DeMere who's an officer under Farragut."

"Farragut? That Southern traitor!" Robert became incensed. "He was born in the Confederate States of America, but now he's a Yankee."

"Settle down, son." Pastor Elliot worked to hide a grin.

Valerie saw Clint staring hard at Benjamin. Realizing she'd placed her hand on Benjamin's shoulder, she slowly removed it.

But his distracted gaze made it clear that was not what bothered Clint. "Remember what we talked about a few days ago, Ben?"

"Yep."

"Did our, um, *client* get that same print?"

"Sure did." His voice rang with a note of regret. "Just tonight, in fact."

"What does that mean?" Valerie asked.

"Let's hope it means nothing." Benjamin turned the page of his photograph book, and despite her curiosity, the topic changed with it.

Ben looked at the amount of money Colonel LaPorte had paid him and felt half tempted not to accept it. True, he'd done what he'd been hired to do, but he sure didn't feel very good about it. He'd violated his oath to stay neutral in this war, and his compromise hadn't produced any new leads regarding Luke's whereabouts.

"You two men have done some fine work here." Colonel William LaPorte flipped through the photographs in front of him. His silvery mustache wiggled thoughtfully as he peered through his spectacles at each albumin print. "Fine work indeed."

"Thank you, sir," Clint said, sitting to the colonel's right at the dining room table.

Ben sat to the older man's left. "Will these images help your cause?"

"Yes, yes, I believe they will." He peeled away his wire-framed specs and narrowed his gaze at Clint, then Ben. "But I'm afraid I have some bad news."

"Oh?" Ben narrowed his gaze.

"I've suspected Edward Fontaine of furtive behavior for some time now. He's made some rather interesting remarks at his gentlemen's club."

Ben could well imagine. The man did love his scotch.

"And now, thanks to you both, I've obtained hard evidence." He held up the photograph of Mr. Fontaine and Captain DeMere.

Ben winced.

"So I called it correctly," Clint confirmed. "DeMere is one of Farragut's men."

"Your camera uncovered the truth. Fontaine has been supplying Union gunboats with food and water and relaying privy information in exchange for his ships being allowed to pass into open waters. His actions have led to the capture of several Confederate vessels. Some of our most highly skilled captains have been killed." The colonel leaned forward. "I can't thank you two enough."

Clint coughed.

Ben shook his head in disbelief. "Colonel, you've known from the start that the Fontaines are friends of ours."

LaPorte sat back again. "If it will ease your conscience, I have an eyewitness account and sworn testimony that states Mr. Fontaine stayed aboard Union ships for days on end before returning to shore. This picture of him and DeMere backs that testimony up."

Ben glanced at Clint and sensed his partner felt the same prickles of unease working their way up his spine.

"The Fontaines' neighbors, Arnold and James Ladden, are involved as well. Both Ladden men are being arrested for treason as we speak. If charged, they'll face the death penalty."

Ben wasn't concerned about the Laddens, especially after hearing Emily's suspicions regarding Valerie's fat lip. The Confederate Army would likely treat Ladden better than Ben ever would. Regardless, he couldn't imagine what her father's arrest would do to Valerie. "What about Edward Fontaine?"

"We'll catch up to him—him and his daughter."

"His daughter? Valerie?" Ben wagged his head. "No. She came home from boarding school less than a month ago. She's been mourning her mother's death. Valerie is not involved, sir."

"Perhaps not, but…" He glanced from Ben to Clint and then back to Ben again. "How can I be certain?"

"If your evidence is merely circumstantial," Ben said, "couldn't our witness on her behalf be enough?"

"No, I'm afraid not. Both your close proximity to the family and the fact Miss Fontaine is Edward's daughter and betrothed to James Ladden will put questions in the minds of my superiors." Regret appeared to tug at his features. "I must issue arrest warrants."

"Sir, can I get you to reconsider?" Everything inside of Ben went taut. He couldn't fathom the emotional distress Valerie would suffer at the hands of Confederate soldiers as they hauled her off to prison. "Valerie knows nothing about her father's involvement with the Union Army."

To his credit, the colonel considered his remark. "I like you two men. I believe you're honorable. So, I'll tell you what I'll do. First, I'm going to finish writing up some other reports and have my lunch. By the time I actually deliver the arrest warrants, it'll be—" He peered at his pocket watch and pursed his lips. "—nearer to evening."

That means I've got about six hours. Ben stood and extended his right hand. He wasn't about to waste even a minute. "A pleasure doing business with you, Colonel."

All right, Lord, show me what to do next.

FOURTEEN

VALERIE PACED THE LENGTH OF HER BEDROOM. After seeing Benjamin last night, she knew now more than ever that she couldn't marry James. It didn't matter that he didn't feel the same intense feelings for her as she did for him. It had even crossed her mind that he still loved Gwyneth Merriweather. Regardless, Valerie knew she loved Benjamin and always would.

But even if she set her feelings aside, marriage to James would mean a life of enduring abuse. Emily was right. She had to talk to her father. *Please, God, let him understand.*

Leaving her room, she made her way downstairs. She hoped James wasn't about. He usually showed up around midmorning. She spied Adalia in the parlor. "Do you know if my father's at home?"

"Last I saw him, he was in his study, dearie." The maid shook her head. "He's acting awfully peculiar." Her expressive gaze sent a forewarning to Valerie.

Somewhat daunted, she approached the library. "Father?" From the hallway she could see the heavy drapes were drawn. It was unusual for this time of day.

In what mind-set would she find him?

Peeking around the corner, she saw the scores of leather-bound books that neatly lined the walls. Two large brown leather chairs seemed to squat in front of the long, polished writing desk near the hearth. No fire burned within its brick confines. But where was her father?

"Are you in here?" Valerie stepped into the room. It reeked of whiskey and stale cigars. "Father?"

She heard a moan and whirled to find him slumped in a chair behind his desk.

Drunk again!

"Father, let me call Ephraim." Valerie wondered if the slender valet was even physically capable of getting her father upstairs.

"No...Vincedupe...send...fovince..."

"Who? What?" Valerie sent a gaze upward at such slurred, nonsensical speech. "Enough, Father; get on your feet. I'll try to take you upstairs myself." She had little doubt that she possessed more muscle than the slight-of-frame valet.

Lord, give me the strength. She moved toward her father and took hold of his right arm, tugging her father upward. He was dead weight.

"You might at least *try* to cooperate." She clenched her jaw in aggravation.

He groaned in reply.

And that was when she saw it—the dark, oozing, red stain on his white shirt. She saw his right hand was covered with the same substance. She drew back at the putrid smell of dying flesh. Her insides rolled. She recognized the scent of gunpowder too.

Oh, God, no! A scream erupted from her as Father crumpled to the floor. All she could do was hold on to his arm to ease his fall.

"What's goin' on in here?" Adalia sounded breathless as she ran into the room.

"Send for the doctor!" Valerie knelt beside his unconscious form. "My father's been shot!"

~ceeΩxΩeee~

"Since you're the brains of this operation, now what?" Clint looked exasperated as he almost jogged to keep up with Ben's long-legged strides across the yard. "I don't want to say I'm going to have to quit—"

"Then don't." Ben halted. His mind was in a whir, wondering what he'd do with Valerie. "We both feel called to document the war. I have to find Luke. That much hasn't changed."

"But Em's with child, and she—"

"Let's send both her and Valerie to Jericho Junction." The words flew out of Ben's mouth before he realized the idea had even formed in his head. It gained momentum by the second. "They're friends, they'll make good traveling companions. My family will look after them until we get home."

"Home?" Clint frowned. "I never thought of settling in Jericho Junction, although when we visited last fall I thought it was a fine little town."

"You've got awhile to think on it, Clint. Meanwhile, Emily will be safe there." He arched a brow. "Doesn't it beat sending her to stay with some distant relative?"

"Point taken." Clint rubbed a hand over his whiskered jaw. "But if Valerie is wanted by the Confederate Army, it won't be safe for Em to travel with her."

Ben walked a few paces on the LaPortes' wide lawn to a tree where someone had carved a set of initials in its trunk encompassed by a heart. He thought of how Valerie said she loved him.

Only a week ago he didn't feel like he had a right to reciprocate because he couldn't offer her the sort of lifestyle to which she was accustomed. He'd been afraid—afraid because of Gwyneth's reaction to Jericho Junction and his family's simpler ways. Now, however, Valerie stood to lose her home and every monetary thing she owned. She faced censure from friends and neighbors. She faced the possibility of harsh treatment from LaPorte's troops. Loving her, Ben felt compelled to offer his name and the protection that went along with it. How could he not? And Jericho Junction was a far sight better than the alternative.

Lord, is this Your will?

Slowly he turned to face Clint. "What if Valerie's name wasn't Fontaine anymore?"

"She'll travel incognito? Brilliant."

"No, no...something more." Ben's mind went back to last night when Em told him about Valerie's lip and her notion to leave New Orleans for some questionable housekeeping job. He thought of how Valerie left boarding school. He kneaded the back of his neck. *Lord, there's only one thing I can think of to make her stay put, and I might even be underestimating her here.*

"Are you talking about marriage?"

"I sure am."

"Then she wouldn't have to lie and worry about slipping if interrogated. Her tickets would be purchased under the name McCabe." Clint tipped his head. "But are you positive? Marriage is a big step."

"I love her." Ben turned and faced his friend. Peace filled his being. "I've never been more positive of anything in my life."

"Adalia has sent for the doctor. He'll be here soon." Valerie secured the pillow beneath her father's head. He still lay on the floor in his study. Valerie hadn't wanted to move him until the physician examined his wounds. He seemed to be bleeding from multiple places. "Father, how on earth did this happen?"

"James was at the club last night...wanted more money."

"More money?" Disgust for the man filled her being. "I'm not prize enough?"

"James is a greedy man, *ma fille*, and I saw him for what he was last night. I told him he'd marry my daughter over...over my dead body."

"So he shot you?"

"The authorities went after him." Father's breathing became labored. "But he escaped. I somehow made it back home."

"Why didn't you go to the hospital?"

"Because...I leave for France...in a week."

Valerie gave a sad wag of her head. "Father, you can't travel in your condition. In fact—" She hated to state it. "Father, your wounds look severe. You might die."

"I'm a good man, *ma fille*. I have done some good things for the United States. Noble things. Brave things."

A curious frown puckered her brow. "United States?"

"I can't support the Confederacy."

Valerie had guessed as much. "Father, please don't talk anymore." She adjusted the pillows behind his head, propping him higher.

"I've been such a sinner—that's the term I heard Pastor Elliot use after your mother died and I fell to pieces emotionally."

"Where were you, Father? When she was sick?"

"Miles away at a meeting. Arnold Ladden was with me. I never knew Marguerite was ill."

Valerie saw the remorse in his dark eyes.

"After she died, Reverend McCabe advised me to believe in something more than myself."

"That's right, Father." Valerie stroked his thick dark hair. "Jesus Christ is the way, the truth, and the life. Remember how Mama explained her faith to you?"

"I laughed at her." His eyelids fluttered closed. "But I loved her so much. When she died, she took my heart with her."

"I know."

"My life without her has been marred by bad decisions. I've hurt you." His voice broke. "Forgive me, *ma fille*."

At first Valerie didn't know what to do with the apology. She'd wished for candidness between them ever since returning from school, but now it frightened her. She peered into his ashen face.

"I–I forgive you, Father." Once those words left her lips, the rest flowed. "Think about what Reverend McCabe told you. Think about everything Mama said. Remember how much she loved you. Know that God loves you even more."

He seemed to rest then.

"God is even here with us right now."

His breathing slowed.

Lord, where is Dr. Dupont?

The sound of heavy booted footfalls in the tiled hallway seemed the answer to her prayer. But then Benjamin entered the study.

"I thought you were...what are you doing here?" She noticed he'd shaved his beard, so the determination on his face was clearly evident.

He stopped short when he saw her there, sitting on the floor behind the desk with her father's bleeding form stretched out in front of her. His expression softened.

"Adalia told me that your father's been hurt." He tossed aside his hat and strode forward, hunkering down when he reached them. The sleeve of his russet frock brushed against her arm. "She also said the doctor is on his way." He took a quick look at Father's wounds and grimaced. "What happened?"

"James shot him."

Sorrow then anger spread across his features. His golden eyes darkened. "The authorities are looking for him. I saw several Confederate soldiers down the block at the Laddens' home." He ran his palm along his jaw. "Valerie, I've got to get you out of here as soon as possible."

"Me? Why?"

Her father's eyes fluttered open and locked on Benjamin.

"Colonel LaPorte has issued a warrant for your father's arrest. On charges of treason. The Laddens too. And you're wanted for conspiracy."

Valerie inhaled sharply. Her hand sailed to her throat.

Questions pooled in Father's eyes.

Benjamin looked at him and explained. "When I photographed a ship last week, Mr. Fontaine, my camera captured you and Captain DeMere."

Valerie knew the one. "The photograph I saw last night?"

Benjamin nodded at her. "I didn't know who that man was until you identified him. But only too late." His gaze moved to her father again. "I'd already given that print and others to Colonel LaPorte."

Dread climbed Valerie's spine.

"I was asked not to discuss my assignment," Benjamin continued, "while at the same time I had no clue what you and the Laddens were up to."

She tried to tie the pieces together. "What exactly did they do that was so treasonous?"

"The Laddens and your father supplied Union gunboats."

"They let my ships pass in return." Father struggled to breathe again. "All except imports." It took effort for him to inhale. "I lost a fortune...and Arnold Ladden invested in...in Fontaine Shipping."

It made sense now. The debt he owed—the one she and her dowry would cover...

Until James decided she wasn't worth it.

Benjamin shifted, lowering one knee onto the floor. "Mr.

Fontaine, as I said, the colonel is charging Valerie with conspiracy. I've got to get her out of New Orleans."

Her father captured her hand. "There's money in my vault," he wheezed. "The key is behind the portrait of...your mother." He struggled to inhale. "Take it...and go."

"Take it where? I have no place to run. Don't you think I would have left already if I had?"

Benjamin reached for her hand. "I have a solution."

She stared at him.

"You could marry me and escape to Jericho Junction."

"Jericho Junction?" Valerie felt paralyzed.

"Dearie, the doctor's here." Adalia bustled into the study with Dr. Dupont in tow. The nimble, middle-aged man took one glance at Edward Fontaine's wounds and shook his head but wasted no time.

"Can we get him up onto the desk? I'll need it as an operating table." He turned to Adalia. "And I'll need some boiling water and plenty of linens."

"Yes, sir." She hurried off.

Dr. Dupont cleared the desktop with one sweeping gesture. Benjamin gathered up Valerie's father and lifted him onto its wide surface. He groaned in such agony that the sound brought tears to Valerie's eyes.

Next Benjamin helped her up from the floor. She saw the large crimson stain where her father had lain on the Oriental rug.

The physician rummaged through his black leather valise. "This operation will take me some time."

"How much time?" Benjamin asked.

"Hours. I suggest you wait with Miss Fontaine in the parlor."

Benjamin didn't reply but took her elbow.

Father moaned in pain.

"I'll be praying for you, Father." Valerie gave his hand one last squeeze.

When they reached the parlor, Benjamin placed his hands on her shoulders. "We can't wait, Valerie. You need to pack up your things quickly. I've got to get you out of here."

"But—"

He moved to the windows and peered outside.

"—what about my father?"

"I'm sure Cousin Max will let you know of his condition. Meanwhile, I've got no guarantee that Colonel LaPorte will keep his word and forestall issuing your arrest warrant. Confederate soldiers are just down the block." Benjamin turned back to her. "If they arrest you, Valerie, you'll go to prison."

Fear shook her.

"Granted, Jericho Junction's nothing fancy. But you'll be safe there. My family will protect you."

"Yes, I–I'll go," she stammered.

"As for what I said earlier, about marrying me...well, Confederates will be on the lookout for Valerie Fontaine. If you travel as Mrs. Benjamin McCabe, you may not be bothered." A sudden resoluteness glinted in his eyes. "And marrying me will also ensure that Ladden never has claim to you again."

Were those the only reasons he was proposing—for her protection? What about love? Perhaps he felt obligated. After all, his photograph incriminated her father.

"You've cited some very practical reasons for marriage."

He stepped toward her and took her hands in his. "What do you say?"

She looked down and ran her thumbs across his knuckles. She wished he'd say he loved her. Pledged his heart as well as protection. She lifted her eyes to his, but she couldn't tell what lay within them.

In any case it seemed her choices were either jail or Benjamin's pity.

"Valerie, please come with me. I've got my wagon out back, so—"

"So it's a good thing I have my trunk already packed."

FIFTEEN

No one looked happy. Neither Emily nor Mrs. Elliot. Neither Pastor Elliot nor Clint. And Benjamin's expression was indiscernible. Even the flowers in the vase on the corner table were wilted and sad.

Valerie lowered her gaze. No orange blossoms in her bouquet. Mama always said a bride should carry a few orange blossoms. But there wasn't a single bloom in her hand. And her dress...no lace, no frills. Just her regular lilac silk gown.

"Valerie?" Benjamin's voice pierced her troubled thoughts.

"I do."

A glimmer of a grin worked on his lips. "Sweetheart, the 'I dos' are done." He guided her around to face him before taking her hands in his. "Time for the vows."

"Repeat after me," Pastor Elliot instructed.

Benjamin's voice was steady as he spoke. "I, Benjamin Daniel, take you, Valerie Charlotte, to be my wedded wife. To have and to hold, from this day forward—"

He sounded like he meant it.

"—for better, for worse, for richer, for poorer—"

Valerie stared into his eyes and read only sincerity in their depths.

"—in sickness or in health, to love and to cherish till death do us part. And hereto I pledge you my troth."

Pastor Elliot turned to her. "Valerie, repeat after me."

She followed the lead, verbally stumbling here and there. But only because she kept glimpsing Robert at the windows. He watched for soldiers who might be on the hunt for her. She felt so frightened she couldn't think straight. And her father...had he survived the surgery?

"Valerie?"

She blinked and looked back at Benjamin. "Yes?" She really ought to pay more attention. This was her wedding, for pity's sake. At least she was marrying the man she loved.

"Cousin Max says I can kiss my bride."

"Oh..." Her gaze migrated from his eyes to his mouth, and a blush warmed her cheeks. The next thing she knew she was in his arms being thoroughly kissed.

When Pastor Elliot cleared his throat, Benjamin released her and grinned rather sheepishly. He opened his mouth to say something, but it was Clint's voice she heard.

"We have to leave if we hope to get the ladies on the steamer."

The necessary marital documents were quickly signed. Emily and Clint penned their names as witnesses.

Then, like the fugitive she was, Valerie hid in the back of Benjamin's wagon on the way to the docks. As they rolled along, she heard the tinkling of glass bottles in which his photographic chemicals were stored. A man's shout caused her to tremble when she imagined Confederate soldiers bore down on them. But soon the voice wafted off into the distance.

The wagon drew to a halt, and Benjamin helped her down and into an awaiting buggy driven by Pastor Elliot. Robert sat beside him.

"I'll meet you at the dock." Benjamin clung to her gloved hand. "I'll get your trunk loaded onto the steamer."

She didn't want him to go, but he pulled away before she could utter a word. The carriage jerked forward, and Valerie pulled her hat closer toward her face. Next she hugged her cape more tightly to herself.

Pastor Elliot drove to the riverfront where stern-wheelers and side-wheelers alike were lined up in a row for miles. Several sets of towering smokestacks coughed out black smoke. He pulled on the reins and the horses slowed to a stop.

"I'll be praying for you." Pastor Elliot assisted her descent from the buggy. "And I promise to stay with your father. Robert and I will go to him straightway."

"How very kind of you." She squeezed his hand with gratitude. "You can't imagine my relief to hear you say that."

"It's my duty and my pleasure." He gave her hand a fatherly pat. "Godspeed, my dear."

"Thank you, Pastor Elliot. For everything." After a hasty good-bye to Robert, Valerie picked her way across the busy thoroughfare. She spotted Emily waving to her in the distance and hurried toward her.

"We'll wait for the boys here where we're out of the way."

Horses trotted by, pulling rattling wooden flatbeds, some loaded high with cotton bales. People milled about, calling to each other. Unsavory-looking characters lurked in the shadows, and Valerie recalled her father's stories about the dangers associated with the wharf.

She turned her back to the goings-on. Fear numbed her. Would someone recognize her? Take her into custody? She felt so conspicuous. *Oh, God, please protect me.*

"That's our boat." Emily pointed to the white, multidecked steamer with shiny red trim. Her name, *Bon St. Marie,* was painted scarlet on the side of the wheelhouse, and she bobbed slightly on the water as her passengers embarked. Her crew noisily wooded up in preparation for the journey.

Valerie marveled at her friend's calm. "Aren't you nervous? Aren't you scared?"

Emily put an arm around her. "Yes. I tend to chatter when I'm terrified."

In spite of herself, Valerie smiled.

"Now, Clint said that we'll take the steamer as far as Vicksburg. From there we'll board a stage that will take us to the train…oh, here he comes now, and Ben's with him!"

Valerie peered over her shoulder and watched the men's approach. Her trepidation ebbed. With Benjamin near she felt decidedly safer.

Clint pulled Emily off to the side, and Benjamin took Valerie's hands. He wore a tender expression as he stared down into her eyes.

"I'm sorry the way things happened this afternoon."

He's sorry he married me?

"We'll fix them when I get home."

"Fix them?" A frown weighed on her brow.

"Yes, but for now, I'd like to give you something. As you know, I didn't have a ring—"

Glancing at her gloved hand, Valerie thought of how Adalia had pressed Mama's wedding ring into her palm as she made her hasty departure. She closed her eyes. How she would miss Adalia.

"But I do want you to have this." Benjamin placed his pocket watch in her hand. "My wedding gift to you."

"Your watch?"

"It was my grandfather's. My most valued possession. Now I want my wife to have it."

"I'll cherish it." She regarded the gold, engraved face cover glistening on her gloved palm in the setting sun.

"Open it."

She pressed down on the mechanism to reveal the beautiful gold hands set on mother-of-pearl. On the back of the cover, she found Benjamin's photograph.

"Take a look at the memento I'll be carrying on my person." He reached inside his coat pocket and pulled out a palm-sized gilt frame. When she peered inside, she saw her picture—and she remembered exactly when he'd taken it. *That day at the army campground.*

She looked up into his face once more, searching his eyes. Why, if he'd taken the time to print her photograph and frame it, could that possibly mean—?

"But I don't have a wedding gift for you."

He tucked the tiny frame away. "We'll settle up when I get home. How's that?" He smiled. "Come on." He led her toward the *Bon St. Marie*. "Let's get you safely on board."

Benjamin handed the clerk her ticket, and he instructed her how to get to her quarters. Valerie did her best to shield her face as she listened. Then Benjamin squeezed her elbow in parting as she lifted her skirts and walked up the plank to the steamboat's deck. When she looked back, she saw him striding over to where Clint stood. She caught Benjamin's eye and waved, but then more passengers embarked. Valerie stepped out of their way and headed to the upper deck and her quarters. Under the circumstances, she didn't think it would be a good idea to stand at the rail and wave farewell.

Entering the room she found it cramped and stuffy. How would she and Emily dress and comb their hair? It was barely enough space for one woman, let alone two. It would prove to be a challenge, but at least their trunks had been delivered.

The steamer began to move, chugging its way up the river. Valerie felt herself relax for the first time in hours. It had been a traumatic day. She wondered how her father fared. The sad realization set in. Even if he lived, he'd face prison—or worse. She closed her eyes. *Oh, Lord, may it be that his soul cries out for You before it's too late.*

Emily walked in. "Well, we're on our way." A show of sadness gathered in her eyes. "Will you come down to the main galley with me and have tea? Clint said most of the passengers are women and children. I think it's safe enough for you."

"Yes, I'd like that."

Emily linked arms with her. "I'm going to miss Clint so much." She rested her head against Valerie's shoulder for a moment. "But he said he'd meet me in Jericho Junction before our baby's born."

Valerie had already figured it would be sometime before July. But, of course, if Benjamin found Luke, it could be sooner.

Arm in arm they made their way to the steamboat's narrow public cabin, which had been set up with small, round tables and chairs for passengers. Within minutes the waiter took their order and returned with a silver teapot, thick porcelain cups, and saucers.

Valerie took a sip and grimaced. It didn't taste anything like the fine black teas or herbal mixtures to which she'd been accustomed. She hoped it wasn't a sign of things to come.

"Catherine Elliot, what are you doing here?"

Valerie brought her gaze up sharply. "Catherine?"

"Hello, ladies." Attired in plain brown traveling garb, she strode forward. "May I join you?" She pulled out a chair without waiting for a reply.

"What are you doing here?" This time Valerie asked the question.

"Do you think I would allow *you* to live my dream of traveling west, teaching, and marrying Ben? Hardly." She folded her skinny frame into one of the wooden armchairs. "I believe it's God's will for me to marry Ben."

"But Ben and Valerie are already married, Catherine," Emily pointed out.

"He only married her so she wouldn't go to jail. The marriage isn't consummated. There's always annulment."

Valerie cringed. Catherine had spoken her worst fears.

"That's enough." Emily reached across the table and clamped on to Catherine's wrist. "We're all Christian women here." Her voice was barely audible. "A slip of the tongue could put any of us in grave danger—and I'm not just talking about *Mrs. McCabe* here."

The subtle threat caused Catherine's mouth to pucker and her eyes to narrow until her features looked pinched.

Valerie toyed with her teacup. The threat was very real for her—even the part about the annulment.

Glancing at Emily, she watched her friend take a sip of tea. She actually looked quite regal with her hair combed neatly back and tucked into a lacy crocheted snood. It matched quite nicely with her burgundy-colored traveling suit.

"So, Catherine," Emily began, "am I to presume that your folks know nothing about your leaving?"

It took several long seconds before Catherine answered. "I am old enough to make my own decisions."

"Next chance we get we'll send a wire." Emily shook her head. "Your parents will be frantic."

"They are aware of my lifelong ambition. I have read every book there is to read on life north of New Orleans and beyond the Mississippi River. My parents will understand that I saw the opportunity and seized it. What harm is there in that?"

Valerie could think of plenty. Closing her eyes, she wished Benjamin were here with his strength and confidence. Catherine's presence caused her heart to drum out an anxious beat. Was this really the way to begin her life as a new bride?

Twilight fell over the army camp in Mississippi as Ben penned a letter to Valerie. He and Clint had made good time after leaving New Orleans more than a week ago. They'd waited around until Ben learned the fate of Valerie's father. Unfortunately, the man didn't live to see the morning.

Ben sent a telegram off to the Widewater Inn in St. Louis. The stop was on the ladies' itinerary. After days of traveling, that particular inn with its comfortable lodging had always been what Ma called "the clean-up stop" before spending one last day on the train, riding in to Jericho Junction. The sad news would be waiting for Valerie when she arrived. He hated to deliver it in such an impersonal manner, but she made him promise to send word as soon as possible. Cousin Max performed a private burial ceremony the next day, and at the same time news spread through the city that James Ladden had been apprehended. He was charged with murder and treason. Ben didn't stick around to find out any details beyond that. He and Clint hit the road after that very afternoon.

Of course, Cousins Max and Amanda were beside themselves when they'd discovered Catherine ran away. In the midst of the hasty wedding and travel plans, no one noticed she'd slipped away. He prayed Catherine's attendance hadn't posed any sort of danger to Valerie and Em.

Boisterous laughter carried on a mild wind. A banjo and harmonica played a lively tune. Temperatures were in the low fifties, and Ben decided a late January winter wasn't half bad out this way. A rabbit scampered through the nearby brush, and a doe picked her way along the edge of the trees.

Ben returned his attention to the letter he wrote to his wife. Wife. Ben suddenly couldn't wait to get home to her and begin their future together. But he had to find Luke first, and, so far, there hadn't been any leads as to his whereabouts, although he and Clint would continue northward in the search.

Ben adjusted the kerosene lamp by which he worked. Again he stared at today's date and realized that if God hadn't intervened, tomorrow would have been the day Valerie married James Ladden. *Thank You, Jesus.*

He penned a couple more lines to Valerie, and all the while his mind couldn't help straying to where she and Emily might be in their leg of the journey. After getting off the packet, they would board a stage that would take them to the train that ran to St. Louis. Clint had neatly mapped it all out. Ben only wished they could stay in one place long enough to get a telegram from home letting them know the ladies arrived safely.

A wistful smile worked the corner of his mouth while his thoughts drifted back to Jericho Junction. He wondered what Valerie would think of the town, of his folks' home. He prayed Jake would mind his cynical self and Sarah would curb her sprightly ways. That aside, Ben trusted his family, knew they were upstanding individuals who loved the Lord. Valerie would be safe with them. He hoped to God that she'd come to love the town the way he did and that she'd heal from all the traumatic events in New Orleans and find happiness there—with him.

A rustling sound in the long, brown grass near to his wagon's door captured his attention. A young soldier suddenly appeared.

"Suh?" He resembled a disheveled lad, with ratty clothes and in terrible need of a haircut. Light brown scruff covered his long chin, and Ben guessed him to be no older than twenty.

"What can I do for you?"

"We-ell, suh, the maj'r tol' me to come see you."

He beckoned the man inside. "Come on. There's room." Ben gave up his chair to his guest and hunkered down, his back resting against the wagon's inner wall. Leaning forward, he held out his right hand. "Benjamin McCabe."

"Sergeant William Samuel Rogers, suh." He clasped Ben's hand in a loose-gripped shake. "Seems you're lookin' for someone?"

"Yes. My brother." Wasn't any secret.

"Maj'r Butterfield says he's a preacher or something?" The young man's drawl was incredibly slow, as if he were half asleep. "I've been thinking for days that mebbe I saw him."

"Where?" Unexpected hope shot through Ben.

"Virginia. At Bull Run." The young sergeant tipped his shaggy head. "That's where the cap'n says you lost sight of your brother, right?"

"Correct." Ben had detailed Luke's disappearance to Major Horace Butterfield some time ago. "Why do you think you saw him?"

"We-ell, you see, I started out in the First Infantry Battalion, Kentucky, but when we reached Virginia, we all got transferred into another battalion. That was before I decided to move into this here company and fight alongside my cousin, Jerome David Rogers."

Ben listened with his forearms dangling over his knees. He didn't find the switching out of regiments too odd. He'd heard similar tales. Plenty of Southern volunteers, particularly the more unrefined and unskilled, migrated from regiment to regiment. It appeared to be part of the South's basic problem—disorganization. "When do you think you may have seen my brother?"

"We-ell, you said he was a preacher, right?"

Tamping down his impatience, Ben nodded. "Right."

"I recollect seeing a preacher like that on the side of the battlefield, and I said to him, 'Sit yerself down, boy, before you get your fool head blown off.' But he didn't budge. He just stood there, real calm like, as if a war wasn't even going on. At first I thought mebbe he was an angel, sent to protect me. He had a Bible in his hand, and I remember thinkin' that, outa the two of us, he had the mightier weapon."

"Do you remember what he looked like?" Ben only dared to hope the description would match Luke's.

Rogers rubbed his jaw with one hand and gazed upward as if trying to see an image in his mind's eye. "A real clean-shaven fella with hair your color."

Ben's heart raced. He closed his eyes. *Lord, could it really be Luke?*

"He gimme this." Sergeant Rogers pulled a tattered card from his pocket and handed it to Ben. "Psalm Twenty-three. I pray it every night, and so far it's kep' me safe." He snorted out a chuckle. "I really did think that other man was some heavenly being, him acting so calm and all—that is, till I heard you were looking for your preacher brother. Then I got to wondering about it and the maj'r sent me to talk to you."

"Luke never did rile easily." Ben inspected the small card, the size of a *carte de visite*. It belonged to Luke, all right. He was known for giving these things out.

"I don't know what happened to him, suh. The fighting got real bad then."

Whatever optimism he felt moments ago came suddenly crashing down. Ben handed the card back to the soldier. "I checked the lists of the wounded and dead, but Luke's name wasn't on them." Looked like he was back to square one. "I've practically combed the eastern sides of the states from Virginia to New Orleans."

"Mebbe check the hospitals, suh."

Ben shook his head. "I just said—"

"Your brother didn't look like no enlisted man. That is, he wasn't carryin' no musket."

"He wasn't—isn't—an enlisted man." Ben said. "Luke's a chaplain."

"Yessuh, and those lists are of enlisted men, ain't they?"

Ben narrowed his gaze, thinking.

"My other cousin, Thomas Albert Thornton, got hisself shot and was loaded into a wagon headed back to Kentucky, seeing that's where our battalion hailed from. Mebbe your brother got collected up in the mix."

"And he wouldn't have appeared on any injured lists because no one would have known who he was."

Rogers shrugged in possibility.

"Except Luke's not irresponsible. He'd have at least sent a wire home to say he was still alive."

"If ya ain't got money, you can't do no wiring."

"A letter then."

"Mebbe it got lost. Wouldn't be the first time."

"But it's been over six months!" Ben was thinking aloud now, playing the devil's advocate when he knew he should be trusting in the Lord instead. But somehow he couldn't seem to help it.

"Six months ain't so very long, considerin' the trek home is mostly wilderness with a few miles of a mountain pass added in."

"Kentucky, huh?" Ben considered the young man who sat crouched over, leaning his lanky forearms on his thighs. "I appreciate your stopping by, Sergeant."

"Well, yessuh." He gave Ben a wide smile before jumping down off the back of the wagon. "I hope you find him, suh."

"Thanks." Ben climbed to the ground after Rogers, intent on sharing this information with Clint, their logistics expert. "So do I." He pumped the young man's hand in a parting shake. "So do I."

Sixteen

IT TOOK A COUPLE OF WEEKS TO REACH FORT HENRY, and the garrison was a pitiful sight to behold. Hands on hips, Ben surveyed the rundown fort as Clint set up their camera on a small patch of dry ground. Outdated and threatened to be overtaken by the Tennessee River before Federal gunboats ever arrived, it was easy to see that the Confederacy wouldn't win any battles here. And if the North won, the victory would open up Union river traffic into the Deep South.

Several soldiers straggled by, and Ben noticed their trousers were soaked to the knees. He wondered when the last time had been since their feet were dry. His own leather boots hadn't been a successful force against the eight inches or so of water that already flooded the fort, and the river was rising from all the rain.

He'd asked around and no one had seen Luke. But that was all right. Ben planned to cross the river and start searching Kentucky, thanks to that lead from Sergeant Rogers back in Mississippi.

Ben now turned to the commanding officer, a slender fellow with weasel-like features from his long brown hair to his pointed nose and beady dark eyes. "If I were you, I'd evacuate this fort and move my troops downriver to reinforce Fort Donelson. Makes more sense."

"You, sir, are not running this war." The commander lifted a haughty brow. "We have our orders from General Tilghman, and we'll follow them."

"At your own peril, I'm afraid. My partner and I have been in Clarksville, and—"

"And you're roving photographers. Yes, I understand."

Ben despised the man's arrogance.

"Take your pictures and then leave."

Ben knew that with the fighting north of the fort, it would be just days before the Union's gunners broke through the Confederate Navy's weak blockades and bombarded the place to smithereens.

"Ben?" Clint waved him over. Once Ben reached him, he said, "We'll develop the plates back in Clarksville. I've got an eerie feeling about this fort."

"Rightly so."

"My self-preservation instincts are high. I'm going to be a father, you know."

"I know." Ben grinned. "You only tell me twenty times a day."

The hyperbole earned him a quelling glare.

"All right." Any remnants of humor vanished. "Let's take our photographs and get out of here."

Dinner at the Widewater Inn consisted of smoked ham and boiled potatoes, served in a creamy sauce with onions and mushrooms. Valerie sat back at the table and dabbed the corners of her mouth with the heavy linen napkin. "What a delicious meal." It had been weeks since she tasted real food—not since they'd left the *Bon St. Marie*. The trip had been rough, mostly waiting in dingy lodges for trains. They had to detour several times because railroad tracks had been destroyed by skirmishes. But now their trip finally neared its end.

Valerie glanced around the inn. Not a single Confederate among the patrons. She figured she'd seen enough gray uniformed men to last the rest of her life. Each time she encountered troops, she almost lost her nerve and broke down on the spot, fearing they were out to arrest her for conspiring with traitors. But Em had pluck and always did the talking. Now that they'd reached St. Louis, chances of encountering more Confederates was slim. Instead, there were Yankees everywhere.

"Good evening, ma'am." A soldier clad in blue tipped his hat as he passed slowly by.

Valerie quickly lowered her gaze.

He walked on.

She sighed in relief. One thing she'd learned about soldiers was they hungered for a woman's attention. It didn't matter much if she was married, and some men were more insistent than others. But so far she, Emily, and Catherine hadn't encountered any real trouble.

Surrounded by Yankee blue, Valerie thought of her father again. Had he survived the operation? Had he been arrested? Hanged?

Shaking off her weighty muse, Valerie noted Catherine's untouched plate. "You really need to take a few bites. You're going to get another one of those nasty headaches if you don't."

"Too late." She winced. "My headache has returned."

"Try eating."

Catherine mechanically brought her fork to her mouth.

"All right. Good. That's one bite," Valerie coached her onward. "Now take another...a piece of potato this time."

Valerie pitied the poor woman. Over the course of the last two weeks, Catherine's appetite had diminished, and she'd grown weak, succumbing to frequent headaches. Valerie thought it was merely a case of nerves, but Catherine maintained her poor health was due to a combination of rich food, poor-tasting food, the soot from the train that often blew through open windows and into the cars, and inadequate sleeping conditions. Emily said

Catherine wouldn't have ever made it traveling with Benjamin and Clint and living out of their wagons.

Catherine chewed slowly on a tiny piece of potato.

"Good. Now take one more bite of ham."

She frowned, her bony shoulders sagged, and she reminded Valerie of a noncompliant little girl rather than the stern schoolmarm she'd been in New Orleans. Catherine's dusty-brown hair looked thinner and more limp than usual, and her face was gaunt and haggard—like a wilted, faded flower on a liriodendron.

Emily returned to the table. She'd finished her meal a good half hour ago and clearly didn't feel like cajoling Catherine into eating. So Valerie took a turn. Em had then left and strolled to the front desk to see if there was any word from Clint and Benjamin. She now waved several slips of paper. "We've each got telegrams, three sent from New Orleans, two sent from Clarksville, Tennessee. "

Valerie tore into the one from New Orleans. She hoped for news about her father. IT'S WITH REGRET THAT I INFORM YOU OF YOUR FATHER'S DEATH. DR. DUPONT DID ALL HE COULD. The telegram was signed by Benjamin. Such sadness overcame her that she couldn't read the rest. She stuffed it and the other piece of paper into the reticule she wore on her wrist.

Emily placed a hand on her shoulder. "Valerie? What is it?"

"My father's dead." She rose quickly from her chair. "Please excuse me." She ran up the steps to the room that she, Emily, and Catherine had rented and closed the door behind her. Leaning against it she sobbed. In spite of all his faults, Edward Fontaine had been her father, and she loved him. Like Benjamin, he had never actually said he loved her, but he'd provided for her all her life. Her needs had been met. Perhaps that was all a woman could ask for from any man.

Valerie touched Benjamin's watch, which now hung around

her neck on one of Mama's gold chains. She kept it hidden inside her bodice. While she never believed in good luck charms, the watch did serve as a reminder of hope and promise.

Emily and Catherine came in about a half hour later.

"Are you all right?" Emily sat down and placed a sisterly arm around Valerie's shoulders.

"Yes, I'm fine. Just sad." But the pain, she realized, hadn't been anywhere near the devastation she'd suffered when Mama died.

"The maid's coming with hot water for the bathtub. A good soaking will lift your spirits."

Valerie wiped the last of her sorrow off her cheeks then offered her friend a grateful smile. "That it will." She watched Emily survey their spacious quarters. It contained one bed and two cots. Their trunks had been brought up already and stood in one corner. The large porcelain bathtub occupied the other, nearer to the hearth. A fire crackled within its bricked confines.

"Catherine, you take the bed," Emily said, glancing at Valerie for confirmation.

"Absolutely. Take the bed, Catherine." The poor woman was ill, after all.

"You've both been very good to me." She collapsed on the mattress, reminding Valerie of a heap of flesh-covered bones. Not an ounce of fat on her. Quite worrisome.

The maid came and filled the tub. They allowed Catherine to have the first bath. Then Valerie helped her into her gown for the night and tucked her in under the covers.

"We'll pray my headache goes away." Catherine's voice sounded weak.

Valerie sat on the edge of the bed. "Father God, You are most gracious. Please touch our sister's body and heal her. Give her strength for the rest of the journey. This I ask in Christ's name…amen."

"Amen!" Emily echoed.

"Thank you." Catherine set a cold hand on Valerie's wrist. "Once I get to Jericho Junction I'll be fine. My cousin, Rebecca McCabe, will know just what to do for me."

"I hope so. Nothing we've done has helped."

"Indeed, and we've tried everything," Emily said, sounding weary.

"You bathe next, Em. Go ahead." Standing from the edge of the mattress, Valerie crossed the room and put an arm around her friend's slender shoulders. "I can wait."

"Oh, thank you. I feel—" She yawned. "—so exhausted."

"It's because of the babe you're carrying."

Emily's features brightened and she ran a hand lovingly over her midsection.

Smiling, Valerie walked to her trunk, unlocked it, and opened it. Adalia had seemingly included *everything*, including Father's lockbox containing the gold he'd mentioned. In her scrambling to leave, Valerie had forgotten about it until she'd unpacked that first night on the steamer. Adalia placed a note inside stating the exact amounts she'd taken in pay for herself, Ephraim, Chastean, and Willie. And what a blessing, her father's gold!

Bittersweet feelings engulfed her. Her father had provided for her yet once more. With this trip's unexpected rooming costs and expenses for their meals, which Valerie had paid for since Emily's and Catherine's funds had been depleted more than a week ago, they would have all three been in a horrible predicament without his provision. Even so, there were still plenty of coins left for Valerie if a need arose. Adalia had also thoughtfully tossed in Mama's herbs and the last of her soap as well as all of Mama's jewelry.

Opening one of the trunk's many drawers, Valerie removed the lavender-rose bar that she and Em had been sharing, although a bath had proved to be a luxury on this journey.

"Valerie?"

"Here it is." She peeled off the protective hankie and handed the perfumed cake to Em.

"What a pleasure and a treat this soap is after a day of traveling." Em had climbed into the tub, the water up to her neck. She'd unpinned her hair and the coppery tresses hung over the end of the tub. "It's a pity, Catherine, that you can't bear the essence of anything on your body."

"It's this headache."

Valerie thought it a shame. Not even some of Mama's herbal teas had helped Catherine. "Perhaps we should summon a physician."

"No, no...this time tomorrow I'll be safe and snug in the McCabes' home."

Nervous flutters filled Valerie's insides. What if Benjamin's family disliked her?

Well, she'd have to cross that bridge when she came to it. For now she prayed Benjamin would find Luke soon and come home. She longed to feel her husband's strong arms around her again.

Valerie lived for that day.

From inside the tub Emily began to sing, and Valerie hummed along. She stood in front of her trunk and unfastened Mama's chain from which Benjamin's watch hung. It had become her habit these past couple of weeks of opening the watch and staring at his photograph, just as she did at this moment. She passed the tip of her forefinger over his face, praying that wherever he was, he thought of her and still maintained his love for her as she did for him.

Unable to help the reflective sigh, she carefully wound the watch. That done, she touched her lips to Benjamin's picture before slipping the precious keepsake into the black velvet drawstring bag that held hers as well as Mama's jewelry. With the velvet pouch safely nestled inside her trunk, Valerie undressed for her turn in the tub.

As she unbuttoned the front of her dress, she felt the weight of a stare. Valerie chanced a peek toward the bed and met Catherine Elliot's intent gaze. An embarrassed flush warmed her cheeks as she realized Catherine had observed her nightly ritual.

"Headache better?" Valerie chose to ignore the incident.

"No." Catherine turned over, her back to Valerie now.

Em climbed from the tub and toweled dry while Valerie got in and washed up. After she too had donned her warmest nighttime gown, she sat on her cot and wrote another letter to Benjamin before extinguishing the lamp.

Beneath her thin blanket, Valerie shivered and envied Catherine beneath a thick, patchwork quilt. She could hear the woman softly snoring. Well, perhaps her headache would go away now.

Her eyes fluttered closed, and her limbs felt heavy with fatigue. *Lord, be with us as we finish our journey tomorrow.*

The next morning Valerie awakened to the sound of the chambermaid lighting a fire in the hearth. On the hard cot and shivering underneath her blanket, Valerie prayed her accommodations in Jericho Junction would be more warm and comfortable. Nevertheless, she'd slept hard during the night. But had she ever been so cold?

Again she shivered as the maid slipped from the room. The flames in the hearth grew higher, and the chill in the air abated. As soon as she dared, Valerie slipped from beneath the thin covering and strode to her trunk where she dressed as quickly as possible. She selected her gown with care, wishing Adalia was here so she could iron away the wrinkles. What Valerie wanted most was to make a good impression on the McCabes. The train would be arriving in Jericho Junction later this afternoon.

Only one more day of traveling...

Valerie pulled the lovely turquoise silk and cotton blend traveling dress over her head and straightened the white bodice. She'd left off her wide hoop skirt for traveling conveniences; however, Emily said women in these parts didn't bother with them unless they were invited to a formal party or ball. Slipping into the matching blue-green jacket, Valerie fastened its only button at the neckline. The jacket hung in an A-shape from her shoulders, and she adored the lace insets in the sleeves.

A moan escaped from Em's lips, and Valerie forgot all about dressing. She whirled around to find her friend perched at the side of the cot. She rushed to her side. "What is it?"

"I think I need something to eat or–or I'll be sick."

Another sign confirming Em's pregnancy. Valerie couldn't conceal a pleased grin. "There's no food here in the room. I'll run downstairs and see what I can find."

The eatery bustled with patrons. Valerie managed to catch a serving woman's attention and explained the situation. The harried older lady was kind enough to slap two biscuits and some honey onto a plate and pour out a cup of tea before trotting off to attend to other customers.

"Oh, Valerie, this is exactly what I needed." Em sipped the tea. "My stomach is settling. I don't know what I'd do without you—or what either of us would do, right, Catherine?"

"Yes, I suppose you've been something of a help to me, although you fawn all over Emily as if she were your spoiled child."

Valerie didn't react or reply, as Em didn't want Catherine to know about her condition quite yet. As far as Catherine's criticism, she'd grown somewhat accustomed to it by now. "Well, I think that was a 'thank-you,' and you're entirely welcome. Both of you." Valerie gave them each a grin before returning to her toilet. She brushed out her dark brown tresses and then pinned each side of her hair back with a small, ivory comb.

On the other side of the room, Catherine was in the process of dressing as well.

"You look as though you're feeling better this morning." Valerie thought Catherine's face didn't seem quite as pale as it had in recent days, although her slow, exacting movements indicated her body's weakened state.

"I'm much better, thank you." The aloofness in her voice sounded stronger, another indication of Catherine's improved health.

"Mama used to say I'd make a fine nurse." Valerie opened the little drawer inside her trunk and removed the black velvet pouch, intending to don Mama's gold chain and Benjamin's pocket watch, then slip it beneath her bodice as always.

"I think you would at that." Emily stood and strode cautiously to her trunk. She'd regained the color in her face.

The morning seemed off to a good start. But then, fishing her hand inside the velvet pouch, Valerie couldn't locate the items she desired. She carried the bag to her cot and dumped out its contents. All her other jewelry seemed present and accounted for, but not the chain or pocket watch.

"It's gone!" A chill swept through her.

"What's gone?" Emily came to stand at her side.

Valerie turned to her friend, feeling confused. "Benjamin's pocket watch. I placed it in here before bed." She held up the now-empty black velvet pouch. "And this morning the watch has vanished!"

"How can that be?" Em picked through the necklaces, broaches, wrist bangles, and earbobs. "But you're right. It's not here."

"You probably lost it yesterday on the train." Catherine's tone held a critical note.

"No." Valerie stood and placed her hands on her hips. She retraced her steps. "I had it last night. I took it off when I undressed." She glanced at Catherine. "In fact, you watched me. You—"

Suddenly Valerie felt like she'd been kicked. She couldn't breathe. She just stared at Catherine, who stealthily moved toward her.

"Are you suggesting that *I* broke one of God's commandments?"

"I'm not making any accusations." Valerie somehow found her voice. Even so thin and weak, Catherine made an imposing, towering figure. Nevertheless, Valerie lifted her chin. "But I know you saw me unfasten my gold chain last night."

She snapped her fingers. "It's coming back to me now. So I did. But isn't it also true that the chambermaid crept in here this morning without our notice?"

Valerie shook her head. "I woke up when she entered. I saw her every move."

Em stepped in. "Perhaps we should put an end to all this speculation and summon the authorities."

"I think so too." Valerie squared her shoulders.

"No time, ladies. We have a train to catch." Catherine eyed Em then Valerie. "But you can file a report with the sheriff in Jericho Junction. I'm sure he'll see that justice is served."

Valerie swallowed the unkind words bubbling up inside. She sensed deep down that Catherine lied. It hurt. After all she'd tried to do to help Catherine. But Valerie knew full well the other woman had observed her tucking the velvet jewelry pouch into the drawer of her trunk. It wouldn't have been difficult for her to sneak into the trunk while Valerie had been sleeping soundly.

How could she?

Em took her hand and pressed it between her palms. Valerie peered into her friend's sweet, round face. She could tell Em's thoughts matched her own.

"Catherine's right." While her tone sounded placating, a knowing little gleam entered Em's eyes. "We'll take care of this matter in Jericho Junction."

Some hours later, the train's whistle belted out three short blasts as it rolled into Jericho Junction. Snow blanketed the wide open fields surrounding the depot and small town. Valerie peered out the passenger car window and took a moment to admire the pristine view, noting the way the indigo sky melded with the cloak of white on the horizon.

"Pretty country, isn't it?" Emily leaned on her arm, catching a glimpse of scenery.

"Mm-hm..."

"Are you excited?"

"Excited and somewhat nervous, I have to admit. But from the way Benjamin talked about his family, I feel like I know the McCabes already." She moved her hand to her chest and the place where Benjamin's pocket watch usually hung. She mourned its loss.

Emily gave her hand a pat, then sat back in her seat and packed away her knitting. Having finished the tiny sweater, she worked on a baby's blanket now.

Valerie sent a glance into the next aisle where Catherine sat. She looked so peaked. Perhaps a good dose of this country air would revive her as she claimed, and maybe her conscience would prick her and she'd return the watch.

The train came to a halt, and Valerie pulled on her woolen cape before trailing Catherine and Emily out of the car and onto the platform. She sucked in a breath of frosty air and shivered. She wasn't accustomed to these frigid temperatures.

Just then a tall man approached. He wore a lined buckskin jacket and used a cane on his left side as he limped toward them. *Jacob McCabe.* Valerie would have known him anywhere. He had Benjamin's rugged features and broad shoulders, albeit his hair was the same color as his brown jacket and his eyes the color of burnt sienna.

"Catherine Elliot?" The man spoke the name with confidence, although his expression seemed uncertain until she stepped forward.

"Jacob?" She appeared equally as unsure.

A wry grin tipped his full mouth. "Well, what do you know?" He wrapped his right arm around her shoulders in a welcoming hug. Valerie was impressed that he stood a good half a head taller than Catherine, quite untypical for most men. Even Benjamin's height barely topped Catherine's nearly six-foot frame.

Jacob released her, and a show of pink covered Catherine's entire face. "Well," she said with a prudent grin, obviously embarrassed by his affection, "thank you for meeting us."

"Aw, now, you don't have to use that formal tone with me. We've known each other since we were kids." He eyed her slim frame. "You look mighty thin and awfully pale. Are you feeling all right?"

"I succumbed to headaches during our journey." Catherine looked embarrassed. "But I'm here now, and I feel better already."

"Good. And not to worry. Ma will fatten you up in no time." He gave her a smile before turning to Valerie and Emily. His dark eyes flitted from one to the other before coming to rest on Emily. "Mrs. Culver, I presume. I believe the last time you and your husband visited Jericho Junction I was riding with General McCulloch."

Jacob is a Confederate. Valerie had forgotten. Sudden nervous flutters filled her insides as she wondered how staunch of a

Confederate he might be—enough to enlist, ride with McCulloch, and risk his life. But she had to believe that Benjamin wouldn't have sent her to Jericho Junction if it wasn't safe.

"Yes. I believe that was the last time I was here." Emily smiled as Jacob took her hand and bowed slightly.

"I'm at your service, ma'am."

Ah, yes, the McCabe charm. Valerie hid a grin.

At last Jacob's gaze came around to her. He inclined his head. "So you're my new sister-in-law." He reached for her hand. "It's a pleasure."

"Likewise."

"The marriage is in name only. Right, Valerie?"

She looked at Catherine with a measure of disbelief. First the watch. Now the humiliation.

Jacob glanced from one to the other.

Emily took the crook of Valerie's arm. "My, but it's awfully cold here on the platform."

"My apologies, Mrs. Culver. How 'bout we load your trunks into our wagon over yonder?" Jake pointed to where a two-seat flatbed wagon was parked on the unpaved road. "My friend Bear is waitin' on us. Once the wagon's loaded, we'll git-along home."

Home. Valerie liked the sound of it.

They walked to the wagon and Jake introduced his friend Bear, whose given name was John Bearman. However, the man truly did resemble a grizzly, which was the precise reason he earned his nickname. *Bear.*

"Pleased ta make yer acquaintances." The large man stared at his dirt-covered boots while he spoke, and Valerie sensed his shyness.

Then the loading of the trunks commenced. Jake helped Bear the best he could with his war-injured leg. But once the men finished, Valerie's teeth were chattering. Obviously her woolen wrap wouldn't get her too far in a Missouri prairie town. Glancing at Em, she noticed the expectant mother didn't seem too bothered by the freezing temperatures, and Catherine was bundled in a warm but uncomely winter coat. Adalia's voice practically haunted Valerie. *These wraps might be the height of fashion, but they sure can't keep a girl warm like a thick wool coat with satin lining.*

Jake must have seen her shivering after he helped her up into the wagon. He shrugged out of his coat and slung it around her shoulders.

"Th–that's not n–necessary. You n–need your c–coat." Although it did appear he wore at least two shirts.

He grinned. "I think my blood's thicker 'n yours right now, sis." He tossed his cane into the front of the wagon and then climbed aboard, sitting next to Catherine in the front. He lifted the horses' reins. "Besides, I can't hardly let you freeze to death your first hour in town."

Emily giggled at the sarcasm, causing Valerie to smile. "You're most kind. Thank you."

Sitting in the backseat beside Em, she steadied herself as the wagon lurched forward. Valerie looked about her as they headed down what had to be the middle of Jericho Junction. Storefronts lined the wide dirt road.

"Off to the right here," Jacob began, "you'll see the darker side of our little town. Every Tuesday Pa and I stand on the boardwalk and share Christ with anyone who is willing to stop and listen. Many times the women from houses of ill repute will even walk up to hear Pa read from the Bible. They'd never dare step into the church on a Sunday morning, but Pa and I feel like we can reach some of them—and we've already made a difference—right there on the street corner."

"Quite commendable." Catherine held on to her hat bonnet as a gust of cold wind blew.

Valerie too admitted to feeling impressed, and she could tell by Emily's expression that she shared the sentiment.

"Now right here you'll see we have a fine hotel."

Valerie grinned, mistaking the comment for a quip, but soon she realized he was serious. Fine hotel? Rustic is the way she'd describe the unpainted, wooden structure.

"We pick up our mail in the lobby. Train drops off satchels of letters and the like each day about this time, and Bear's the one who unloads 'em off the train and transports 'em to Eli, the clerk in the hotel. Eli sorts it all out, and we just go pick it up. There's also a nice little restaurant inside the hotel called JJs. It's respectable." He paused while another wagon rattled by. "What we're passing by here is Sheriff Nuttleman's office. If the sheriff's not in, should you ever need him, he's probably preoccupied at the other end of town. There's a saloon down that way, and every now and then a gunfight'll break out."

At once Valerie decided the sheriff sounded too busy for her small issue of Benjamin's missing pocket watch. Besides, she was reasonably sure who took it. She let go a heavy breath and stared at the back of Catherine's head.

They rode by more businesses. The livery and blacksmiths. Taylor's General Store. Doc Owens's office. A barber shop and the bank. At the end of the road stood a pretty little church, the parsonage beside it, and a larger home next to it. Recalling Benjamin's description of the McCabe property, she knew they'd arrived.

The wagon creaked and shook as Jacob steered the horses up a long side drive that wound around the back of a yellow, two-story house. A large dark brown barn and several other outbuildings came into view. A dog ran toward them, barking and jumping.

Chickens clucked and flew out of the way. Then another gust of frosty wind slapped Valerie's cheeks.

However, it couldn't begin to match the cold stare Catherine sent her once the wagon halted.

SEVENTEEN

THE BACK DOOR SWUNG OPEN, AND AN ATTRACTIVE older woman, in her fifties, perhaps, strolled from the house. The cut of the copper-colored dress she wore accentuated her full figure, and she moved with matriarchal confidence. Her hair, a pepper color, had been drawn back into a tidy bun. Valerie figured she was Benjamin's mother.

Jake climbed down and helped Emily alight.

"So nice to see you again, Emily," the woman said, giving her a hug.

"Thank you for allowing me to stay here awhile."

"You're most welcome."

Jake assisted Valerie next. She handed back his jacket after her feet touched the frozen ground.

"Ma, this here's Ben's wife, Valerie. And Valerie, if you haven't guessed, this is my mother, Rebecca McCabe."

"Nice to meet you, ma'am."

"Ma'am?" Her brows shot up. "Oh, no. None of that 'ma'am' nonsense."

Valerie heard Jake's chuckle just before she became enfolded in a snug embrace.

"Call me Becca, most everyone does. Of course, as my daughter-in-law, I'd love to hear you call me Ma, but when you're ready." She held Valerie at arm's length. Sincerity shone from the depths of her cerulean eyes. "Welcome to the family, honey."

"Thank you." She glanced at Emily, who replied with an affirmative nod.

"She's darling, isn't she?" Becca glanced at Jake before her gaze fell back on Valerie. "After that telegram from Ben, we weren't sure what to expect."

"A New Orleans socialite is what we thought we were getting."

And another Gwyneth? Valerie pressed her lips together before the question escaped.

Then Catherine rounded the wagon. "Hello, Cousin Rebecca!"

The woman's gaze narrowed. "Don't you 'Hello Cousin Rebecca' me, young lady." Stepping forward, she reached for Catherine's hand. She pulled her toward the house. "Don't you realize how devastated your mother, my favorite second cousin, has been since you ran off?"

"Now, Cousin Rebecca—"

"Sick with worry. Your father too."

The farther away they walked, the more muffled Becca's voice became. Valerie noticed then that Jake stood nearby, Bear right behind him.

"I reckon Catherine deserves that tongue-lashing." He turned to Valerie. "Guess I'll go ahead and explain the living arrangements. You'll be here in the big house, sis," he said with a smart grin, "and Mrs. Culver, you're staying with Leah."

"Wonderful." Emily smiled. "I met Leah last fall and we got along fine."

Jake nodded, adding for Valerie's benefit, "She and her husband Jon reside in the parsonage, except Jon's away in the army. Leah could use some full-time company."

"We understand congratulations are in order with the birth of the baby," Emily said.

Jake suddenly resembled the proud uncle he was. "Little Josiah. He's a wonder, all right."

From out of the corner of her eye, Valerie glimpsed movement. She turned to see a young lady running toward them from the parsonage. Her long blonde hair billowed behind her. *Sarah McCabe*. She smiled.

Sarah reached them and expelled a winded sigh. She eyed Valerie curiously as Jake made the introductions.

"I think your new sister-in-law is about frozen, Sarah." Jake grinned. "Why don't you take her and Mrs. Culver into the big house while Bear and I get these trunks unloaded?"

"All right. I can make some tea." She led the way. "C'mon. Follow me."

Valerie and Emily traipsed behind the bouncy girl into the McCabes' house. They entered through the back where a mudroom preceded the spacious yellow kitchen. Following Sarah's example, they hung up their outer wraps before stepping inside.

A tantalizing smell reached Valerie's nose. She glanced to her left and spied the cast iron stove on which a pot of something simmered.

"I'm cooking venison stew for dinner tonight." Becca seemed to read her thoughts. She was standing at the long counter that ran the length of one wall. "I hope you'll enjoy it. We've still got potatoes in the root cellar, and I'm adding the carrots and corn we canned last fall. Leah's baking the biscuits. She'll be over with the baby later."

"I can't wait to meet her, and the dinner sounds marvelous." Valerie's stomach rumbled with hunger.

"I don't suppose you've ever canned anything, huh, Valerie?" Catherine had seated herself in a chair at the large round table.

"Well, actually, no, I never did. My mother didn't grow vegetables. But I helped her dry herbs for teas and soap."

"Speaking of tea," Sarah said, "I set the kettle to boiling."

"Thank you." Valerie exchanged a smile with the girl and hoped they'd be friends.

"Wait until you try some of Valerie's Psalm 55 soap!" Emily pulled out a chair and sat down. "It's ever so fragrant and leaves a lady's skin feeling rose-petal soft."

"My, my." Becca looked interested. "Psalm 55 soap, huh?"

"Named for my mama's favorite psalm. So with every batch she made, she'd write a piece of that psalm on a silk ribbon. Then after the bars were cut and set, she'd tie the ribbon around each one and give them away or put them upstairs in the guest room." Valerie recalled how fine Benjamin had smelled that night they rode off to the Donahues' party.

"A ribbon of scripture..." Becca poised in thought. "Psalm 55..."

"Cast thy burden upon the Lord," Valerie quoted, "and he shall sustain thee." She'd written the verse on ribbons more times than she could count.

"I wonder if we could use some of the Psalm 55 soap in our ministry, Valerie."

"Oh." Valerie felt flattered and pleased. Mama would have been happy.

"Jake told us a little about how he and Reverend McCabe preach on the corner every Tuesday."

"Well, yes, but I see some of those working girls go in and out of Taylor's General Store. What if I stood outside the store and handed out soap?"

"I'd help you, Becca." Valerie smiled. "That's exactly how Mama would have wanted her soap to be used." She sat down in the chair next to Emily.

"I would too!" Sarah stirred the pot on the stove.

A broad grin spread across Becca's face. "Well, then, I'll talk to Daniel about it."

"Back to the original subject of canning." Catherine ran her finger along a scar on the tabletop. "I canned vegetables and fruits last fall and made preserves. Mama couldn't help me. The rheumatism in her hands was bothering her at that time."

"Oh, my poor, dear cousin." Fretting over her lower lip, Becca shook her head. "And on top of living in chronic pain, she's had to endure the loss of her eldest daughter, who ran away."

"I'm not so terrible." Annoyance drew together Catherine's features until they looked taut and pinched. "Valerie left boarding school without permission, and all the trouble in New Orleans was her fault."

Valerie sucked in a startled breath.

"Catherine." Emily leaned close to her. "We discussed this on the steamer. You're not to—"

"We're not on the steamer anymore. And I'm tired of you behaving like my superior. We're at the McCabes' now. They're *my* family. They have a right to know, so maybe it's high time the whole sordid truth came out."

"Are you referring to the incident concerning Ben's pocket watch?" Emily lifted the corners of her mouth.

"You mean the watch that the chambermaid stole? No. I'm speaking about Valerie's father's treasonous ways and how his death is all her fault."

"Stop it, Catherine. Please." Valerie shot up from her chair. The wounds in her heart reopened, and the smug expression on Catherine Elliot's face cut her even deeper.

The teakettle whistled, and Sarah took it off the burner.

"And she's not really a McCabe. Ben only married her to keep her from going to prison."

Valerie closed her eyes and heard the gasps that emanated from every woman, including herself. "Please, let me explain—"

"It's not like that at all." Emily stood. "Clint and I witnessed the ceremony."

"Was it a beautiful wedding?" Sarah wanted to know. She poured the water into the teapot. "A church filled with people and white roses everywhere?"

"No, it was held in our parlor." Catherine snorted derisively. "The room looked like a disaster because the Culvers and Ben had been staying with us, and of course Robert created one mess after another."

Valerie barely recalled it. She'd been in shock from holding her dying father in her arms and learning the Confederate Army wanted her on charges of conspiracy. She only remembered bits and pieces. Had she missed something? Perhaps the part about her marriage being in name only? Ben had said they'd "fix it" when he came home. Maybe Catherine was right.

Spinning on her heels so the McCabes wouldn't see the hurt and frustration that welled in her eyes, Valerie hurried out of the kitchen, through the mudroom, and outside. She almost collided with Jacob and Bear, who were carrying in the trunks. Jake leaned heavily on his cane while with the other he gripped the trunk's handle.

Valerie opened the door for them.

"Looks like you came out just in time."

She glimpsed Jake's friendly smile before averting her gaze so he wouldn't see her tears.

Once the men entered, Valerie let the door close. She hugged herself and took a few steps out where chickens pecked their way across the yard. It occurred to her then that she had nowhere to run. She felt trapped. Had God brought her all this way only to allow her to suffer the same fate as in New Orleans?

An orange tabby suddenly bounded toward her and rubbed

itself against the soft leather of her boots. Valerie lifted the fat cat into her arms. It nuzzled her and purred.

"Why, you're a friendly thing, aren't you?" She stroked its soft fur as the door behind her opened.

The ground crunched, and the sound grew near. Valerie turned to see Sarah come to stand beside her, wearing no coat, only her dark blue linsey-woolsey with its white crocheted collar. She'd obviously followed Valerie out.

"If you married my brother, then you're a McCabe. I don't care what Cousin Catherine said. Ben is my favorite big brother, and I know he wouldn't marry someone just to lend out our name. I mean, if that's all it took, you could have just fibbed and said your last name was Lincoln."

The girl made a point that Valerie never stopped to consider.

"That's Sunset, Sunny for short." Sarah inclined her head toward the cat. "She's going to have kittens soon."

Valerie smiled in spite of herself. "I wondered why she was so plump."

"That's why. Jake says I spoiled her when she was young. It's true. I always carried her around and even snuck her into the house and let her sleep with me."

A laugh bubbled up inside of Valerie as she recalled Benjamin's story about Sarah wandering off to hold kittens when she was a small child.

"And if Sunny likes you, then you must be a good person. She's sort of picky about who she lets hold her. She hisses at Jake."

This time Valerie couldn't conceal her mirth. "Thank you, Sarah, for lifting my spirits." The cat squirmed and Valerie set her down. "I can see why Benjamin spoke so highly of his youngest sister."

Sarah's smile spread wide across her face. She took Valerie's arm. "I think our tea is ready."

~~eeθⅩℓℓℓ~~

Hours later Daniel McCabe walked in, and from her place in the drawing room where she sat near the hearth, Valerie thought he looked as tall as an oak. It was easy to see from whom Benjamin and Jacob had inherited their height and broad shoulders.

He greeted Emily as he moved farther into the room, and Valerie stood, smoothing down the skirt of her traveling dress.

He stepped in front of Valerie. "And you must be the latest addition to our family."

As she looked up into his golden-brown gaze, so much like Benjamin's, her tongue felt suddenly adhered to the roof of her mouth. Confusion enveloped her. Was she part of this family, or was annulment part of the way Benjamin planned to "fix" things when he returned?

Reverend McCabe chuckled. "I can see you've had a long day already." He gave her a genuine, fatherly hug that caused tears to spring into her eyes again.

Emily came alongside her. "It's been an emotionally draining journey."

"I can imagine. We expected you weeks ago." Reverend McCabe put his hands on his hips. "But Jake reminded me that with this war going on—" He inhaled, then expelled a sigh, relief perhaps. "Praise the Lord you're safely here now."

"Amen!" Em said.

Valerie gave him a smile and thanked God also for Emily's bit of backbone since hers seemed weak and vulnerable at the moment.

"And Catherine—" Reverend McCabe walked to where she sat on a bench, diddling on the pianoforte's keys.

She pushed to her feet and hugged him. "Cousin Daniel."

"It's a good thing you're not my daughter—" He held her at

arm's length. "—or I'd take you over my knee, no matter how old you are."

Crimson spanned the width of Catherine's face.

Sarah giggled behind her hand. "Don't worry, Catherine. Pa won't really do it. He threatens to take me over his knee a couple of times every week."

Reverend McCabe's features softened as he glanced at Sarah but turned stern as he regarded Catherine again. "Catherine, what you did caused great concern among this family and your own."

"I can't imagine why. Living out here is my dream. I wrote and told Cousin Rebecca and corresponded with Leah."

"Yes, I heard." Reverend McCabe crossed his arms. "But that still doesn't—"

"Well, somebody had to see after those two." Catherine pointed to Valerie and Em. "After her scandal in New Orleans, Valerie's been emotionally unstable."

"I have not!" Valerie's jaw dropped at the derogatory image Catherine painted.

"And Emily's in the family way."

"That's true," Emily said shyly.

"You're really expecting?" Sarah stood. "That's happy news! When is your baby due?"

"July, I suspect."

"Well, congratulations." Reverend McCabe gave her a smile.

"Josiah will have a playmate," Sarah said. "I hope you and Mr. Culver will stay in Jericho Junction."

"I wouldn't mind—"

Taking a step back, Valerie marveled at the way Catherine had so expertly shifted everyone's attention after dropping a most unsavory remark about her character. Valerie hadn't been "emotionally unstable" when she'd paid for Catherine's accommodations and helped with her headaches.

Another woman entered the parlor. She had soft brown hair and kitten-gray eyes. She wore a simple gown with a jeweled neckline and cradled a baby.

"Leah!" Catherine strode forward and bent to peer at the infant.

"Hi, cousin, so nice to see you again. It's been a long time." She smiled at the bundle in her arms. "May I present Josiah Matthew Henderson."

"He's beautiful. May I?"

"Of course." She handed off the child to Catherine, who sat back down on the bench.

Valerie watched curiously. She'd never seen Catherine interact with children, although she knew the woman taught school. But as for babies, Catherine never seemed interested...until now.

"Well, hello, Emily." Leah gave her a welcoming hug.

"Leah, how good to see you again."

"I understand we'll be housemates for a while. I'm looking forward to your stay."

"Thank you."

"Mrs. Culver's expecting, Leah," Sarah blurted.

Leah's face lit up with happiness. "Congratulations!"

Emily flushed with pleasure, and her gaze caught Valerie's. "Your new sister-in-law." She tugged on Valerie's elbow.

Leah's gaze moved to Valerie, who didn't miss the sweeping glance of momentary inspection. She smiled. "How very nice to meet you."

"Likewise."

"She's nothing like Gwyneth," Sarah sprouted. "What a relief, huh?"

"Sarah!" Leah whirled on her younger sister. "That remark was uncalled for."

"Well, it's true."

Reverend McCabe cleared his throat in mild reprimand.

Sarah shrugged. "I'm merely stating a fact."

Valerie had to come to Sarah's defense. "It's all right. Benjamin told me about Miss Gwyneth Merriweather and the way she hated Jericho Junction. I can assure you, I'm quite different."

"Although your background is similar," Catherine pointed out. "Up until now you've enjoyed maids, servants, wealth…it will be an enormous adjustment for you out here."

"I won't deny it. I have much to learn." Valerie moved toward the window and peered outside. Dusk settled around the frozen landscape. No street lamps. No noise of neighboring buggies passing by. She turned back to the McCabes, Catherine, and Emily. "But I plan to give it my best try."

"That's all anyone can ask of you." Leah came forward and reached for Valerie's hands. "We'll all help you."

"I appreciate it." The offer meant a lot.

"But I'd advise against doing chores for her." Catherine's tone rivaled a schoolmarm's. "She's lived a spoiled, pampered existence, and now she's got to learn the basics like milking cows, gathering eggs, and cooking, just to name a few."

"And I'm willing." Valerie couldn't argue, although she loathed Catherine's derogatory tone.

Leah squeezed her hands in a silent promise.

"I'm sure no one here would blame you," Catherine said, "if in a few days or a week you wanted to leave. St. Louis might be a better fit for you, Valerie…or Jefferson City."

"I'm not leaving." Valerie squared her shoulders.

"And, I should say, we're not letting her go." Jake ambled in with Bear right behind him. "Ben would skin me alive if he came home and his wife wasn't here."

Catherine shifted on the piano bench.

Valerie hid a smile.

"Oh, I didn't mean any harm." Catherine's voice sounded smooth as butter. "I was merely pointing out that no one would blame Valerie if things here didn't work out."

"But we're not slave drivers here." Reverend McCabe smiled at Valerie, and tiny crinkles appeared at the sides of his golden-brown eyes. He glanced at Catherine. "Stop trying to scare this poor girl off."

"Oh, Cousin Daniel—" Catherine waved a hand at him.

"I'm glad you're feeling better today, Catherine." Valerie walked to the settee and sat down. "And I'm so very relieved to see those nasty headaches of yours are gone."

"Me too." Emily lowered herself down beside Valerie.

Catherine flicked them an annoyed gaze before peering at the babe still in her arms.

"Headaches?" Reverend McCabe sat in an armchair and leaned forward, a frown now creasing his brow. "I want to know all about them, Catherine. It might be that Dr. Owens will need to be summoned in the future, and we need to know about your ailment."

"I don't have an ailment, Cousin Daniel, so you needn't worry. It must have been a virus." Icy-blue eyes stared hard at Valerie, then Em. "I'm just fine." Catherine ground out each word.

In that moment Valerie sensed the gauntlet had been thrown down. A challenge loomed on the horizon like tomorrow's dawn. While some people enjoyed a stimulating contest, Valerie wasn't up for it. All she yearned for was love, peace, and happiness in her new home. She didn't want to battle Catherine.

And yet somehow Valerie knew this duel was one she couldn't afford to lose.

~ueelxelee~

Ben had grown tired of the cold and relentless rain. His bones ached. After almost two weeks of traveling into Kentucky, he and Clint had discovered no new developments in Luke's disappearance. Ben was rapidly losing heart. The one fact he was learning fast was that men went missing every day. It made him wonder if he'd ever see his brother alive again.

Ben reined in his horses and jumped from his wagon's bench. He walked to where Clint stood several feet behind him. "This town seems a good enough place to stop for the night."

"I figure we're in Stanford—southeast of Lexington."

Ben grinned and motioned to the livery. "That's what the sign says. Stanford Livery." He chuckled.

Clint didn't look like he was in the mood for any humor as the rain fell on his already soggy hat and drenched raincoat. "I'll meet you over there."

"Right."

They both checked their animals and wagons into the livery, then walked a short distance to the inn. They ordered separate quarters and hot baths but elected to eat supper while the housekeeping maids readied their rooms.

"So where to next?" Ben stared at the flickering taper on the stuffed tabletop. They sat near the crackling hearth, and the warmth radiating from it felt good. He was still soaked from front to back and, sadly, getting used to it. "I'm about to give up any hopes of finding Luke. It's beginning to seem pointless."

"That's because you're cold and tired. Tomorrow morning you and I will both feel better."

Ben thanked God for Clint and his good ol' common sense. "I expect you're right."

"As usual." Clint grinned. "But I do believe God spared our lives by getting us out of Clarksville when He did."

"Agreed." Ben recalled the news of the Union's victories at Forts Henry and Donelson. He mourned the loss of life. Over one hundred Confederate casualties from the Fort Henry battle, and more than ten thousand from Fort Donelson. Last Ben heard, officials were still counting.

More than ten thousand Confederate soldiers dead, captured, or missing! The numbers were staggering—and nearly three times more than the total number of men lost at Bull Run.

And men went missing all the time. Those words kept playing over and over inside his head.

"Oh, God," he silently prayed, "I don't think I could stand it if Luke's dead."

As if in reply, Psalm 91 came to mind. *A thousand shall fall at thy side, and ten thousand at thy right hand; but it shall not come nigh thee.*

"Don't look now," Clint muttered. "We might have company."

Ben watched with a wary eye as a couple of Union officers swiped off their dark blue caps and claimed the table next to theirs. Hidden in his saddlebags was a letter from a certain Confederate colonel; things could get ugly if those fellows decided to do a search and seizure. However, neither Ben nor Clint would give them any reason.

One officer regarded them intently and nodded a greeting.

Ben inclined his head in a brief reply.

"Looks like you men have been out in the weather too." The officer hesitated before taking his seat.

"Yes, sir, we sure have." Ben thought he appeared harmless enough, probably seeking chums with whom to split a whiskey bottle or additional card players. Ben wasn't interested in either, and he knew Clint shared his sentiments, so he didn't invite the men to sit at their table.

The second man swiveled around in his chair and narrowed his gaze. "You're not in uniform…what's your business?"

"Freelance photographers, sir."

"You don't say?" The first officer grinned. "I had a feeling you weren't regulars here."

"No, sir." Clint twisted his torso and faced the other men. "We're new in town."

The two soldiers appeared interested. Then, after a look at each other, they simultaneously moved their chairs over to Ben and Clint's table.

"Sergeant John Withers." The dark-haired, bearded gentleman offered his right hand.

Ben took it and introduced himself. Clint did likewise.

"And this is Sergeant Douglas Strauss. We're with the First Ohio Infantry."

"Nice to meet you both." Clint's voice sounded steady, calm.

Ben relaxed some more, knowing his partner didn't sense danger either.

"We sort of took the night off to eat some real food and get warm." Strauss stroked his long, red-orange beard and grinned as the serving girl passed. His eyes lingered. "Nice to see a pretty face too."

Withers didn't seem to notice his pal's leering. "Now where'd you two say you were headed?"

"As of now, no place specific. I'm actually searching for my brother Luke McCabe. He's a chaplain. Went missing after Bull Run."

Both officers shook their heads.

"That's a shame," Withers stated with remorse. "Men seem to vanish after every battle."

"So I understand." The comment didn't help Ben's morale in the least.

"In the meantime," Clint added, "we're photographing the war as it happens around us. We send pictures and articles to various publications."

"You ought to come and photograph our regiment." Withers smiled with pride. "We've set up camp near where the old Fort Logan once stood—about a mile east of here."

"We'll ride out tomorrow." Ben looked at Clint, who nodded in agreement.

"You say your brother's a chaplain?" Strauss narrowed his pale green eyes. "There's a young man in our camp..." He shook his head. "Naw..."

"Please. Go on." Ben leaned forward with interest.

"Well, this fellow sort of resembles you. He talks about God a lot."

Ben's exhaustion fled.

"But the boy's a few cards short of a full deck. Doesn't know his real name or where he's from. Nobody does. Seems he just started marching with us one day."

"You talkin' about PB?" Withers tipped his head and peered at his buddy from beneath one bushy brow.

"That's the one." Strauss nodded with a smirk.

"Peebee?"

"Private Preacher-boy," Strauss said with a smirk. "Most of us just call him PB for short." He shrugged. "We had to call him something."

Ben shook his head. "Luke's intelligent. Hardly 'a few cards short of a full deck.'"

"I'll say one thing about PB." Withers's expression turned serious. "The boy knows how to handle a gun. Last Saturday night a few men bet they could outshoot him. Well, they lost their wager and ended up sitting through PB's Sunday morning preaching. Sang hymns and everything." The sergeant snorted a laugh. "But I guess that's not the worst thing that can happen when a man loses a bet."

"Reckon that's the truth." Ben could well imagine Luke showing off his skills with a gun in order to get men to hear God's Word. Sort of like Elijah when he challenged the prophets of Baal. "How old would you say this PB is?"

"No more than twenty." Strauss stroked his mangy beard again and hailed the serving girl.

Ben still pondered the reply. The age matched Luke's. "I'd like to ride back with you tonight and meet this man. May I?"

"Fine by me," Strauss said. "Then tomorrow maybe you men can take some photographs. That'll boost the men's spirits and bide some time until we receive our next orders."

"Good." Ben glimpsed Clint's nod. "We're up for it." And he was more than ready to check out this sharp-shooting, God-loving "PB" the men spoke about tonight.

EIGHTEEN

D ON'T GET YOUR HOPES UP."

"Hard to do, Clint. This fellow could be Luke." Ben led his horse along the muddy camp road where Fort Logan once stood with blockhouses and cabins all surrounded by a high stockade. Dismantled now, but in a way, Ben felt as though he were treading on hallowed ground. This was, after all, Daniel Boone country—well, close enough. While Boone traveled north and founded Boonesboro, Colonel Benjamin Logan founded Fort Logan by the creek, and the town of Stanford grew out of that during Revolutionary War time. There wasn't a McCabe alive who didn't regard Boone as a legendary figure. And although a frontiersman in Kentucky, Boone lived his final years in Missouri, and not too far from Jericho Junction either. Ben was always proud to claim Daniel Boone as a Missourian—at least in part.

He smiled inwardly. Ol' Ivan would be pleased to know the education he'd paid for hadn't been completely wasted. Nearing the soldiers' tents, Ben and Clint tethered their horses and then strode the rest of the way into the camp. Strains from a fiddle could be heard off in the distance.

"I never figured I'd find Luke in a Union infantry camp." Ben looked hard at each man they passed.

"You haven't found him yet." Clint grabbed the sleeve of Ben's coat and pulled him between two tents. "From what Withers and Strauss said, Captain J. T. Marshall's quarters are over here."

Ben trudged along, mud splattering over his boots and onto

his trousers. When they reached the tent they found the captain sitting at a makeshift table writing in what appeared to be his logbook.

The man looked up. Wariness masked his well-defined features, and Ben guessed the man to be somewhere in his forties.

"What can I do for you gentlemen?" The captain rose slowly to his feet.

Ben quickly introduced himself and Clint. "I'm searching for my brother. We were told about a young man who's called PB around here, and I'm wondering if he might be Luke McCabe."

"PB?" The captain tucked his chin, looking thoughtful. Several agonizing seconds passed. "All right. I see no harm in it. I'll send for him."

Stepping back as the captain came around and ducked under the tent flap, Ben prayed—and prayed hard. So many questions scampered across his mind. If this was Luke, why didn't he know who he was, where he came from?

Captain Marshall returned, carrying a couple of stout, wooden stools. "Have a seat, men."

They did. Then the waiting began. Captain Marshall wasn't one for small talk—he quickly bent his head to his book and absorbed himself in his work again.

Finally a young man entered the tent. "You wanted to see me, sir?"

Ben sat forward. He sounded like Luke but…different. His gaze quickly wandered over the soldier's baggy blue shirt, too-snug jacket, and dirt-covered black pants. He held a Union-blue cap in his hands. Between the shadows dancing off the tent walls and the man's full beard and shoulder-length hair, Ben couldn't tell for sure.

The captain sat back in his chair. "What's your name, son?"

"Everyone calls me PB."

"Your *real* name?"

The young man shifted his stance. "Don't know, sir."

Ben moved to stand, but Clint's hand pressed down on his shoulder.

"Where you from, soldier?" the captain queried.

"You asked me that question some time ago, sir, and I still don't have the answer."

Captain Marshall's gaze shifted to Ben and Clint, and suddenly the young man became aware of their presence. "It's probably battle fatigue. That's how we figure, anyway. I haven't discharged him because he's not a rabble-rouser. He's able-bodied, and he's proved himself proficient with a weapon."

Ben pushed to his feet, and this time Clint didn't stop him. "Luke? Luke McCabe?" He moved closer, his heart thumping. But when their gazes met, he knew for sure. "Luke!" He set his hands on his brother's shoulders and peered deeply into his blue eyes. "Don't you know me, Luke?"

His brother's bearded jaw moved, as if he wanted to say something but couldn't. He blinked a few times and his breath came and went in rapid sequence. Finally he muttered, "Ben."

With a joyous hoot, Ben gave his brother's shoulders a shake followed by a bear hug. "Thank God I found you. I found you!"

"Ben…" Luke's tone beheld a note of disbelief. "Ben!" He clutched him.

"Can't you remember where you've been?" Ben stepped back. "You disappeared at Bull Run."

"Bull Run…" Luke's voice was quiet, a distant echo.

And then he saw it. "What's this?" He reached out and pushed strands of Luke's stringy hair aside, revealing a jagged reddish scar—a wound, poorly stitched and looking still infected with dirty hair pressed up against it.

Luke touched the side of his head, then looked at his fingertips. "It's nothing. Just a cut or something."

Captain Marshall had come up behind Ben. Clint stepped in behind him. They all stared at the side of Luke's face, but it seemed no one wanted to say what had to be going through all their minds. *Head injury.* "I wasn't aware of your wound, son." Captain Marshall folded his arms. "You might have mentioned it."

"Like I said, it's nothing." Luke seemed embarrassed. "Most days I forget it's even there."

"When did you get it? How?"

Luke hesitated. "Don't know," he finally said.

Ben turned to his brother's commander. "Captain, if it's all right with you—"

"Take him. Maybe there's a doctor in town."

"My thoughts exactly."

"There's not a trained physician among us here in this camp."

"Hey, wait," Luke began to protest. "No. I'm not leaving my regiment."

Ben's heart twisted when he glimpsed the determination in his brother's eyes.

"You're hereby ordered on medical leave," the officer said.

"Captain—"

"I'm not saying you can't return. Just…" He flicked a glance at Ben and Clint. "Get your head fixed up. Once you remember your own name, I'd be proud to have you back."

Luke conceded, but grudgingly so. "Come on." Ben steered him around toward the tent's entrance. "We'll start by getting you cleaned up and a good night's sleep."

"You have beautiful dresses." Sarah handed another gown to Valerie.

Taking it, she hung it in the tall, knotty-pine chifforobe. She'd been told Jacob made the piece of furniture. "Thank you. My mother and I always had such fun shopping for clothes." Sadness tweaked Valerie's heart, but she felt surprised how much the pain had lessened. Maybe she could begin relishing the memories of Mama now.

"Is your mother sad that you left New Orleans?"

"My mother died last year."

"I'm sorry to hear that." Sarah gave her a compassionate look before holding out another gown. "What about your father?"

That wound was still raw. "Murdered. A month ago." She could barely eke out the words.

Sarah looked horrified.

"I didn't mean to upset you. Please forgive me if I have."

Swallowing hard, Valerie shook her head. "Nothing to forgive. I'm not so weak-kneed that I can't handle the truth."

Sarah pulled another garment from the trunk. "Who–who killed your father?"

"A horrible man." Valerie's gaze roamed around the bedroom, the whitewashed walls, the multicolored quilt on the double bed. Simplicity described the décor, but she'd rather be here than in any sort of luxurious suite James might have provided. "I shudder to think how I might have been forced to marry the brute if Benjamin hadn't intervened."

Sarah's blue eyes widened, her mouth fell open.

"It was an arranged marriage, one I heartily opposed." Valerie recounted the story, purposely leaving off the part about her father being a Yankee spy.

"So you and Ben got married, and he sent you here until he gets home?"

"Yes. He plans to settle in Jericho Junction."

Sarah shrugged. "He'd do a better business in St. Louis."

Valerie wondered about that.

"I know Catherine said that your marriage to my brother is in name only, but I still don't believe Ben would have taken wedding vows unless he meant them."

"I'm sure you're right." Would he or wouldn't he? Valerie realized how little she really knew her husband.

Glancing across the way, she saw Sarah watching her closely.

"Tell me about you." Valerie decided to shift the attention off herself. "What do you like to do? What exciting things are taking place in your life?"

"Exciting? This is Jericho Junction, Valerie."

She laughed as she hung up a few more garments.

"But there's a St. Valentine's Day party tomorrow night."

"Sounds like fun." Valerie found it hard to believe that last year at this time she was at Miss C. J. Hollingsworth's without a care in the world.

"The whole town's invited, although there won't be many men in attendance because of the war. But that doesn't bother me because I never want to get married anyway."

Surprised, Valerie arched a brow. "Why not?"

Sarah shrugged and held out another dress. "I want to be independent. I'm going to live in a big city like Chicago or New York and teach music."

"Hmm—" Valerie couldn't help a grin. "I think you're much too pretty to remain unmarried. Some man's bound to snatch you up."

"He'll have to go through my pa, big brothers, and Bear first, and that isn't likely to happen. Not here in Jericho Junction anyway."

"Is Bear a family member?"

"No, his parents died when he was my age. He didn't have anywhere to go, and he was friends with Jake. So he moved in and stayed in this room with Jake and Luke. Ben had already left with Ol' Ivan."

"Yes, I've heard about Old Ivan."

Sarah nodded. "Anyway, things got crowded quickly, so Jake and Bear built the lean-to off of the kitchen. There are four bunks in there." She expelled an audible sigh. "I reckon you can say I have four big brothers. One's adopted but just as protective as the others."

Suddenly Valerie saw the dilemma. "Well, if a man truly loves you, he won't feel intimidated in the least."

Sarah rolled a shoulder. "I'll bet you had a lot of suitors." She fingered a green, beige, and pink striped silk gown.

Valerie realized how useless the dress would be here. "I had a few beaus. Mostly the sons of my father's acquaintances. None of the relationships developed, though, because of my lack of interest."

"But Ben got your attention, eh?"

"Immediately."

The expression on Sarah's face said she was pleased to hear it. "If you were wearing a dress as pretty as this one—" She held up the gown. "—then you would have captured Ben's eye, that's for sure."

Considering her, Valerie noted their body shapes weren't dissimilar. An idea struck. "Say would you—?" She came to stand next to Sarah and inspected the dress in the young lady's hands. "Well, I wonder if you'd be willing to work out a trade."

"A trade?"

"Yes." Valerie smiled. "One that might come in handy for you tomorrow night."

~~eeꝃꝃ꠷ee~~

Bright and early the next morning, Ben walked Luke over to the local physician's clinic. The man worked from inside his large home.

"So what do you think, Dr. Birmingham?" Ben folded his arms as he watched the stout man with a full gray beard finish examining Luke's wound.

"I'd think whoever sewed this boy up didn't know the needle from the thread." Moving back, he met Ben's gaze. "Infection's set in. Needs to be taken care of."

"What are you going to do to me?" Luke struggled to sit upright.

The doctor held his shoulder down. "I'm going to incise that wound and clean it out before the infection kills you." He turned to Ben. "This'll take some doin'."

Luke managed to crunch himself halfway up. He pointed at Ben. "You're stayin' close by, I hope."

"I'll be here the whole time." He looked back at the doctor. "What about the amnesia?"

"Can't say for sure. Only time will tell. The fact that he recognized you last night is a good sign his memory's coming back."

The physician gathered his instruments. A bottle of chloroform stood on a nearby tabletop. "Now, be still, son."

Luke wetted his lips. "Well, I guess it's the way it has to be then." He lay back down on the examination table. "Hey, Ben?"

"Yep?"

"Just don't let him take out my brains, OK?"

Ben chuckled. "What brains?" After seeing his brother's grin, he watched as Dr. Birmingham worked.

When it was all done and Luke was still sleeping off the effects of the chloroform, he slipped into the small parlor where Clint waited.

He looked up from the book he'd been reading. "Is Luke going to be all right?"

"Some minor surgery to clean out that wound, and he should be fine—physically." Ben lowered himself into the adjacent armchair. "No telling when his memory will return, but there are hopeful signs." *Please, God, heal his mind and body.*

An older woman wearing spectacles entered the room. She carried a tray containing cups of coffee and a plate of heart-shaped cookies.

Ben and Clint stood to their feet.

"I'm Mrs. Birmingham, the doctor's wife. Please be seated. I brought you refreshments. You'll do me a favor by tasting my cookies. They're for a St. Valentine's Day bazaar at church tonight to raise money for our soldiers."

"Yes, ma'am." Ben helped himself, and Clint did the same.

"Cookies are delicious." Clint took a second bite.

"My compliments." The sweet taste of the frosting lingered on Ben's palate.

Looking pleased, Mrs. Birmingham left the room.

"I forgot it was St. Valentine's Day."

"Me too." Ben sat back and took a drink of his coffee.

"In Boston there were enough reminders, the flower shops, the parties. A fella couldn't forget this day in that city."

"And heaven help the man who did."

They shared a chuckle.

Silence fell between them, and thoughts of Valerie consumed Ben. He missed her—missed her pretty smile. The way she looked up at him with adoring blue eyes. Reaching into his shirt pocket, he pulled out the photograph he'd kept close to his heart. Valerie. Smiling. Laughing at Emily's wisecracks that day she'd ridden out to the army camp with him. Maybe he'd add a line just for her on the telegram he planed to send his family, informing them that Luke was alive, and hopefully well, soon.

"You know what I think?"

Ben gazed over at Clint. "What's that?"

"I think it's time we start making the trek home. I'm going to be a father soon, you know."

"I know. I know." Ben sent a glance toward the ceiling before pocketing the photograph. "I'd like nothing better, especially after that massacre at Fort Donelson." He shook his head. "I seem to be growing disillusioned with our undertaking of photographing this war."

"And here I thought it was only me."

"Naw. Home sounds awfully good, especially with a new bride waiting for me. Even so, I can't leave Luke. He has to be in agreement, and he seems determined to return to his regiment."

"What are you going to do if he refuses to head home with us?"

"I'm praying that won't happen."

"Well, we've got a few extra months to spare. Just as long as I'm home when my baby's born in July."

Ben rested his head against the parlor's blue papered wall and prayed Luke will have recovered by then. As much as he'd like to head home right now, he knew he couldn't leave. He just couldn't lose track of his brother again.

NINETEEN

N OW, WHY DON'T I BELIEVE THAT YOU PURCHASED THAT outfit at a New Orleans's boutique?"

Valerie raised up the steaming pot she held. "Did you want your coffee in your cup?"

Jake's brown eyes twinkled with amusement. "As opposed to in my lap?" He laughed. "Yes, ma'am." He slid the thick white porcelain cup her way.

After filling it, Valerie moved to where Bear sat on the other side of the dining room table. He smiled until their gazes met. Then all traces of humor fled.

"More coffee?"

"Yes'am." As big as the man was, he looked scared to death.

Valerie hid her grin. Jake's ribbing didn't bother her a whit. However, she did admit to feeling humbled as she slipped Sarah's A-line calico over her head before donning the beige muslin pinafore. In New Orleans calico was referred to as "slave cloth," and Valerie would have never imagined herself wearing it. But Sarah had recently sewn this dress and another one just like it, and they'd make good work dresses. Sarah eagerly traded both of them for Valerie's striped silk gown, which she planned to wear to the party this evening.

Reentering the kitchen, Valerie replaced the coffeepot onto the stove. Becca and Catherine stood at the counter, finishing breakfast preparations. An interesting-smelling mix sizzled in an iron frying pan.

"Can I do anything else to help?"

"We've taken care of everything." Catherine flicked a glance in her direction. "Besides, you're a guest."

Valerie flinched at the backhanded dig.

"Now, Catherine, she's a McCabe and part of this family." After the soft reprimand, Becca sent Valerie a smile. "I had just thought I'd go easy on you for a few days. But I must say, your eagerness to help around here is commendable."

"Surprising too, since you've never worked a day in your life." Catherine turned and carried a bowl of food to the dining room.

Valerie bit down hard.

Becca glanced her way. "I sense discord between the two of you."

Not trusting herself to say more than necessary, Valerie nodded.

"Let's you and I talk more about it later."

"All right."

Reverend McCabe strolled in, dressed in a mushroom-colored shirt and brown trousers. "Good morning. It's shaping up to be a lovely one indeed." He placed his hands on Becca's shoulders and kissed her cheek. "Happy St. Valentine's Day, my love." Next he whispered something close to her ear that made her smile.

Valerie looked away, embarrassed to have witnessed the display of affection, and yet the sight warmed her heart. Her parents had rarely touched, and certainly never in front of anyone else. Out of the two, Valerie hoped her marriage would resemble the McCabes'.

"I made your favorite breakfast this morning," Becca said. "A good ol' fry-up and biscuits and gravy. It's just about ready."

"Ahh…" He looked pleased and placed a hand on his midsection. "You're a woman whose worth is far above rubies."

"Oh, you are a darling man." She turned and hugged him.

"Have a seat in the dining room, and Valerie will bring you a cup of coffee."

"Thank you." He looked over and gave Valerie a smile.

The back door banged closed and Sarah appeared through the mudroom. She carried a pail of white liquid.

"Lilac and Tulip aren't cooperating today. The milking took a lot longer, and Jake refused to do it for me." An aggravated frown creased her brow. "I hope I'm not late for school now." Handing off the pail to her mother, she trotted across the kitchen, but not without a sunny smile for everyone she passed.

"Did our youngest wake up a bit late today?" Reverend McCabe folded his arms.

"Yes." Becca poured the milk into a glass container. "But if she hurries, she can enjoy some breakfast before leaving for school."

Valerie collected another cup and saucer and then lifted the coffeepot and poured out the strong-smelling brew. She carried the cup of coffee into the dining room and set it before Reverend McCabe, then noticed Catherine talking to Jake, although she snapped her mouth shut when Valerie entered the room. But too late. Valerie caught snippets and heard the words "jail" and "traitor," and it didn't take a genius to figure out what Catherine was up to. Jake, of course, had ridden with a Confederate brigadier general in the army.

Fear nibbled at her soul, but she reminded herself that Benjamin wouldn't have sent her here if she'd face danger from his family.

Back in the kitchen Becca handed her a large bowl of fry-up that Valerie carried into the dining room while Becca brought in the biscuits.

"Well, I think we're all set."

A glimpse at Catherine's cavalier expression made her nerves fray. Just days ago, she cajoled this woman into taking some nourishment so she wouldn't grow even more ill from those awful headaches she suffered, and now Catherine backstabbed her.

She walked back into the kitchen, thought things over, and decided to skip breakfast and seek refuge over at Leah's for a while. In the mudroom, she found her woolen wrap and threw it around her shoulders. Then she left.

Outside the temperature felt well below the freezing mark, and Valerie shivered as she walked the narrow pathway through the snow. The parsonage was a whitewashed, clapboard structure, as was the attached church building. Reaching the door, she rapped on it loudly.

Leah pulled it open with a laugh. "Nobody knocks around here. C'mon in."

"Thank you." She gave Leah a smile. A faint smell of corn bread lingered in the air.

"You probably ate already, huh?" Leah took her cloak and hung it on a wooden peg behind the door.

"I'm not hungry. But if you've got some tea, I'd love a cup."

"Of course." Leah frowned a little as her gaze fell on Valerie's attire.

Valerie smiled. "I traded Sarah one of my silk gowns for two of her work dresses."

"Well, that explains it." Leah gave a short laugh. "I was wondering…I mean, a woman like you who comes from such finery—"

Valerie shrugged. "But I have a new life here in Jericho Junction now."

Leah seemed to think about that reply a moment before a smile curved her lips. "Well, in that case, would you be interested in more trading?"

"I would indeed."

"Let me get that teakettle boiling first. Why don't you make yourself comfortable? Emily's in the dining room."

Valerie strode through the doorway and found the dining room around the corner. She discovered Emily sipping a cup of coffee. When her friend saw her, her face lit up.

"Good morning. Are you missing your husband as much as I'm missing Clint on this St. Valentine's Day?"

Valerie nodded and took a seat. "But it's more than that. I'm also dismayed by Catherine's behavior." She lowered her voice until it was but a whisper. "I think she told Jake that I'm wanted for conspiracy." Valerie wetted her lower lip. "You don't think he'll turn me in to Confederate authorities, do you?"

"No. Of course not." Her words belied the troubled look in her hazel eyes. "Ben said you were safe here. He knew Jake was home when he said it."

"Oh, Em—" Valerie put her face in her hands.

"That Catherine Elliot—" Emily ground out. "After all you've done for her, how can she turn around and be so cruel!"

"Who's cruel?" Leah walked in, set a cup and saucer in front of Valerie, and reclaimed her seat.

Valerie and Emily exchanged glances.

"You're referring to Catherine, aren't you?" Leah guessed. "I noticed there was something going on at dinner last night. What it is?"

Figuring she'd find out in time anyway, Valerie disclosed the facts as she knew them, adding one bit of speculation. "And I think she took the pocket watch Benjamin gave me as a wedding gift."

"Ben's pocket watch? The one Grandpa gave him?"

Valerie looked across the table at Leah and nodded. "I've been sick about it."

The kettle screeched, and Leah went in to take it off the burner.

"Where's that precious baby?" Valerie had enjoyed holding Josiah last night.

"Sleeping. Isn't he a love?"

Leah returned and set the teapot on the table. Valerie would let it steep a few minutes.

"You know," Leah began, "I have a couple of dresses that are too small for me now that I've given birth to Josiah. I would be happy to give them to you if you'd like two more work dresses."

"I'd be happy to have them. Thank you. I have a green satin gown that would probably fit you."

"Wouldn't Jonathan like it if I dressed up for him his first day back home?"

"Why, he'd fall in love with you all over again."

"Then you've got yourself a deal, sister." She left to get the garments, and Valerie poured her tea.

"Leah's got a few dresses I can borrow when I start showing." Emily sipped from her cup. "She loves to sew and practically made a whole new maternity wardrobe."

"Anybody home?" Jake's voice suddenly boomed from the kitchen. The sound of the door closing followed.

Valerie brought herself up straighter in her chair.

Leah reentered the room. "In here, Jake." She set the dresses over the back of a chair. "Don't be afraid of him, Valerie. My brother's a good man."

She wanted to believe it.

Jake filled the entryway, making an imposing figure. He still wore his buckskin jacket. He didn't even acknowledge Emily or Leah. His gaze honed in on Valerie. "You and I need to talk, sis."

Prickles of unease moved down her limbs. "Whatever you have to say to me, you can say in front of Emily and Leah."

"What I have to say to you is private." He inclined his head toward the kitchen door. "Come on."

Valerie squared her shoulders. She was not about to be bossed. "What if I refuse?"

Jake's expression said like he half expected that reply. Reaching into his jacket pocket, he pulled out a piece of paper. "I have a telegram here from my big brother asking me to look after you till he gets home." He held it out so Valerie could read it for herself.

Unfolding it, she scanned the message. SENDING MY BRIDE TO JJ. WATCH OVER HER FOR ME. ACCLIMATION WILL BE DIFFICULT. MAKE SURE SHE STAYS PUT. WILL WIRE FUNDS FOR HER NEEDS SOON. BDM

Refolding it, Valerie nibbled her lower lip. What did he mean by "make sure she stays put"? Did Benjamin think she'd run off? Where would she go? Didn't he know she loved him and couldn't see a future without him?

Bewildered, she handed the telegram back to Jake.

"On a side note here, we waited for you at breakfast. None of us could figure where you'd run off to. Finally Pa prayed over the food because it was getting cold. You might want to let someone know in the future when you decide to take off like that."

Remorse fell over her. "My apologies." She felt bad that everyone waited on her and here she sat at Leah's house. "I guess I'm not used to being a part of a family."

"In time you'll get the hang of it. Now, c'mon."

"There's more?"

"There's a lot more." He leaned on his cane while holding his hand out to Valerie. "We'll go talk in Pa's office."

Valerie figured there was no harm in a discussion since Benjamin asked Jake to look out for her. She refused to take his hand and brushed by him, waiting for his first move. She gave a single wave to her friends before following Jake down a hallway. They passed three bedrooms before they reached a closed door. Jake opened it and allowed Valerie to enter first.

"Straight down and to your right," Jake said.

Another hallway and Valerie did as he bid her. Making the turn, she found herself walking onto the platform in the front of the church on which the pulpit stood. The place was cold as its heating source hadn't been lit. Across the way, she could see another open doorway near the choir loft.

Jake pointed in that direction.

Valerie strode across the distance and entered the quaintly decorated office. Warmth enveloped her, and she spied a glow in the corner wood-burning stove. A braided rug covered much of the scuffed floor. Drawings, obviously made by children, were hung on one wall while a beautiful quilt with a large scarlet cross in its center occupied the space behind a cluttered desk.

"Please, come in and be seated." Valerie jumped, hearing Reverend McCabe's voice. He stood before one of the mismatched upholstered chairs arranged off to the side. "Sorry for startling you."

She replied with a smile. Gathering her skirts, she sat down and folded her hands.

Jake took the chair beside hers, moving his cane out of the way.

"Becca will be joining us shortly," Reverend McCabe announced. "But she said to begin without her."

"I'm feeling a bit intimidated." *Not to mention vulnerable*, but she didn't say that aloud.

"We have nothing against you, Valerie. In fact, we'd like to get to know you. You're family now." Reverend McCabe had that same disarming manner as Benjamin, and it made Valerie miss her husband more than ever. "We're also hoping you can help us."

"Help you? How?"

"Allow me to start." Jake shrugged out of his jacket. "Last year I had the privilege of riding with General McCulloch's army."

"Yes, Benjamin told me."

"After I got wounded, I was so angry and bitter and consumed with hatred for the Yankees. I wished I could kill every one of 'em."

Valerie shuddered at the admission.

"Then around Christmastime, things changed for me. God showed me that each man has a soul, and despite his political views, Christ came to Earth and died for him—like He died for me. I was humbled. I realized too that owning another individual, a slave, is just plain wrong. Viewpoints and skin color don't matter to the Savior. He brought salvation to all mankind."

"Sounds like Yankee thinking to me." Valerie grinned and watched as he rubbed his hands together.

"Maybe so. But the point is, when I forgave, I was forgiven. My anger faded. I'm telling you all this because I can spot an angry and bitter person readily enough."

"Me?" Valerie brought her chin back, shocked. She wasn't any of those things Jake described.

"No, sis." His expression softened. "Catherine."

"Oh…" Valerie's tension ebbed, and suddenly she felt grateful that the McCabes hadn't been fooled by Catherine's subtle belittlements.

Reverend McCabe sat forward. "We've talked to Catherine, and now we'd like to hear your side of the story."

"I see." Valerie presumed her character had been maligned, and now she had a chance to defend herself.

She spilled the entire story, how it began New Year's Day when Benjamin brought her to the Elliots and ended that tragic afternoon when her father lay dying in her arms. "I had no idea that he and the Laddens were Federal spies." She turned to Jake. "Please believe me."

He nodded. "I do."

"Are you...well, you wouldn't turn me over to Confederate authorities, would you?"

Sitting back he narrowed his gaze. "I just said I believed you. Now you have to trust me."

She sent him a tight grin. "Trust doesn't come easily to me anymore."

"Understandable, seeing all you've been through." Reverend McCabe wore a tender expression. "But I promise that you will be perfectly safe here. We'll do everything in our power to see to it."

"Thank you."

"Now, getting back to Catherine. Did you know she planned to run away from home?"

"No. She showed up on the steamer, accusing me of cheating her out of her dreams to marry Benjamin and live here in Jericho Junction. She said she was seizing her God-given opportunities. But then she took ill the rest of our journey. I cared for her. Emily helped, of course, but she hasn't been feeling well herself because of being in the family way."

Becca walked in, smiled at Valerie, and sat down in the last vacant chair. "Please continue. Don't let me interrupt. I had to see Sarah off to school and take care of the dishes."

Reverend McCabe smiled at his wife then inclined his head, and Valerie went on.

"Well, as you may know, we encountered delays because of trouble with the railroad, and Emily and Catherine ran out of money, so I paid the rest of their way and mine." She quickly amended the statement. "Actually, God provided for all of us. I take no credit for it. I only tell you this because Catherine seemed to be my friend when she needed me. But then she turned on me as soon as we set foot in Jericho Junction. But maybe even the night before then." Valerie added her suspicions about the pocket watch theft.

"This is all quite troubling, not to mention disappointing." Reverend McCabe shook his head. "We've known Catherine since the day she was born."

"We're aware too of her dreams to live out here," Becca added. "She feels called to teach." She looked at her husband. "I'm sure you could put a good word in for her at the school. You're on the board."

"I can't do that, Becca. I have a moral obligation to make certain our teachers are upstanding and forthright individuals." Reverend McCabe shook his head. "I'm afraid teaching is out of the question until Catherine gets her heart right with God."

Valerie lowered her gaze. On one hand she felt the consequences were just deserts, but another part of her felt sorry for Catherine.

"Unfortunately, we can't send her back to New Orleans. The fighting has intensified along the way, and it wouldn't be safe. She'll have to stay here, and we'll all have to help her realize that her jealousy and bitterness might end up destroying her."

Valerie inhaled a short breath, praying she'd overcome her anger toward Catherine lest it permanently mar her life.

"She mentioned your marriage to Ben being in name only." Becca's voice was soft. "Was that the agreement between you and my son?"

"I–I don't know. I think I was in shock that day. I barely recall the ceremony. But maybe—" She remembered Benjamin's kisses, which didn't feel like he meant the marriage to be in name only. She shook her head. "Oh, I don't know."

Glancing down, she fingered Mama's wedding ring, now hers. The sad truth was, if Benjamin didn't love her, Valerie almost hoped for an annulment. She wouldn't be able to stand the pain of living day in and day out with him, knowing her love would never be reciprocated.

"My feeling is," Reverend McCabe said, "that when a man and a woman vow to spend the rest of their born days together, they ought to have a biblical reason not to uphold those vows."

Valerie looked up and met his stare.

A hint of a smile lifted the corners of his mouth. "Let's end our meeting in prayer, shall we?"

Closing her eyes, Valerie suddenly felt more confused about her marriage than ever.

Evening came, and Sarah couldn't wait to dress for the St. Valentine's Day dance. Valerie smiled at her eagerness. She curled and pinned Sarah's hair before tying it off with pretty pink ribbon. If Adalia were here, she'd have done a far better job, but Valerie thought the style was becoming.

She stared over Sarah's shoulder and into the mirror. "Who is that gorgeous creature looking back at us?"

"Why, I'm sure I don't know." Sarah batted her lashes.

"Hmm…well, whoever she is, she'll be asked to dance the whole night long."

Sarah scooted around and peered up into Valerie's face. She frowned. "Only by boys and old men."

"Never know. Leah said some local soldiers might attend."

Hopefulness shone on Sarah's face, and Valerie enjoyed the way her younger friend seemed pleased with her reflection. "Now it's time to show you off to your family."

Standing, Sarah held out her skirts and pirouetted. "I've never worn a dress this fine in all my born days."

Valerie replied with a grin and stole a last minute to hang up garments in Sarah's wardrobe. She glanced around to be sure she hadn't missed something. This bedroom, which Sarah shared with Catherine, appeared as feminine as could be with its pink and yellow printed paper and white wainscoting that covered the lower half of the walls. All the furniture had been painted white, and the room's accents were rose, from the covers on the two matching canopy beds to the frilly lacy curtains adorning the tall windows.

"Do you think I look like a wealthy young lady in a big city? Would I have fit in at the balls you attended?"

Valerie returned her attention to Sarah. "New Orleans balls are formal affairs. Elsewhere, I'm not sure." She refrained from saying that the dress Sarah wore was an everyday silk and nothing remarkable, at least not in Valerie's former social circles. Still, Sarah would have turned heads because of her flawless peaches-and-cream complexion, startling blue eyes, and her soft blonde hair. Her figure curved in all the right places, and the dress accentuated the fact. "But if you made an appearance at one of the Sunday afternoon socials held at my boarding school, I think every lady there would be green with envy."

Sarah's features heightened. "Really?" She ran her hands down the striped skirt.

"I mean it."

"Then I'm ready to show myself to the world." She smiled sweetly. "Beginning with my family."

Valerie followed Sarah downstairs and into the drawing room where everyone waited.

Reverend McCabe stood at once. "Well, now look at you, my little girl." He seemed a bit sad. "Hardly little anymore."

"Or a girl, either."

"I stand corrected." Her father kissed her cheek.

"You're beautiful, honey." Becca hugged her.

Emily and Leah stood by smiling, but Catherine folded her lanky arms and frowned.

"A good Christian woman does not adorn herself in a way that might catch a man's eye. Her beauty shines from within."

"I think so too, Catherine." Sarah glanced down at her attire. "But it's not wrong for a lady to want to look pretty once in a while. Right, Pa?"

"As long as she's modest," Reverend McCabe added, "and conducts herself in a moral, upstanding way, you're right. I see no harm in wearing a pretty dress."

"But a dance, Cousin Daniel?" Catherine shook her head. "Shameful things." She cast a glance at Valerie. "Daddy used to preach against dancing."

"I know. Your father and I have discussed the topic many times, and I'm of a different persuasion. But I would submit to you, Catherine, that our shindigs aren't anything like the balls and parties in New Orleans. Tonight, for instance, there'll be plenty of chaperones about, and no alcoholic beverages will be served."

Valerie thought that alone made a difference.

"This dance is a chance for townspeople to get out and see one another since the cold winter weather keeps plenty of them isolated." Reverend McCabe smiled. "We clap and stomp our feet to the fiddlin', and I must say it gets one's blood moving again."

Catherine replied with a prudish jerk of her chin.

Just then Jake hollered from the back of the house. Everyone's attention turned, and he came in with a hurried limp. "Pa, Ma...everybody—"

"What is it?" Becca stepped toward him.

"It's Luke." Jake still sounded winded.

Silence filled the room.

"Picked up the telegram at the hotel minutes ago. He's alive!"

Hoots of happiness erupted from the group. Embraces were plentiful. Leah cried tears of joy and hugged her baby tighter to her.

Becca's eyes grew misty before she squeezed them shut. "Oh, God, thank You!"

Happiness engulfed Valerie. "I knew Benjamin would find him. I just sensed it all along."

"You were right." Emily locked arms with her. "Sometimes I thought Ben's search for Luke was, to use the cliché, like looking for a needle in a haystack." She appeared chagrined. "My faith was weak."

"We all had times of doubt, my dear," Reverend McCabe said. "I for one prayed for the best and silently feared the worst."

Jake said, "As far as faith goes, God knows if it's even a speck—the size of a grain of a mustard seed—it's still mountain-moving faith."

Sarah threw her arms around Valerie and jumped up and down, giggling.

"Stop it, silly." Valerie laughed while being jostled.

"I'm so happy! My brothers are coming home!"

Which meant Benjamin would be home soon. Valerie felt her smile wane, feeling uncertain.

"Hey, now, wait just one minute." Jake took hold of Sarah's arm and pulled her toward him. He glanced over her apparel. "Where do you think you're going, looking like that?"

"Like what?" She tipped her head.

"Like...pretty."

Sarah blushed. "Thanks, Jake. I'm going to the dance." She moved her hips so her skirt flowed side to side.

"Oh, no, you're not." Jake's eyes flitted to his father. "Pa?"

"She has my permission to go, son. Your mother and I will both be there too."

Jake narrowed his gaze as he looked back at Sarah. "Maybe I'd best go along as well."

"No!" Sarah turned to her father. "Tell him he can't go, Pa.

He'll scare away any gentleman who comes within five feet of me."

Reverend McCabe chuckled. "Jake's a grown man. I can't tell him where he can and can't go."

"Then I'll tell him." Sarah squared her shoulders and stood up to her brother. "You can't go. I forbid you to follow me around tonight."

Jake chucked her under the chin. "Don't worry, baby sister, you won't even know I'm there." He moved toward Catherine. "Will you accompany me tonight?"

"What?" Shock stole over her.

"Come along with me to the dance. I can't very well show up by myself. With all the single women in Jericho Junction, I'll be mobbed."

"You poor thing," Valerie drawled with a laugh.

He sent her a quelling glance.

Leah set a hand on Catherine's shoulders. "Go and protect this poor man since I'm not going."

"I'm not either," Valerie said.

"Me either." Emily sounded just as decided.

"Well…I—"

"Say no, Catherine," Sarah begged. Her jaw muscle worked and her cheeks flushed in anger. "I don't want Jake there to spoil my fun."

"Hmm." Catherine eyed Jake. "Perhaps I'd better go along to keep peace between the two of you."

"There's the spirit, Catherine." Jake chuckled.

Valerie hid a smile, but she could feel Emily's shoulders shake as she laughed.

"Oh, you two—" Becca stepped between them. "Jake, I'm still in awe over the news about Luke. Will you let me read the telegram for myself?"

"Sure, Ma." He handed over the piece of paper. "Oh, and that reminds me—" He pulled several envelopes from the inside pocket of his jacket. "I picked up the mail too." A letter arrived for Mrs. Benjamin McCabe." He held it out to Valerie.

"Let's all sit down," Becca said. "Valerie can read us the news from Ben."

She hesitated, and Becca noticed.

"Forgive me, honey." She placed a hand on Valerie's arm. "I'm being presumptuous. Maybe it's personal and you'd rather not share it."

"Well—" Valerie hoped to see words of love from her husband.

"Why don't you read it first and then decide whether you'd like to share it?"

With an incline of her head, Valerie walked into the kitchen and sat down at the small table. She noticed the letter was dated a month ago.

Dearest Valerie,

I am writing to you from Mississippi, and if you're reading this, it means you arrived in Jericho Junction. I hope you will come to love the town and my family as much as I do.

Clint and I left New Orleans last week. I trust you received the wire I sent to the Widewater Inn about your father's death. You have my deepest sympathies. Please know that Cousin Max stayed with him until the end. He promised, and I hereby do as well, to uphold you in prayer.

Meanwhile, we have been following a Confederate regiment as we press northward and search for Luke.

Valerie quickly read the rest. Benjamin had written about his travels, detailing the army regiment's routine. It read like an impersonal newspaper article, and the disappointment she felt knotted in her chest. Why couldn't he have penned the words "I love you"? Why couldn't he have told her of his feelings and his plans for them? Even in closing he wrote "Sincerely yours."

Some St. Valentine's Day this turned out to be!

Rising from the chair, Valerie strode back to the drawing room and gave Benjamin's letter to Becca.

"Nothing in here you can't read."

Valerie spun on her heels and ran upstairs to her room, closing the door behind her. Disillusionment rained from her eyes, and she wondered if, like her father, her husband would be a remote figure in her life. Obviously Benjamin didn't love her and only married her out of guilt and pity. His kisses might belie her beliefs, but his words—or lack thereof—affirmed them. The McCabes were obviously against an annulment...

Oh, God, show me what to do!

TWENTY

"I WAS IN SOME HOSPITAL. I REMEMBER THINKING I WAS going to die for sure. I wasn't scared. Just in a whole lot of pain. A headache like nothing I ever felt."

"Well," Ben drawled, "good thing that bullet sideswiped your head. Things could have been worse."

"Go on." Luke gave him a brotherly shove.

Ben smiled as they walked up Main Street in Stanford, heading for the post office. It was good to see his brother coming around. "I'm guessing maybe you were injured at Bull Run. Otherwise you'd have found Clint and me after the battle."

"I reckon so."

Per the doctor's orders he'd had a shave and a haircut. He now resembled the kid brother Ben knew so well. And that sorry wound on his face had begun to heal up nicely too, thanks to Dr. Birmingham's skill.

"Don't know how I got hooked up with the First Ohio, though. Seems one day I was just there in camp."

Ben detected a far-off note in Luke's voice—one he'd come to recognize in the last week as a good sign. A piece of memory always seemed to come back after Luke mentally chewed on something awhile. He now knew his name and remembered family members in Jericho Junction, along with most of his past. But this last year's events still eluded him, specifically the time-table that marked his disappearance.

"So tell me more about this new wife of yours," Luke said with a grin. "Hope she's nothing like the last woman you brought home.

"You remember Gwyneth, huh?" Ben tossed him a glance. He'd given Luke one of his white shirts, a tan vest, and coordinating trousers to wear until they could wash his clothes. He looked right respectable today. "I shouldn't have pursued that woman. Any fool could see she wasn't the right one for me. Finally *this fool* saw the light—praise the Lord for that."

"Amen."

Ben shook his head. "But in answer to your question, no, Valerie's nothing like Gwyneth. She's sweet and caring. Loves the Lord." He smiled wryly. "And she adores me."

"Love is blind."

The quip earned Luke a sock in the arm.

He laughed. "So, what are your plans for the future, now that you're a married man?"

"Well, funny you should ask. I've been thinking along those lines for some time now."

"I noticed."

"Once I get home—" Ben grinned. "—I plan to take my wife in my arms and kiss her like she's never been kissed." He shared a chuckle with Luke. "And then I hope to find a house somewhere, one with a pretty yard and little white fence, and Clint and I are talking about opening our own photographist studio—just like the one we saw in New Orleans."

"Got to have townspeople for a photographist studio, don't you?"

"The people are going to come. Jericho Junction has been growing steadily."

"That's right. I remember last fall when Pa told us about it, how there'll be a need for more businesses and how Mr.

Crenshaw at the bank is willing to help—leastwise he was before the war."

Entering the post office, Ben checked for a telegram. Nothing. It bothered him that he didn't hear back from Jericho Junction. He prayed Valerie was all right. He wished she'd wire a few words to him. Clint had received a message from Em telling him she felt fine. Not to worry. Of course he did anyway, being a first-time expectant father.

"Well, I reckon no news is good news." Luke clapped him between the shoulder blades.

"You sure are filled with platitudes today." Ben sent him an annoyed glance, although he had to admit it was a miracle that his brother stood by his side.

As for Valerie, it wouldn't be long until he was home.

As she looked off into the east, Valerie recalled her father once saying, "Red sky at morning is a sailor's warning. Red sky at night is a seaman's delight." She smiled to herself, thinking the dawn waxed scarlet across the horizon. Perhaps they'd see rain today.

Reaching the barn, Valerie hoisted the lantern onto a nail. "It's me again, Tulip." She ran her hand along the cow's side, then sat down on the low stool and adjusted her skirts. Next she blew into her palms before rubbing them together. Milking a cow wasn't exactly Valerie's favorite pastime, but she promised to help Sarah with the chore. After several near-catastrophic attempts, Valerie had learned to warm her hands before grasping Tulip's teats. She'd also figured out how to pull down just right and squeeze in order to fill the awaiting pail underneath the animal's udder. In the last two weeks, she'd chased chickens around the yard and overcome her fear of the rooster in order to gather eggs—which proved more than Catherine could say. The rooster pecked at her, and Lilac and Tulip, the cows, kicked her. Valerie just tried to stay out of the poor woman's way.

She let go of a sigh of regret. It seemed Catherine would never forgive and forget. The McCabes continually reasoned with her, and Jake had talked to her a couple of weeks ago when she'd accompanied him to the St. Valentine's Day dance. Sarah and Leah made attempts and reached out. Emily scolded her. No words could soften Catherine's defenses now that hatred had fortified them. But the real cannonball came when Catherine had been denied a teaching position at Jericho Junction's school. Her world was rocked off its axis—

And Valerie knew exactly how that felt!

Someone's whistling reached her ears, signaling that she and the animals weren't the only ones in the barn. With Tulip's milking completed, Valerie lifted the pail and headed toward Lilac's stall. The whistling grew softer, but she didn't know who it belonged to. By the timbre she guessed it was either her father-in-law or Jake. Curious, she set down the pail and followed after the tune "Amazing Grace."

"Hello!"

No answer. Obviously he hadn't heard her call.

Valerie made her way around the wagon. "Good morning!" She walked into a part of the large barn she'd never seen before. A golden glow from the back corner drew her. Soon she found herself in a small room, surrounded by unfinished wooden furniture. A lantern hung from a large iron hook and Jake stood several feet away, rolling up his sleeves. When he spotted her, he ceased his whistling.

"Mornin'." His gaze fell over her. "What are you doing up so early?"

"I told Sarah I'd help with the milking this morning."

He shook his dark-brown head. "You're helping to spoil that girl."

Valerie rolled her shoulders. Right now the smooth, sanded surface of a chest of drawers held her attention. "So this is where you hide out."

He grinned.

"You're quite a good carpenter, you know. I've admired some of the pieces you made in the house."

"High praise, coming from a woman who's lived her life surrounded by fine furniture."

She folded her arms and tipped her head. "Do you hold that against me, Jake? I keep thinking you compare me to Gwyneth Merriweather, and that's not fair."

Jake rubbed his jaw in momentary thought. "Maybe you're right. I apologize."

"Accepted." Valerie liked Jake even though he could be exasperating at times. Her gaze suddenly honed in on the beginnings of a rocking horse. "Are you making this for Josiah?"

"Yes, but it's a secret. I want to surprise Leah—and Jon too—next Christmas. Josiah will be old enough to enjoy the toy by then."

"I'm sure he'll love it. You're a thoughtful uncle. In fact, I think you're a thoughtful man. I'm surprised some woman hasn't snatched you up for her husband."

He laughed. "And what woman do you think would want a man with a bum leg?"

"Jacob—" Valerie was taken aback by the question. "The rest of you is fine, and not many men are as talented as you are with woodworking." She felt like teasing him for a change. "And you're handsome and charming…exasperating too. Bossy…and did I mention exasperating?"

"Yes, well…my list of attributes is endless." He smiled at his sarcasm.

"If I weren't so in love with Benjamin, I'd probably be interested in you."

His gaze met hers, and she saw a mix of alarm and curiosity in his stare.

"My point is you're not as undesirable as you think. Even if you are...exasperating."

"Hmm...thanks."

Valerie gave her head a toss for good measure. "A bum leg is the least of your problems."

"I get it. I get it." He held both hands up in surrender.

Valerie liked the feel of victory.

With a grin, Jake moved to sit on a tall stool. He picked up a piece of wood and turned it in his palm. "If you're so in love with Ben, why did you refuse to send him a telegraph message?"

She thought it over. "Two reasons, really. I have far too much to say to Benjamin. It wouldn't fit on a telegram. Second, I want to confront him face-to-face."

"Confront him?"

Valerie nodded and squared her shoulders. "The truth is, I fear your brother married me out of a sense of obligation. If he wants an annulment, I'll give it to him. If not, I have a list of demands."

"List of demands, huh?" Jake shook his head. "I thought you heard Pa when he said a vow is vow."

"I heard. And I prayed about it. Unfortunately, there's nothing in the Bible about annulments. It's a legal matter, and the Lord said that we should follow the laws of the land. On a personal level, I refuse to be locked into a loveless marriage."

"Whoowee! This ought to be interesting when Ben gets home." Jake narrowed his gaze. "But how do you know Ben doesn't love you?"

"He had plenty of chances to tell me, and he didn't." She frowned. Or did he? She'd been in such a state of shock that day.

"Are you happy here in Jericho Junction?"

"I'm adjusting. Don't you think so?" Valerie dropped her hands into the pockets of her smock. "I've been working hard."

"That's for sure. No one can say you're not pulling your weight." He chuckled. "But you're not such a good cook."

"I'm learning." Valerie shifted her weight, recalling the burned biscuits last night and the near disaster a few days ago when she'd tried to bake a cake. Thankfully Leah came to her rescue since Becca was away and Catherine proved little help.

"My poor brother might starve to death before you master the oven."

"Oh, hush." Valerie wasn't worried. Em said Ben knew how to cook well enough to survive, and they could always come and visit here. Becca reminded her of that fact often. "Speaking of ovens—" Valerie paused and sniffed. "I smell something." She suddenly remembered the lantern she'd left unattended. "Oh, Lord, no!" She whirled around and ran but only made it a short distance before she saw the smoke and flames. "Jacob!" She screamed. "The barn's on fire!"

For a man with a permanently injured leg, he moved quickly. He steered her toward the rear side door. "Run and get help."

She fled the barn and sprinted across the yard. A mix of guilt and confusion roiled inside of her. She'd left the lantern on the other side of the barn, near Tulip's stall. The fire came from the stacks of hay bales adjacent to the wagon.

"Reverend McCabe! Bear! Help! Fire! Fire!"

Her cries successfully roused the household. Emily and Leah ran from the parsonage too.

"Is everyone accounted for?" Reverend McCabe shouted out the question.

"Jake's still in the barn." Panic assailed her as Valerie looked to where black smoke now billowed from the double doors. Bear filled buckets with water from the rain barrel.

"Where's Catherine?" Becca's eyes darted around.

"She's not upstairs in our room," Sarah said. "I just came from up there."

A sick feeling wafted over Valerie. Had Catherine been in the barn too?

"Jake!" Reverend McCabe fought the smoke while Becca clung to his shirttails. "Son, can you hear me?"

"You can't go in there, Daniel!" Becca cried.

Bear pushed a bucket into Valerie's chest, nearly knocking the wind out of her, but she managed to hand off the bucket to Becca, who tearfully passed it to her husband.

"Jake! Catherine!" Reverend McCabe walked in far enough to toss the water at the flames. He returned, coughing from the smoke until the next bucket was given to him.

"Pa! Look!" Sarah went running toward the same door that Valerie had exited. "Pa, it's Jake...and Catherine!"

Valerie gaped at the sight. Through the haze of smoke came Jacob, and he carried Catherine's limp form in his arms.

That evening a somber atmosphere filled the drawing room. Valerie puttered with her needlepoint while Em, Leah, and Sarah busied themselves with their sewing. Bear stayed outside to tend to the last of the fire. Jake helped. His burns hadn't been serious, thank God! However, despite all efforts, the barn was a complete loss. The fire took the lives of livestock and the McCabes' wagon, harnesses, and farming equipment. All of Jake's carpentry projects went up in flames as well.

And then Catherine...the doctor and Becca were upstairs with her now. It appeared her burns were extensive.

"I felt the baby move this morning." Emily set her knitting down. She apparently wanted to lighten the mood. "It was the most exciting thing, like a smooth, rolling sensation. I guess that's the best way to describe it." She smiled.

"Must be doing somersaults in there," Leah teased. "Probably a boy."

Emily had a dreamy expression on her face. "I wouldn't mind giving Clint a boy. Not one bit. But I wouldn't mind a girl either."

Valerie wondered if she and Benjamin would ever have children. She wanted to be a mother someday. Each time she watched Leah cradle little Josiah, she desired a baby of her own.

"Perhaps we should all say another prayer for Catherine," Sarah said, changing the subject. "I keep remembering how bad she looked when Bear carried her upstairs."

"She tried to kill Valerie." Emily raised her chin. "It's hard to feel pity for someone so loathsome."

Disbelief shook Valerie's being. "Tried to kill me? Do you really think it's possible?"

Emily's expression was one of regret. "Yes, I do."

"We don't know if the fire was set on purpose," Leah put in. "Let's give Catherine the benefit of the doubt."

Valerie tried, but she couldn't help but wonder...was Catherine really capable of attempting murder?

"Either way, this is the time when we must pity her." Leah folded her sewing and laid it in her lap. "You know, just because a woman is a preacher's daughter and listened to sermon after sermon while growing up doesn't mean she actually heard a word of them and believed God's Word."

Sarah came to sit on the arm of Valerie's chair.

Leah continued, "So even more's the reason we must pray for Catherine."

Valerie felt somewhat guilty for having jumped to conclusions.

Heads bowed, Leah began, asking the Great Physician to heal Catherine's body, mind, and soul. Emily prayed next.

But when it came time for Valerie to pray, she found it difficult to ask for mercy for someone who may have wanted her dead. And when the words did enter her heart, they weren't for Catherine per se. "Lord, please help me forgive so bitterness doesn't rule my heart. Give me a meek and gentle spirit so I can be of help in Catherine's convalescence—"

Sarah wrapped up the short prayer session. Then just as they finished praying, Becca and Dr. Owens walked into the room.

Everyone stood.

"Catherine's going to lose her right hand." Tears glistened in Becca's eyes.

Valerie covered her mouth to retain her gasp. Her gaze glided to the pianoforte, and she thought of how Catherine would never play again.

"There's significant tissue, vascular, and muscle damage to the right hand. It warrants amputation." Dr. Owens, a bearded, gray-haired man, didn't seem to mince his words. "It must come off to save the patient's life. The surgery will be first thing in the morning. Meanwhile, Miss Elliot has a long recovery ahead of her. She's suffered burns to her chest, belly, and thighs. If not properly treated, the burned area could become infected, and that may threaten Miss Elliot's life."

"Is she awake?" Emily asked.

"She is awake and in a lot of pain," the physician replied. "I've given Mrs. McCabe a bottle of laudanum to ease some of the discomfort. But there will be much more to come."

Valerie winced, imagining it.

"We're all going to have to take turns caring for Catherine." Angst and sorrow bore down on Becca's features. "Can I have everyone's solemn promise that you'll help Catherine get better?"

"We promise, Ma, don't we?" Leah glanced around. Everyone's head bobbed in agreement.

Valerie's included.

Becca left to see Dr. Owens out.

"That poor woman, burned so terribly." Leah lowered herself back onto the settee. "I hope it's found out Catherine didn't intentionally set the fire. I hate to think she'd do something so hateful."

Becca returned to the room and paused at the entryway. Her gaze fixed on Valerie, and tears gathered in her eyes. "Oh, honey..." She strode across the room and pulled Valerie into an embrace. "I almost lost my son, Catherine, and–and a daughter today."

Valerie held the woman as she cried it out. "I'm all right, Becca." No one had fretted over her like this since Mama did when she was a little girl. "Calm down. I'm all right. And we'll keep praying for Catherine."

Leah, Sarah, and Em came and put their arms around Becca too.

They stood there, bundled, all wrapped up in each other. Valerie had never experienced anything like it. She rather enjoyed the feeling of being a part of something so uniquely special—

Something called a family.

Twenty-one

REINS IN HAND, BEN steered his team down the unpaved road that wound through Tennessee. He and Luke followed the 1st Ohio Infantry to the lower part of the state. Up ahead the drum beat out the time to the soldiers' march. His photographic wagon clattered behind them. He breathed in deep of the fresh crisp March air, then blew it out on a sigh. His heart begged to keep going on to Missouri, but his brother struggled with leaving his comrades.

"You and Clint sure about this?"

"We're sure." They'd stopped in Nashville long enough to send and receive a telegram. The reply from Pa had been disturbing. BARN DESTROYED IN FIRE. JAKE AND CATHERINE INJURED. LIVE-STOCK ALL LOST. PRAISE THE LORD EVERYONE ELSE OK. Ben gave his younger brother a side-glance. "I want to be home. But I don't want to risk getting separated from you again. That head injury of yours isn't all the way healed. I just appreciate the fact that Clint chose to stick with me—at least for a couple more months if that's what it takes."

Luke didn't reply, and Ben prayed he'd have a change of heart. He wasn't contractually bound as he never officially enlisted. And this regiment was marching to Pittsburg Landing, where they'd engage the enemy. If he had to go, Ben decided to make good use of it. He figured that since he'd helped the South by working for Colonel LaPorte, he'd now do his part for the North by docu-menting everything leading up to the battle and photographing what he could during and after the fight. He knew of several publications that might be interested in purchasing his and Clint's articles and pictures. But he and Clint both would toss aside the opportunity in a second if Luke wanted to go home too.

Finally, his younger brother spoke up. "I can't explain it, but I need to be there for these men, pray with them before the battle. I told Captain Marshall that I'm not willing to fight alongside them, but if I must, I must. I'm a chaplain, concerned for all souls, Fed and Reb alike. Captain Marshall called me an 'unwilling warrior.'"

Ben gave a short laugh. "Guess that describes a lot of us, eh?" He wasn't willing to pick up his gun and kill another man either, war or no war, although he'd do it in self-defense.

"Well, as a matter of fact, I started thinkin' on it for a future sermon, about being an unwilling warrior. As Christians we're supposed to 'fight the good fight,' as Paul wrote, but many of us aren't willing. We want life to be like that Sunday afternoon when we're sittin' on the front porch—" He made a faraway gesture with his hand. "—with smells of Ma's fried chicken coming through the open window."

Ben groaned. "Boy, don't make me more homesick than I already am!"

Luke laughed. "Sorry 'bout that."

"But I get your point."

Up ahead, some of the men sang "The Girl I Left Behind Me" as they marched along, and Ben's heart ached as he missed Valerie for the umpteenth time today.

He shifted his weight on the hard bench. Maybe some temptation was in order. "What say you about us getting home for Easter Sunday? Pa always delivers a fine message from the pulpit. It'll fire you right up."

"Always does. Hmm. I reckon I'll have to see what happens in the next few weeks."

"So you're not opposed to it?"

Luke sent him a frown. "Opposed? No. I want to go home as bad as you. But God's not done with me here yet."

"Fair enough." Ben started thinking, praying. He'd discuss logistics with Clint later, but if there was even a remote chance they'd make it, Ben wanted to try. "Home by Easter Sunday." He grinned. "Has a nice ring to it."

Valerie finished preparing the dozens of bars of soaps that the McCabes planned to hand out in town today. They prayed some of the working girls would accept more than the gift of a lavender-scented bar. Attached to each ribbon was verse sixteen of Mama's favorite psalm. *As for me, I will call upon God; and the LORD shall save me.* It seemed an appropriate message for this Saturday before Easter.

"Are those all set to go, sis?" Jake entered the kitchen and stood with hands on hips, gazing at the kitchen table. It was nice to see the bandages gone from his hands and forearms where they'd been burned.

"I just got done." Valerie lifted the basket off the table and gave it to Jake.

"And you don't mind staying with Catherine?" Becca asked. "I know you've been avoiding her."

"I haven't wanted to upset her, but if she agreed to let me sit with her, I'm fine with it."

"She'll probably ask for laudanum." Becca pulled on her gloves.

"I can administer it." The drug was all Catherine asked for— that and water. She refused to answer questions or talk about what happened. At first, Dr. Owens thought perhaps her vocal cords had been singed. But her requests came out loud and clear.

Jake pursed his lips and gave his head a shake. "I don't agree with it, but the doc says to give her as much as she wants."

"She's in so much pain." Valerie had spent countless nights listening to Catherine moan in agony. "Her wounds can't heal if she's writhing."

"I reckon...well, we won't be gone that long, and if something should happen, we're just right up the road."

"I know, Jake." Valerie widened her eyes. "You're a regular mother hen."

Becca laughed.

"And you're getting as sassy as Sarah. See! The way you rolled your eyes just now!" He shook his finger at her. "That's got to stop."

"Oh, Jake, really." Becca tugged on his arm. "Let's go."

"Good-bye, Jake." Valerie smiled sweetly just to irk him.

He narrowed his gaze, but she saw the grin working its way across his mouth.

Once he left, she sighed in relief. The man needed a wife in the worst way to soften him up a bit—Emily and Leah both said so. And Valerie knew that softer side of him existed. She'd glimpsed it the night he learned General McCulloch was killed in a battle in Arkansas. Jake said he would have ridden days to attend the man's funeral, but his father needed him here. A new barn needed to be built by the fall.

And then the news came about the battle near the Shiloh Baptist Church in Tennessee. It was a Union victory, and Jake hadn't been himself. Not because the North won another fight, but he worried—as they all did—about the well-being of Benjamin, Luke, and Clint. Days later, a telegram arrived stating they were unharmed. Valerie had never felt such relief. It reminded her how very much she loved Benjamin. After the news, Jake returned to his normal, exasperating ways.

With everyone gone now, Valerie crept up the steps. Since the fire and her hand surgery, Catherine occupied the room in which Valerie had resided. Valerie moved in with Sarah. Peering in the doorway, she saw that Catherine slept peacefully. Only a thin sheet covered her. Valerie turned to go.

"Wait."

Valerie slowly pivoted. "I didn't mean to wake you."

"I was merely resting my eyes." Catherine's voice sounded raspy. "Come in. I've been wanting to talk with you. Privately. You never came."

"I've kept my distance for obvious reasons. But I felt comfortable enough to stay with you for a few hours today." Valerie stepped into the room. It smelled of disinfectant combined with the sickening odor of decaying flesh that somehow defied Dr. Owens's painful debridements. But the window had been cracked open to allow for some air circulation.

"Please sit."

She did, but cautiously so. She had no reason to trust Catherine, except in her incapacitated state she seemed harmless enough. She took in her appearance. Becca had cut her brown hair in an effort to conceal the part that was badly singed, which made Catherine's large eyes even more prominent. The gauntness of her face spoke to her lack of appetite, and Valerie feared Catherine was dying.

"I never meant you any physical harm. That day of the fire. I saw you walk around the wagon, and I became suspicious. I put the lantern down and followed you. I eavesdropped on your conversation with Jake, and I was jealous of you again. I thought it should be me who was well liked and treated as a sister. You stole my place."

"Catherine, I've told you—"

"Wait." She sounded winded and worked to catch her breath. "I marched off, forgetting I'd set the lantern down on the ground. I kicked it over, and the kerosene splashed up onto my dress, catching fire. I tried to extinguish it, but it ignited the dried hay. Then suddenly it was everywhere. The fire. I coughed and choked on the smoke and ran for the side door. I bumped into something, and that's the last I remember."

"You ran smack dab into Jake." Valerie had heard his version. "But why have you kept your silence these past weeks?"

"I didn't think I could live with myself if I admitted that it was my fault the barn burned to the ground. The McCabes must have lost so much, livestock and property. Am I right?"

Valerie didn't see any point in lying. She nodded.

"I knew it. And all because of my stupidity."

"It was an accident." Valerie reached out and stroked Catherine's forearm, careful to avoid the heavily bandaged area that covered what was once her right hand. "The McCabes love you."

"But you hate me?"

"No, I don't. And now that you've told me what happened, you need to tell everyone else."

Catherine turned her face away. "I don't think I can bear the guilt and shame."

"You didn't mean to—"

"But in a way I did. Can't you see?"

"So you still hate me? After all that's happened? After all I did for you?"

Catherine turned her head away, and anger coursed through Valerie's being. But before she could say more, raucous hoots and shouts followed by laughter drifted in from outside. It wasn't even noon yet. Could men from the saloon be spilling out into the street already? Only twice since she'd come to town had she known of any trouble, and both times the sheriff took swift care of it.

Valerie stood and crossed the room. Looking out the window, she couldn't see far enough away to figure what happened. In any case, the disturbance had ceased.

She whirled back around and touched the neckline of her calico. It was then she remembered—

"What about Benjamin's pocket watch?"

Catherine closed her eyes. "Yes, I took it."

"Can I have it back?" Hope filled her.

"I'd return it if I could." She winced as she swallowed. "While you slept that night at the Widewater, I took the watch, walked to the end of the hallway, and tossed it out the window. If I couldn't have it, I didn't want you to have it either."

Valerie's jaw slacked. But then, what could she expect from a woman whose hostilities ran so deep?

"Don't you hate me now?" Catherine's tone teetered on mockery. Her eyes looked like ice.

"No, I don't hate you." Was Catherine trying to drag her into her cesspool of resentment and bitterness? Well, she refused to go there!

"It was a despicable thing for you do to, Catherine. Benjamin's watch was precious to me. But I don't hate you." She pitied the woman more than anything.

"Just wait until Ben gets home. Then you'll see that I was right about your so-called marriage. You'll hate me then—and you'll hate him."

"Never."

A frightening chill passed through Valerie. She turned and closed the window, but it didn't seem to be coming from outside. Something had changed inside this room—and not for the good. "I think I should go. Call me if you need anything more."

"Valerie, wait."

She halted her strides.

"My laudanum…" The words sounded forced through great pain. "Would you give me some more?"

She strode to the bureau and poured some into the spoon. After feeding the liquid to Catherine, she replaced the utensil on the saucer and pushed the cork back into the cruet.

"Just give me the bottle, and I won't have to trouble you again."

Valerie almost complied but suddenly realized an overdose would be fatal. Valerie wondered how she'd forgive herself if she was a party to Catherine's demise. For safekeeping, she tucked the bottle into her dress's front pocket.

Never forgive…

But unforgiveness was worse than poison.

Understanding filled her. Enslavement came in many deceivingly pretty packages. Fear. Guilt. Jealousy. Envy. Greed and covetousness. Revenge. Father and James succumbed to theirs. After all, God said the love of money was the root of all evil. The McCabes obviously knew all about such bondage. That's why they tried to rescue the working girls on the edge of town.

"You're no trouble, Catherine." Feelings of benevolence stirred inside of her.

She strode to the side table and picked up the Bible. Gently she leafed through the pages until she found Psalm 55. "This was my mother's favorite passage of Scripture. I'll read it to you."

Catherine didn't object.

Valerie cleared her throat lightly. "Give ear to my prayer, O God; and hide not thyself from my supplication…"

The woman dozed off before Valerie reached the third verse.

Having straightened the drawing room, Valerie practiced the coming Sunday's music on the pianoforte. She couldn't imagine what was keeping the McCabes. Had there been trouble in town?

Surely she'd have heard by now if there was. She stood and walked to the windows. Maybe she ought to run next door to Leah's. She and Em were home today.

Valerie took to the stairs and checked on Catherine. Still asleep. She replaced the bottle of laudanum on the bureau, but set it far enough back that it remained out of Catherine's sight and reach.

Back downstairs again, Valerie walked to the kitchen, and just when she reached the mudroom, the door opened. She stepped back when the darkly clad man entered.

Recognition set in. "Benjamin?" She felt frozen in disbelief.

He slid off his wide brim hat and inclined his head. "Mrs. McCabe, I presume." His gaze traveled over her, and a smile inched across his face. "I see you've adjusted to life out here quite well."

She glanced down at her work dress. She looked a sight and hardly resembled the exquisitely clad woman he put on the steamer in New Orleans.

He opened his arms, and without another thought, she ran to him. She heard his laugh as she threw herself into his embrace. It felt good to hold him tightly and press her nose into his neck. *He's home!* It seemed too good to be true.

He squeezed her and spun her around in the kitchen. When her feet finally touched the floor again, Benjamin leaned in for a kiss. Reality caused her to tense, and Valerie stopped him by touching her fingers to his lips.

"We need to talk," she said in the most determined voice she could find.

"All right." Surprise and skepticism were etched into his features. "Everything OK?"

"Well, yes, but—" Gazing into his clean-shaven face and getting caught up in that golden-eyed gaze of his, Valerie fought to recall her complaint.

After a grin, Benjamin got his kiss.

"I love you." The words leaked from her heart.

He released her. "Now there's something I want to talk to you about."

"Oh?" She did her best not to feel hurt.

"Later," he promised. Then his eyes moved over her, and he shook his head. "Just look at you."

Embarrassed, Valerie patted a few hairpins into place.

"I'm not as pretty as when you last saw me in New Orleans."

"No, you're not. You're beautiful." He touched her cheek, then kissed her again.

The door opened. "Sorry to bust in on you like this."

Valerie stepped backward and saw a young man standing in the mudroom. He resembled Benjamin except his eyes were as blue as Becca's.

Valerie smiled. "You must be Luke."

"Yes, ma'am."

When he inclined his head, Valerie glimpsed the purplish scar that ran down along the side of his face.

Benjamin narrowed his gaze at him. "I told you to give me ten minutes."

Luke shrugged carelessly. Then he removed his hat and smiled at Valerie.

"Luke, meet my lovely bride."

She righted the skirt of her calico, wishing she'd known they were coming home today.

"Valerie, this is my brother Luke."

"It's a pleasure." She reached for his hand. "I'm so happy to meet you. I've prayed for you, and it's a blessing to see you're alive and looking well."

"Thank you." Luke jabbed Benjamin with his elbow. "She's even prettier than you said."

He replied with a tolerant grin. "Don't you have something else to do?"

"No." Luke wagged his head, obviously goading his big brother.

But the jokes and quips had to stop. "Gentlemen, there's a gravely ill woman upstairs."

They both straightened to their full height, their expressions serious now.

"Ma told us about Catherine." Benjamin's gaze softened. "I don't mean this tritely when I say we'll keep her in our prayers."

"I know." Valerie believed him.

"And Ma's on her way in. She was right behind Luke." Benjamin sent his brother an annoyed glance.

Luke chuckled.

With an arm around her waist, Benjamin guided her to the stairs. "So you've got a few minutes to go pack."

"But—" Questions whirled inside her head as she looked up into his face.

"We're going to do that talking you mentioned."

"All right." Valerie ran up a few steps and then paused. "Should I pack for a long trip or short?"

He leaned against the balustrade and grinned. "I reckon that depends on what happens after our talking."

"Hmm, I see." Valerie guessed his intentions. "Am I correct in assuming I'm going to have your attention all to myself tonight?"

"Only if you hurry before the rest of my family gets home."

Not wanting to waste a moment more, she whirled around and ran up the stairs as fast as her legs would carry her.

TWENTY-TWO

I
T'S A SORRY SHAME ABOUT CATHERINE." BY THE FLICKER-
ing glow of the small lamp on their table, Valerie saw Benjamin shake his head sadly.

"What do you think about my bizarre encounter with her this
afternoon?"

"Sounds like Catherine isn't quite ready to forgive and be
forgiven."

"That's what I thought too. What about your pocket watch?
Are you angry?"

A wry grin curved his mouth as he retrieved something from
out of his waistcoat's inner pocket. Valerie recognized Mama's
gold chain and then his watch.

"How did you—?" She reached for it, inspecting it beneath the
glow of the candles on their table. Opening it, she saw Benjamin's photograph and held the precious keepsake to her heart
a moment before slipping it over her neck. "Oh, Benjamin, how
did you find it?"

"Clint, Luke, and I stopped at the Widewater Inn last night. A
serving woman who had worked at the place for decades found
my watch lying in the alley when she took out the garbage.
She knew it was mine because of the photograph inside. She
recognized me. So she tucked it away until one of us McCabes
happened through there again."

Valerie sighed as enormous relief engulfed her. "Thank you."

"Thank the Lord, not me."

"I thank you both." She smiled.

Benjamin stretched his arm across the table and took her hand. "You sure are a sight for these sore eyes."

"You mean because you took in so much after that battle at Shiloh? We heard thousands of men died on both sides."

Sorrow fell over his expression. "Over twenty-three thousand casualties is the last number I heard."

Valerie tightened her grip on his hand. "I thank God you and Clint and Luke all made it through safely."

He brought her fingers to his lips.

A blush warmed her cheeks.

He released her hand, and she let her gaze wander for a moment so she could collect her thoughts. The hotel's small eatery was surprisingly busy tonight, and at the other end of the rustic room a small ensemble of guitars and banjos made melody. Strains of the melody "Lily Dale" reached her ears.

"Do you remember the first night we met?"

Valerie returned her gaze to Benjamin. "Of course I do."

"Well, the way I see it, I got cheated that night at the Donahues'."

A frown set on her brow. "How so?"

Benjamin slid back his chair. Its legs scraped against the plank floor. "I never got the chance to dance with you." Standing, he held out his hand.

Smiling, Valerie took it, and Benjamin pulled her close to him. There wasn't a designated area for dancing, so couples claimed a spot anywhere.

Benjamin hummed and occasionally sang to the song as they swayed to the music.

She peered up into his face and met his stare. She marveled at how a mere connecting of gazes still caused her pulse to react and her knees to feel weak.

But what did he feel?

He stopped singing and leaned his head against the side of Valerie's. "I missed you."

"I missed you too." Valerie silently whispered a prayer of thanks while asking for courage too. She needed to present her demands and insist that Benjamin give her an answer. Did he love her? She'd like to think so. If he didn't, then they ought not to be dancing so closely and Benjamin shouldn't be nibbling on her neck in that way that made her shiver all over.

"I sense your thoughts are elsewhere." He leaned back.

She lowered her gaze, embarrassed that he'd read her thoughts so well.

The tune ended, and disappointment coursed through Valerie. She would have enjoyed lingering in his arms awhile longer.

Without a word, Benjamin led her through the eatery and toward the stairs leading up to the room he'd rented. Before dinner he had allowed Valerie to use it privately to change her dress. Now, however, it seemed she'd need that courage she only moments ago prayed for.

Inside, the tiny room was furnished with a desk, a small wardrobe, a chair, and a bed covered with a flimsy, white spread. Valerie wondered how she ought to begin to convey the matter that weighed so heavily on her heart.

Benjamin shrugged out of his dress coat and undid his tie. The waistcoat came off next.

"What are you doing?"

"Getting comfortable." He sent her a glance. "Feel free to do the same."

Valerie flushed with embarrassment. "I do not feel free to do any such thing." Turning toward the window, she strained her eyes to look past the gauzy drapes. She made out the train station across the way.

A minute later she felt Benjamin's hands on her shoulders. "Sweetheart, you don't have to be so shy. We're married now."

She faced him, noticing the pearly buttons of his crisp, white shirt. "And what does that mean, exactly? 'We're married.' Forgive me, but I can't recall our bargain."

"Bargain?"

"Yes, the one we apparently made. I wasn't myself on our wedding day, if you can even call what we had a wedding. I barely remember taking our vows. So I've been wondering what sort of marriage this is."

Benjamin arched a brow. "There's more than one kind of marriage?"

Valerie folded her arms and reminded him of what he'd said before putting her on the steamboat.

"Well, sure, I was sorry about the way things happened. You deserved a beautiful wedding ceremony with all the trimmings. As for the fixing it part of my statement, I thought maybe you'd like to have a celebration here in Jericho Junction."

"I'll think about it." She wasn't sure it was necessary.

"I'm sorry you don't recall our vows." He looked wounded.

"Emily said we both recited them, but the whole day is something of a blur for me."

"Understandable." He seemed pensive for several moments. "But I hope you don't feel I coerced you into marrying me. You said you loved me, therefore—"

"I didn't feel coerced, although I've rather wondered if you're the one who felt pressured into marrying me. After all, your photographs implicated my father. You may have felt guilty...and coerced."

"Hardly. I prayed about marrying you and felt God opened up the way to make it happen. I don't mean to put a happy spin on tragic events, but taking you to be my wife was one of the finest days of my life."

The admission warmed Valerie's heart. "So you didn't marry me out of pity?"

"I'm really not that noble." His eyes lit up from the grin on his face. "I married you, Valerie, because I love you."

"You do?"

Benjamin slipped his arms around her waist and placed a kiss on her forehead. "I'm sorry you ever doubted it."

"But that night in the kitchen, when I said I loved you, you didn't reply. You could have."

"I felt I had no right." He pulled back far enough so he could look into her face. "I knew I'd never be a man who could afford to lavish you with expensive items."

"I never cared about wealth."

"Maybe not, but I couldn't get past my fear that you'd one day hate me because I couldn't measure up to your expectations."

"And now? Do you still harbor that fear?"

"No, because marrying me far outweighed your alternative."

Valerie angrily pushed him back. "That's the most absurd thing I've heard. Benjamin, do you realize that by not stating your feelings you allowed my father to betroth me to James Ladden?"

"I talked to your father, Valerie, and he refused to change his mind." On a long breath, Benjamin cupped her head and drew it to his chest. She could hear his heart beating strong and sure. "I do love you so much, and I'm sorry what you suffered at the hands of that lousy excuse for a man. I wanted to step in, but each time I felt God tell me to be patient and wait."

"I felt God tell me the same thing." Her irritation at him waned, and she relaxed in his embrace. "That's why I didn't leave home even when the urge to flee was so overwhelming."

"I wouldn't have allowed you to marry him, Valerie. I didn't know what to do, but I would have thought of something."

Knowing that soothed away her concerns.

"Part of me worried you might want to flee from Jericho Junction, that you'd hate me for sending you here."

"Remember our carriage ride through New Orleans when I said I'd follow the man I love to the ends of the earth?"

"I remember the instance quite well." A smile entered his voice. "Actually, I plan to hold you to it." He released her and his tone took on a businesslike quality. "Now, then, I understand you have, um, a *list of demands* you'd like to run by me."

She gaped for a long moment, wondering how he knew. Then it dawned on her. The ruckus in town earlier…

"Your brother Jake is the most exasperating man I know."

"Yes, he mentioned your high opinion of him." Benjamin couldn't curb his chuckle.

He folded his arms. "All right, so let's hear 'em."

"Actually, I think you've met all my demands." She felt humbled to admit it. "And quite effectively, I might add."

He replied with a satisfied nod. "So it's all right to proceed with the honeymoon? I thought tomorrow morning you'd like to take the train back to St. Louis with me. The Culvers too. You see, Clint and I left our wagons there because we couldn't wait another day to be home with our wives."

"Oh, Benjamin…"

He gathered her in his arms. "We'll go to the theater and visit some shops."

"Sounds like a grand honeymoon."

"I love you, Valerie."

"I love you too." Up on tiptoes, she wrapped her arms about his neck and kissed his jaw. Then she whispered in his ear, "All I ever wanted is to be completely yours."

EPILOGUE

May 1866

I T'S THE BIG DAY. ARE YOU NERVOUS?"

"More curious than nervous." Valerie searched her husband's face. "What are you up to? What's this big surprise you've been talking about? Is Sarah coming home?"

"No, it's not Sarah."

Momentary disappointment descended. Valerie and the rest of the McCabes, and most of Jericho Junction too, had recently given Sarah a tearful send-off. She'd left home to fulfill her dreams of big city life. Valerie hoped Sarah wouldn't regret her decision. She'd soon learn that city living had its downfalls too and that happiness resided in one's heart, not in any particular place.

Benjamin set one arm around Valerie's shoulders, while in the other he carried their ten-month-old son, Daniel. Valerie held on to the hand of their daughter, Maggie. The darling girl had been named after Valerie's mother, Marguerite, and "Maggie" was the nickname that stuck. At three years old, Maggie had become a marvelous little helper—and Valerie figured she'd need all the assistance she could get once this new baby arrived in September.

She leaned against Benjamin. "Tell me your surprise."

"Just wait." He kissed her temple. "You'll see in a few minutes."

She nibbled her lower lip in thought. "It has to be a person, or we wouldn't be waiting here at the train station."

"I'd say that's a good likelihood." He chuckled.

Valerie rolled her eyes and sighed. "You McCabes love your surprises, don't you?"

"I reckon so."

Valerie's gaze moved to their little boy, secure within the confines of his daddy's strong arm. His large blue eyes were wide as he took in the activity around him.

Once the war ended, the westward movement brought throngs of people through their little town, which was rapidly expanding. The McCabe-Culver Photography Studio was often lined with customers desiring to have their pictures taken. Other times Benjamin and Clint took their cameras outdoors if customers desired a photograph or two of themselves with their team of oxen before heading West.

"Mama, where's the surprise?" Maggie stared up at her.

"No idea, honey. But Daddy knows."

"Daddy?" She moved to him.

"Soon. You'll see soon."

A few minutes passed, and Benjamin led them over to a recently vacated bench. Valerie eased herself down, and he sat beside her. He positioned Daniel on one knee while Maggie climbed up into his lap. Valerie did her best to hide her smile. Maggie had her daddy wrapped around her little finger.

Benjamin hadn't at all been disappointed his firstborn proved to be a girl, although Clint, having already celebrated the birth of his son, teased him about pink this and pink that for months afterward. But now it was Clint's turn to have a newborn daughter. Only days ago, Emily delivered their third child, a baby girl.

Placing a hand on her rounded belly, Valerie's thoughts came forward, and she scanned the crowd. She tried to think of an individual from her past who'd want to come for a visit. Certainly not Elicia Donahue. Valerie heard she'd married a Union major, a physician, and settled in Baton Rouge.

"There she is!"

"Where?" Valerie looked at Benjamin, then tried to follow his line of vision. "Benjamin, who is 'she'?"

A moment later Valerie saw her and sprang to her feet. A squeal of delight escaped her.

"Well, look at you, dearie! All plump and rosy-cheeked, y'are!"

"Adalia!" She had looked beyond the older, gray-haired woman. "I can't believe I didn't recognize you." She gave her special friend as much of a hug as her midsection allowed. "This is a surprise. A grand surprise. I never thought we'd meet again."

"Oh, ye of little faith." Adalia chuckled loudly. "And look who I brought with me. None other than my own true love, Dalbert Dempsey. He came for me after the war. Sailed all the way from England, he did." She leaned close to Valerie. "You were right about true love."

She smiled broadly as she greeted the rotund man whose hat seemed too small for his head.

Removing it, he bowed. "A pleasure to make your acquaintance, Mrs. McCabe."

Benjamin stepped in beside her and shook Mr. Dempsey's hand. Next he kissed Adalia's cheek. "I trust you two had a good trip."

"We had a lovely trip." Adalia pinched Daniel's chubby cheek. "Such a handsome fellow...and look at this little princess." She bent and spoke to Maggie. "Why, I remember when y'mama was your age. You're just as pretty too."

Benjamin introduced the children. Then he caught Valerie's gaze, winked, and smiled.

"We'd best take our guests on home." He nodded his head toward the wagon.

Home. For Valerie the word still held an incredible, beautiful note.

They'd purchased a house about a half mile outside of town. Jake and Luke recently helped Benjamin build on an addition as their family was growing quite rapidly. Valerie decided she'd miss Jake and Luke when they left for the Arizona Territory.

"May I escort you, my lovely?" Benjamin offered his free arm.

A soft breeze wafted through the budding treetops as Valerie threaded her hand around his elbow. She gave it a tug, and he inclined his ear to her. "Thank you, my love," she whispered.

"You're entirely welcome."

While Daniel rode on his daddy's other arm, Maggie clasped onto Adalia's hand.

"My Uncle Jake made me a rocking horse."

"Is that right?" Adalia sent Valerie a wink. "Can I ride it?"

"No, you're too big." Maggie giggled.

"How 'bout a ride for me?" Mr. Dempsey teased.

"You're too big."

Adalia chortled as they walked to the wagon. "Y'certainly are blessed, dearie."

"Yes, I am." They reached the wagon. "How long can you stay?"

"Long enough to help you with the wee one that's on the way."

"Wonderful, although I might have to share you with Emily. The two of us have our hands full."

"Well, now I'm here, dearie. You can relax."

"Mr. Dempsey is going to help Clint and me this summer," Benjamin put in. "It just so happens he repairs photographic equipment."

"Learned the trade in England," said the man, "so I could support m'darling wife in New Orleans once I found her again."

Benjamin helped Valerie into the backseat of the wagon.

Maggie came up next and sat down beside her. Valerie righted her bonnet and adjusted her skirt, and then Benjamin handed over Daniel. Snuggling their son in her lap she glimpsed the tall grave markers in the cemetery. Catherine had succumbed to her burns just days after Benjamin, Luke, and Clint returned. Her death still saddened her, just as her father's and Mama's did too at times. But whenever sorrow knocked at her door, Valerie hugged her husband and children a little more and a little tighter.

Adalia clambered aboard.

Valerie smiled. "We have a lot to catch up on."

"Years' worth, to be sure." The older woman righted her skirt, then met her eyes with a kind look. A knowing look. She reached to touch Valerie's hand. "I say we put the kettle on for tea when we get home and let the catchin' up begin."

With a slap of the reins the wagon jerked forward. Valerie squeezed her hand. "Yes, let the catchin' up begin."

Coming in October 2010—

UNCERTAIN HEART

Book 2 in the Seasons of Redemption Series

ONE

Milwaukee, Wisconsin, June 1866

STEPPING OFF THE TRAIN, HER VALISE IN HAND, SARAH McCabe eyed her surroundings. Porters hauled luggage and shouted orders to each other. Reunited families and friends hugged while well-dressed businessmen, wearing serious expressions, walked along briskly.

Mr. Brian Sinclair... Sarah glanced around for the man she thought might be him. When nobody approached her, she ambled to the front of the train station where the city was bustling as well, what with all the carriages and horse-pulled streetcars coming and going on Reed Street. Sarah had all she could do just to stay out of the way. And yet she rejoiced in the discovery that Milwaukee was not the small community she'd assumed. Not a farm in sight. In fact, Milwaukee wasn't all that different from Chicago where she'd visited and hoped to teach music in the fall. The only difference she could see right off was that Milwaukee's main streets were cobbled, whereas most of Chicago's were paved with wooden blocks.

Sarah squinted into the morning sunshine. She wondered which of the carriages lining the curb belonged to Mr. Sinclair. In his letter he'd stated that he would meet her train. Sarah glanced at her small watch locket: nine thirty. Sarah's train was on time this morning. Had she missed him somehow?

My carriage will be parked along Reed Street, Mr. Sinclair had written, the letter in which he'd offered Sarah the governess position. *I shall arrive the same time as your train: 9:00 a.m.* The letter had then been signed: *Brian Sinclair.*

Sarah let out a sigh and tried to imagine just what she would say to her new employer once he finally came for her. Then she tried to imagine what the man looked like. *Older. Distinguished. Balding and round through the middle.* Yes, that's what he probably looked like.

She eyed the crowd, searching for someone who matched the description. Several did, although none of them proved to be Mr. Sinclair. Expelling another sigh, Sarah resigned herself to the waiting.

Her mind drifted back to her hometown of Jericho Junction, Missouri. There wasn't much excitement to be had there. Sarah longed for life in the big city, to be independent and enjoy some of the refinements not available at home. It was just a shame the opportunity in Chicago didn't work out for her. Well, at least she didn't have to go home. She'd found this governess position instead.

As the youngest McCabe, Sarah had grown tired of being pampered and protected by her parents as well as her three older brothers—Benjamin, Jacob, and Luke—and her older sisters, Leah and Valerie. Sarah thought they all had nearly suffocated her—except for Valerie. Her sister-in-law was the only one who really understood her. Her family members loved her too, of course, but Sarah felt restless and longed for some time now to be out on her own. So she'd obtained a position at a fine music academy in Chicago—or so she'd thought. When she arrived in Chicago, she was told the position had been filled. But instead of turning around and going home, Sarah spent every last cent on a hotel room and began scanning local newspapers for another job. That's when she saw the advertisement. A widower by the name of Brian Sinclair was looking for a governess to care for his four children. Sarah answered the ad immediately, she and Mr. Sinclair corresponded numerous times over the last few weeks, she'd obtained permission from her parents—which had taken a heavy amount of persuasion—and then she had accepted the governess position. She didn't have to go home after all. She would work in Milwaukee. Then, perhaps in the fall, there'd be an opening at the music academy in Chicago.

Now, if only Mr. Sinclair would arrive.

In his letter of introduction he explained that he owned and operated a business called Sinclair and Company: Ship-chandlers and Sail-makers. He had written that it was located on the corner of Water and Erie Streets. Sarah wondered if perhaps Mr. Sinclair had been detained by his business. Next she wondered if she ought to make her way to his company and announce herself, if, indeed, that was the case.

An hour later, Sarah felt certain that was, indeed, the case!

Reentering the depot, she told the baggage man behind the counter that she'd return shortly for her trunk of belongings and, after asking directions, ventured off for Mr. Sinclair's place of business.

As instructed, she walked down Reed Street, or South Second Street as it was also called, and crossed a bridge over the Milwaukee River. Then two blocks east and she found herself on Water Street. From there she continued to walk the distance to Sinclair and Company.

She squinted into the sunshine and scrutinized the building from where she stood across the street. It was three stories high, square in shape, and constructed of red brick. Nothing like the wooden structures back home.

Crossing the busy thoroughfare, which was not cobbled at all but full of mud holes, Sarah lifted her hems and climbed up the few stairs leading to the front door. She let herself in, and a tiny bell above the door signaled her entrance.

"Over here. What can I do for you?"

Sarah spotted the owner of the voice that sounded quite automatic in its welcome. She stared at the young man, but his gaze didn't leave his ledgers. She noted his neatly parted straight blond hair—as blond as her own—and his round wire spectacles.

Sarah cleared her throat. "Yes, I'm looking for Mr. Sinclair."

The young man looked up and, seeing Sarah standing before his desk, immediately removed his glasses and stood. She gauged his height to be about six feet. Attired nicely, he wore a crisp white dress shirt and black tie, although his dress jacket was nowhere in sight and his shirtsleeves had been rolled to the elbow.

"Forgive me." He sounded apologetic, but his expression was one of surprise. "I thought you were one of the regulars. They come in, holler their orders at me, and help themselves."

Sarah gave him a courteous smile.

"I'm Richard Navis," he said, extending his hand. "And you are...?"

"Sarah McCabe." She placed her hand in his and felt his firm grip.

"A pleasure to meet you, Mrs. McCabe."

"Miss," she corrected.

"Ahhh..." His deep blue eyes twinkled. "Then more's the pleasure, *Miss* McCabe." He bowed over her hand in a regal manner, and Sarah yanked it free as he chuckled.

"That was very amusing." She realized he'd tricked her in order to check her marital status. *The cad.* But worse, she'd fallen for it! The oldest trick in the book, according to her three brothers.

Richard chuckled, but then put on a very businesslike demeanor. "And how can I help you, Miss McCabe?"

"I'm looking for Mr. Sinclair, if you please." Sarah noticed the young man's dimples had disappeared with his smile.

"You mean the captain? Captain Sinclair?"

"Captain?" Sarah frowned. "Well, I don't know..."

"I do, since I work for him." Richard grinned, and once more his dimples winked at her. "He manned a gunboat on the Mississippi during the war and earned his captain's bars. When he returned from service, we all continued to call him Captain out of respect."

"I see." Sarah felt rather bemused. "All right...then I'm looking for Captain Sinclair, if you please."

"Captain Sinclair is unavailable," Richard stated with a twinkle in his eyes, and Sarah realized he'd been leading her on by the nose since she'd walked through the door. "I'm afraid you'll have to do with the likes of me."

She rolled her eyes in exasperation. "Mr. Navis, you will not do at all. I need to see the captain. It's quite important, I assure you. I wouldn't bother him otherwise."

"My apologies, Miss McCabe, but the captain's not here. Now, how can I help you?"

"You can't!"

The young man raised his brows and looked taken aback by Sarah's sudden tone of impatience. This couldn't be happening. Another job and another closed door. She had no money to get home, and wiring her parent to ask for funds would ruin her independence forever in their eyes.

She crossed her arms and took several deep breaths, wondering what on earth she should do now. She gave it several moments of thought. "Will the captain be back soon, do you think?" She tried to lighten her tone a bit.

Richard shook his head. "I don't expect him until this evening. He has the day off and took a friend on a lake excursion to Green

Bay. However, he usually stops in to check on things, day off or not...Miss McCabe? Are you all right? You look a bit pale."

A dizzying, sinking feeling fell over her.

Richard came around the counter and touched her elbow. "Miss McCabe?"

She managed to reach into the inside pocket of her jacket and pull out the captain's last letter—the one in which he stated he would meet her train. She looked at the date...today's. So it wasn't her that was off but him!

"It seems that Captain Sinclair has forgotten me." She felt a heavy frown crease her brow as she handed the letter to Richard.

He read it and looked up with an expression of deep regret. "It seems you're right."

Folding the letter carefully, he gave it back to Sarah. She accepted it, fretting over her lower lip, wondering what she should do next.

"I'm the captain's steward," Richard offered. "Allow me to fetch you a cool glass of water while I think of an appropriate solution."

"Thank you." Oh, this was just great. But at least she sensed Mr. Navis truly meant to help her now instead of baiting her as he had before.

Sitting down at a long table by the enormous plate window, Sarah pulled off her gloves and waited for him to return. *He's something of a jokester,* she decided, and she couldn't help but compare him to her brother Jake. However, just now, before he'd gone to fetch the water, he had seemed very sweet and thoughtful...like Ben, her favorite big brother. But Richard's clean-cut, boyish good looks and sun-bronzed complexion...now they were definitely like Luke, her other older brother.

Sarah let her gaze wander about the shop. She was curious

over all the shipping paraphernalia. But before she could really get a good look at the place, Richard returned with two glasses of water. He set one before Sarah, took the other for himself, and then sat down across the table from her.

He took a long drink. "I believe the thing to do," he began, "is to take you to the captain's residence. I know his housekeeper, Mrs. Schylterhaus."

Sarah nodded. It seemed the perfect solution. "I do appreciate it, Mr. Navis, although I hate to pull you away from your work." She gave a concerned glance toward his books, piled on the desk.

Richard just chuckled. "Believe it or not, Miss McCabe, you are a godsend. I had just sent a quick dart of a prayer to the Lord, telling Him that I would much rather work outside on a fine day like this than be trapped in here with my ledgers. Then you walked in." He grinned. "Your predicament, Miss McCabe, will have me working out-of-doors yet!"

Sarah smiled, heartened that he seemed to be a believer. "But what will the captain have to say about your abandonment of his books?" She arched a brow.

Richard responded with a sheepish look. "Well, seeing this whole mess is *his* fault, I suspect the captain won't say too much at all."

Sarah laughed in spite of herself, as did Richard. However, when their eyes met—sky-blue and sea-blue—an uncomfortable silence settled down around them.

Sarah was the first to turn away. She forced herself to look around the shop and then remembered her curiosity. "What exactly do you sell here?" She felt eager to break the sudden awkwardness.

Well, *exactly*," Richard said, appearing amused, "we are ship-chandlers and sail-makers and manufacturers of flags, banners, canvas belting, brewers' sacks, paulins of all kinds, waterproof horse and wagon covers, sails, awnings, and tents." He paused for a breath, acting quite dramatic about it, and Sarah laughed again. "We are dealers in vanilla, hemp and cotton cordage, lath yarns, duck of all widths, oakum, tar, pitch, paints, oars, tackle, and purchase blocks...*exactly*!"

Sarah swallowed the last of her giggles and arched a brow. "That's it?"

Richard grinned. "Yes, well," he conceded, "I might have forgotten the glass of water."

Still smiling, she took a sip of hers. And in that moment she decided that she knew how to handle the likes of Richard Navis—tease him right back, that's how. After all, she'd had enough practice with Ben, Jake, and Luke.

They finished up their cool spring water, and then Richard disappeared for a while, saying he'd hitched up the captain's horse and buggy. When he returned, he unrolled his shirtsleeves, and finding his dress jacket, he put it on. Next he let one of the other employees know he was leaving by shouting up a steep flight of stairs, "Hey, there, Joe, I'm leaving for a while! Mind the shop, would you?"

She heard a man's deep reply. "Will do."

At last Richard announced he was ready to go. Their first stop was fetching her luggage from the train station. Her trunk and bags filled the entire backseat of the buggy.

"I noticed the little cross on the necklace you're wearing. Forgive me for asking what might be the obvious, but are you a Christian, Miss McCabe?" He climbed up into the driver's perch and took the horse's reins.

"Why, yes, I am. Why do you ask?"

"I always ask."

"Hmm..." She wondered if he insulted a good many folks

with his plain speech. But in his present state, Richard reminded her of her brother Luke. "My father is a pastor back home in Missouri," Sarah offered, "and two of my three brothers have plans to be missionaries out West."

"And the third brother?"

"Ben. He's a photographer. He and his wife, Valerie, are expecting their third baby in just a couple of months."

"How nice for them."

Nodding, Sarah felt a blush creep into her cheeks. She really hadn't meant to share such intimacies about her family with a man she'd just met. But Richard seemed so easy to talk to, like a friend already. But all too soon she recalled her sister Leah's words of advice: "Outgrow your garrulousness, lest you give the impression of a silly schoolgirl! You're a young lady now. A music teacher."

Sarah promptly remembered herself and held her tongue—until they reached the captain's residence, anyway.

"What a beautiful home." She felt awestruck as Richard helped her down from the buggy.

"A bit ostentatious for my tastes."

Not for Sarah's. She'd always dreamed of living in a house this grand. Walking toward the enormous brick mansion, she gazed up in wonder.

The manse had three stories of windows that were each trimmed in white, and a "widow's walk" at the very top of it gave the structure a somewhat square design. The house was situated on a quiet street across from a small park that overlooked Lake Michigan. But it wasn't the view that impressed Sarah. It was the house itself.

Richard seemed to sense her fascination. "Notice the brick walls which are lavishly ornamented with terra cotta. The porch," he said, reaching for her hand as they climbed its stairs, "is cased entirely with terra cotta. And these massive front doors are composed of complex oak millwork, hand-carved details, and wrought iron. The lead glass panels," he informed her as he knocked three times, "hinge inward to allow conversation through the grillwork."

"Goodness!" Sarah felt awestruck. She sent Richard an impish grin. "You are something of a walking text book, aren't you?"

Before he could reply, a panel suddenly opened, and Sarah found herself looking into the stern countenance of a woman who was perhaps in her late forties.

"Hello, Mrs. Schlyterhaus." Richard's tone sounded neighborly.

"Mr. Navis." She gave him a curt nod. "Vhat can I do for you?"

Sarah immediately noticed the housekeeper's thick German accent.

"I've brought the captain's new governess. This is Miss Sarah McCabe." He turned. "Sarah, this is Mrs. Gretchen Schlyterhaus."

"A pleasure to meet you, ma'am." Sarah tried to sound as pleasing as possible, for the housekeeper looked quite annoyed at the moment.

"The captain said nussing about a new governess," she told Richard, fairly ignoring Sarah altogether. "I know nussing about it."

Richard grimaced. "I was afraid of that."

Wide-eyed, Sarah gave him a look of disbelief.

"Let's show Mrs. Schylterhaus that letter…the one from the captain."

Sarah pulled it from her inside pocket and handed it over. Richard opened it and read its contents.

The older woman appeared unimpressed. "I know nussing about it." With that, she closed the door on them.

Sarah's heart crimped as she and Richard walked back to the carriage.

"Here, now, don't look so glum, Sarah...may I call you Sarah?"

"Yes, I suppose so." No governess position. No money. So much for showing herself an independent young woman. Her family would never let her forget this. Not ever!

Suddenly she noticed Richard's wide grin. "What are you smiling at?"

"It appears, Sarah, that you've been given the day off too."

Coming in October

ANDREA BOESHAAR CONTINUES THE ENTERTAINING
AND INSPIRATIONAL SAGA OF THE McCABE FAMILY IN
UNCERTAIN HEART

Secure in her job as a governess for Captain Sinclair, Sarah knows first hand the life she has always desired: a life of luxury, culture, and social privilege. But then she meets Richard Navis, the captain's steward, and those dreams seem to vanish in the salt air. Sarah loves his teasing tenderness, and she admires his commitment to the Lord. So why would Richard want to leave behind his career to buy, of all things, a farm?

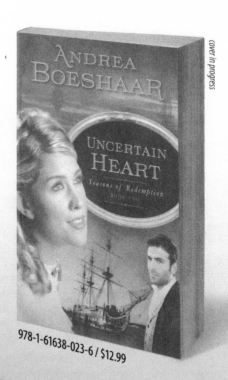

cover in progress

978-1-61638-023-6 / $12.99

LOOK FOR IT
IN BOOKSTORES
OCTOBER 2010

REALMS
A STRANG COMPANY
9190